Eric Wilder

Oyster Bay Boogie

Gondwana Press

Edmond, Oklahoma

Other Books by Eric Wilder

Gondwana Press
1802 Canyon Park Cir. Ste C
Edmond, OK 73013

For information on books by Eric Wilder
www.ericwilder.com

Front Cover by Gondwana Graphics

ISBN: 978-1-946576-13-2

Acknowledgments

I wish to thank Donald Yaw and Linda Hartle Bergeron for beta reading, editing, and providing valuable input involving timeline and character development.

For Marilyn

Oyster Bay Boogie

A novel by
Eric Wilder

Chapter 1

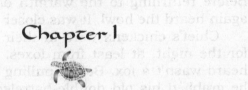

Grogan La Tortue had never spent an entire night in a bed, at least not alone. The man everyone called Chief was an American Indian and quite literally the last of the Atakapas. Native American blankets and animal skins covered the straw pallet where he slept. His Chihuahua Coco didn't seem to mind.

Late spring, the rain, and a gentle breeze had created almost perfect sleeping weather. Light rain beat a gentle cadence on Chief's teepee. It didn't matter because the distant howl of some creature he didn't recognize kept Chief awake. It bothered him that his dog Coco hadn't also heard it.

Chief brushed his shoulder-length gray hair out of his eyes, got up from the pallet, and relieved himself in the privy behind the teepee.

Chief's property sat on a hill overlooking the Gulf of Mexico. The moon was full, damp clouds partially cloaking its yellow luster. When the moon burst from the shadows, he gazed across the island. Chief could smell the storm moving in from the Gulf. The warm rain felt good on his bare back.

A hulk of a man, Chief's shoulders rippled when he drew a bucket of water from the well. The water was cool and tasted good. Chief's grandfather had lived more than a hundred years, attributing his long life and good health to the mineral water from the well. His grandmother had touted the water as having magical restorative powers. Chief had no doubt her words were valid. Before returning to the warmth of his pallet, he again heard the howl. It was closer this time.

Chief's chickens were in their coop and safe for the night, at least from foxes. The howl he'd heard wasn't a fox. Before pulling the covers up, he grabbed his old double-barreled shotgun and rested it beside him on the dirt floor.

Chief's cat Buttercup was out tomcatting, and he worried about her. He knew she didn't like the rain and wondered why she hadn't joined him and Coco on the pallet. Though he closed his eyes, sleep resisted his efforts. Finally, he descended into the gentle rapture of a vivid dream.

Dark smoke engulfed the island. Chief stood outside his teepee. Somewhere in the distance, someone cried for help. The cries grew louder as Chief floated down the hill. Though he sensed the crackle of flames, he couldn't smell the smoke.

When the smoke cleared, he was standing in

the sand, looking out at the vast cove where boats and yachts once docked, their occupants gambling inside the casino set on stilts over the water. The old wood-framed building, flames spewing from open windows, was on fire. A young woman's head and upper body protruded from a third-story window.

"Help me," she screamed.

The scream awakened Chief to another sound: a howl outside the teepee. He saw a black claw from the glow of the fire pit as it tore through the animal skin. Rising into a sitting position, Chief pointed the shotgun at the claw and pulled both triggers, the ensuing blast waking his Chihuahua.

Coco bounded off the pallet, growling as he raced through the flap of the teepee.

"Dammit!" Chief said.

After grabbing a handful of shells, he followed the tiny dog through the flap. When he stepped on a sand burr, he realized he'd forgotten his moccasins. Coco's distant growls reinforced that he had no time to return for them.

The moon had temporarily disappeared behind the clouds. Chief missed the trail leading down the hill, tripped on a vine, and rolled to the bottom. His breechcloth did nothing to protect him from the burrs and bull nettle through which he'd rolled. His raw and itching skin meant little now as Coco's growls grew farther away.

Chief could see blood in the sand and large footprints when the moon burst from the clouds. The indentions in the sand looked like those of a giant dog, or maybe a wolf. Whatever had made the prints wore no shoes. Chief had little time to process the information as he heard the commotion of a fight up ahead.

Half-naked and without his shotgun, Chief had no other plan than to join the fray

3

barehanded and try to rescue Coco. Forgetting his lacerated skin, he raced ahead, reaching the bridge connecting the island to the mainland as the shadow of some erect creature crossed the structure. Chief watched it disappear into the underbrush.

Coco's barks and growls had gone quiet. The rain had also stopped leaving Chief's skin in a tormenting burn. Ignoring the discomfort, he frantically searched the bushes on the side of the trail beside the road leading to the Majestic, the island's Prohibition-era hotel and casino, stopping when the beam of a large flashlight shined in his face.

"Chief, is that you? What in holy hell are you doing out here this time of night?"

"It's me, Jack. I'm looking for Coco."

Jack was short, probably no taller than five-six or seven. He was wiry, closely shaven, with brown hair buzzed almost to his scalp. From the odd shape of his mouth, It was hard to tell if Jack was smiling or frowning. Chief stood at least a foot taller than the smaller man and weighed at least a hundred pounds more.

With Jack was Oscar, his English bulldog whose shoulders were as broad and muscular as Chief's. Oscar wagged his short tail when Chief reached down to rub his head.

"I had an intruder at the teepee," Chief said.

"I heard a shotgun blast. Was that you?"

"Something tried to tear into my teepee. When I unloaded the shotgun, Coco ran after him."

"Who was it?"

"Not who, what?"

"The hell?"

"Help me find Coco, and I'll tell you the rest of the story."

"Oscar," Jack said. "Find Coco."

Oscar's flat nose went to the sand. He ran

4

down the trail from where Chief had come. Jack and Chief chased after him until he stopped and barked at the brush beside the path.

"I'll get my machete," Jack said.

Before Jack could go for his big knife, Oscar bulldozed his way into the brush, returning with the scruff of Coco's neck in his mouth.

"Oh shit!" Chief said. "Please, God, don't let him be dead."

"Let's get him to the lighthouse," Jack said. "We can't check him out in the dark."

Chief cradled the little dog in his arms as he followed Jack up the hill to the lighthouse overlooking the bay. The door to Jack's house was ajar. Jack hadn't bothered shutting it.

"Give him to me," Jack said. "I was the part-time medic on more ships than I can count."

Chief was stoic. Jack had never seen him cry and had only rarely seen him smile. Expecting little emotion from the hulking man, he laid Coco on the kitchen table and began wiggling his head and legs.

"Nothing's broken," he said. "Get me a washrag."

"Is he breathing?" Chief asked as he handed Jack a damp washcloth.

"He had the holy hell knocked out of him," Jack said.

Coco opened his eyes and struggled to his feet. Though wobbly, his tail was wagging when Chief rubbed his head.

"You scared the hell out of me, you little bastard."

"He doesn't look half as bad as you do," Jack said. "Use my shower and get cleaned up. I'll put iodine on your cuts when you return."

"It's not the cuts that are bothering me. I took a roll in bull nettle."

"Sit here," Jack said. "I'll get the tweezers."

Thirty minutes passed as Jack methodically extracted tiny poisonous spines from Chief's body.

"I think I got them all," Jack said. "I'll apply cortisone and iodine when you come out of the shower."

"What am I going to wear?"

"Hell, Chief, none of my clothes will fit you. You'll have to put your breechcloth back on."

"It's filthy and full of sand burrs."

"Then throw it in the washer. A towel will do until it's washed and dried."

The aroma of Jack's chowder greeted Chief when he exited the bathroom. Sitting at the kitchen table, he ate a bowl as Jack doctored his cuts and scratches. Coco and Oscar were lying together in Oscar's doggie bed next to Jack's old stove. Both were asleep as if nothing had happened. The rain had returned, the storm from the Gulf resulting in high wind, thunder, and lightning.

When Chief's breechcloth was clean and dry, he put it on and sat on Jack's couch with a blanket wrapped around his shoulders.

"Feel better?" Jack asked.

"Not as good as I would if I had a mug of your firewater."

Jack poured each a mug of rum from a bottle he kept in the cabinet over the stove. The hint of a smile crossed Chief's face as he leaned his big head against the couch.

"What the hell were you and Coco chasing out there?" Jack said.

"I think it was a Rougarou," Chief said.

"What the hell is that?" Jack asked.

"Navahos call them Skinwalkers, a human who can take the shape of an animal."

"You mean like a shapeshifter?" Jack asked.

"Yes. Whatever tore into my teepee was bigger

6

than me and had the claws of an animal."

"What kind of animal?" Jack asked.

"Though I didn't get a good look, it was howling like a wolf."

"Get out of here!" Jack said.

"Coco thinks he's a lion and went after him. He's lucky to be alive."

"If you didn't get a good look at him, how do you know how big he was?" Jack asked.

"Wait'll you see his tracks in the sand," Jack said. "Whatever the thing is, he's a monster."

"Pardon me if I don't believe you," Jack said.

"Magic is real. Doesn't matter if you believe it or not. It is what it is."

Jack was squirming as he sat at the table of the tiny kitchen. "You think whoever tried to break into your teepee was magical?"

Chief nodded. "That's not all. I had a dream."

"What?" Jack said.

"The Majestic was on fire, a woman I didn't recognize trapped on the top floor."

"No one's lived in the Majestic for decades," Jack said.

"Then why does my dream worry you?"

"I had a call from Mr. Castellano today."

"The man who claims to own the island?" Chief asked.

"The biggest mob boss in the south," Jack said. "He doesn't like it when things go wrong."

"Why do you work for a crook?" Chief asked.

"Mr. Castellano pays me well to take care of things. That and my navy pension provides the grog you enjoy so much."

"You didn't answer my question. Why does my dream worry you?"

"Mr. Castellano has found someone to come live here and restore the Majestic to its former glory."

"You're kidding me?" Chief said.

7

"I wish I were. The last thing two old hermits like you and me need is a crowd of people taking over the island."

"That's a fact," Chief said.

"I would lose my job if the Majestic burned, and it won't make Mr. Castellano happy to learn a shapeshifter's roaming the island."

"Then don't tell him," Chief said.

"The rain has stopped," Jack said. "Show me the footprints."

Oscar and Coco didn't awaken as Jack and Chief followed the powerful flashlight beam down the path from the lighthouse. They halted when they reached the bridge to the mainland.

"The only way onto the island is across the bridge," Jack said.

"It's low tide," Chief said. "He could have waded across."

Chief was correct, the water beneath the bridge shallow enough to see the bottom. Jack was staring at something in the water.

"What is it?" he said.

"Looks like an old crate," Chief said. "Must have washed up in the storm."

Chief waded into the shallow water, dragging the crate to shore.

"Too heavy to carry back to your place," he said. "We'll have to get it with the ATV."

"Any idea what it is?" Jack asked.

"Don't know," Chief said. "The stenciling on the crate is faded. I think it says Dominican Republic."

8

Chapter 2

Coco didn't awaken during Chief's return to his hill overlooking the Gulf. The rain continued, and Jack had lent him an umbrella. The first thing he noticed when he entered his teepee was the large hole in the wall made when he'd unloaded the shotgun on the intruder. Rain and wind continued blowing through the hole. Chief decided not to worry about it, covering his head with a blanket.

The sound of a horn honking woke him some hours later. From the wagging of Coco's tail, Chief knew it was Jack waiting in the ATV at the foot of the hill. When Chief exited the privy, Jack was coming up the path, Oscar in front of him.

"Hell, man," Jack said. "You going to sleep all day?"

"Wouldn't be a bad idea," Chief said, "seeing as I got no sleep last night."

"We got work to do. I brought the ATV."

"I'm not deaf. I heard the horn."

"Then get your butt in gear. We'll haul the crate to my house, and then I'll fix us a navy breakfast."

Always hungry, Jack's offer of food riveted his attention.

"Let me feed the chickens and Buttercup. She was tomcatting all night and is still asleep on the pallet."

"You and that cat," Jack said.

"You don't like cats?"

"There are half a dozen feral cats that hang out behind my house. They live in the storage shed and eat my grub just like you do. Haven't had a mouse since I moved in. Doesn't mean I want them sitting in my lap and purring."

"Bet they feel the same way about you," Chief said.

The four-wheel-drive, all-terrain vehicle was waiting at the foot of the hill. Jack had lowered the top, Chief contorting his massive frame to fit in the front seat. The 90-horsepower engine started on the first crank of the key. Oscar and Coco loved it, their tails wagging as they sat in the backseat.

A hazy orb poked rays of sunshine through the clouds as Jack drove past the Majestic.

"What a place that must have been back in the thirties," Jack said.

"That casino almost kept me from being born," Chief said. "Grandpa went there one night before he and Grandma married. Got hooked up with a lady of the night."

"What happened?" Jack asked.

"Grandma forgave him. I wouldn't be here now if she hadn't," Chief said.

"Was your granddad as big as you are?"

"Nope," Chief said. "He was six inches shorter than Grandma. My dad wasn't tall either."

"You never talk about your parents," Jack said.

"Maybe I'll tell you someday when we've both had a bit too much of your grog. Not now."

Jack let the matter drop as he parked the ATV near the bridge where they'd found the crate.

Chief lifted the container into the bed behind the backseat. Instead of returning to the front seat, he stood with his hand shielding his eyes from the sun.

"What the hell, man? What are you looking at?" Jack asked.

"I saw a flash in the water."

"Just a seashell. Let's go," Jack said.

Chief didn't obey. Instead, he pulled up his jeans over his knees and waded into the water under the bridge. He needn't have bothered because even his hair was wet when he returned to the ATV.

"Found something," he said.

"Another crate?" Jack asked.

When Chief opened his hand, the objects in it glinted in the sunlight.

"Gold coins," Chief said. "Grandpa always told me there was a fortune in Spanish gold buried somewhere on the island."

"Jesus!" Jack said. "An entire doubloon and a piece of eight. Got to be worth a lot of money."

"You think I'm going to split it with you?" Chief said.

"If I'd found them, I would have split it with you."

"Sure about that?" Chief asked.

"Hell yes, I'm sure," Jack said.

"I'm mighty hungry," Chief said. "I'll decide after breakfast."

Jack carried the doubloons as Chief lugged the crate into the little white house and sat it on the floor.

"Hope you have a crowbar," Chief said.

"Nothing much I don't have in my toolbox," Jack said.

Chief took the crowbar and began loosening the lid. When it popped open, Jack laid it against the wall and then ripped open the waterproof covering with a kitchen knife. The crate contained liquor bottles, and Jack held one up to the light.

"What's it say?" Chief asked.

"151 proof rum, Whistling Winds Distillery, Dominican Republic, bottled 1929."

"Then the rum is. . ."

"Close to a hundred years old," Jack said, finishing Chief's sentence.

"They look like they were just bottled."

"The waterproof cover did the trick," Jack said.

"Open it," Chief said. "Let's see how it tastes."

"You crazy? No telling how much this crate of hooch is worth."

"Nothing if it tastes like shit," Chief said. "Open it, and let's find out."

Jack continued grumbling as he opened the bottle and filled two mugs. They both took a sip.

"What do you think?" Jack asked.

"Best rum I ever tasted in my life," Chief said.

"Got that right," Jack said. "I've drunk rum from all over the world. None even comes close to this."

"What'll we do?" Chief asked.

"Eat breakfast while we think about it," Jack said.

The aroma of baking biscuits and bacon and eggs soon filled the cozy kitchen Jack always referred to as his galley. Chief's stomach growled, and his mouth watered as he waited at the plank table. As they tore into breakfast, complete with strong coffee laced with Dominican rum there was no conversation. Chief was working on his third helping of bacon and eggs when Jack pushed away from the table.

"I think we need to take a road trip," he said.

"Road trip to where?" Chief asked.

"New Orleans. Seems to me we have a few things to celebrate."

"Sounds good to me," Chief said.

"Lots of shops on Canal buy and sell things. We'll split the money and then eat someplace where I don't have to cook."

"You sick of cooking?" Chief asked.

"No, but I love it when someone else does the cooking for me."

"I'm all in, Jack. Raw oysters, all we can eat, cold beer and barbecue shrimp," Chief said. "Can't wait."

"You got it," Jack said. "And then a visit to a Bourbon Street tittie bar to watch the naked girls until we get drunk and obnoxious, and they kick us out."

"Not that drunk and obnoxious," Chief said. "I don't ever want to spend another night in the French Quarter drunk tank."

"Right about that," Jack said. "It wasn't exactly the Hotel Monteleone."

"At least they just let us sleep it off and didn't charge us with a crime," Chief said.

"No jail this time," Jack said. "If you start getting rowdy, I'll herd your ass out of the joint."

"Who's going to herd yours out?" Chief said.

"Let's don't worry about it until it happens."

"What about Oscar and Coco?" Chief asked.

"The doggie door leads out back, and there's plenty of room inside the fence to run around. Those two dogs won't go hungry or thirsty and will probably never miss us."

Chief was already half-drunk as they crossed the bridge to the mainland and headed toward New Orleans. Using the dashboard as a tom-tom, he sang an Indian war song until Jack turned up the radio in his old red pickup.

"Lighten up, Chief. If you even think about scalping someone, I'm bringing you home. Got it?"

13

"I can't remember the last time I scalped anyone," Chief said.

"Because you never have," Jack said. "That doesn't stop you from talking about it when you get sotted. You're so damn big you scare everyone half to death when you do."

"Raw oysters and wild women are the only two things on my mind right now," Chief said.

"Then quit hogging that bottle of rum. This country road makes me thirsty."

Chief took a swig before handing the bottle to Jack. Pastures filled with cattle and cattle egrets were their only company along the rural road. The sky was still cloudy, pelicans flying overhead looking for their nests. The radio station Jack had found was playing an old Hank Williams song. He and Chief knew the words and were soon singing along. The road grew wider when they reached St. Bernard Parish.

"I'm glad you know the way," Chief said.

"You're Indian," Jack said. "You people are supposed to have extrasensory perception."

"On foot or horseback," Chief said. "Not in a truck."

"Then it's a good thing it's all but impossible to get lost in New Orleans."

Chief almost laughed. "Huh? You have a hard time finding your ass with both hands."

Jack ignored Chief's retort. "Any more rum in that bottle you're bogarting?"

"Not much. Lucky we brought two bottles. Where are you going to park this old heap, so it doesn't get impounded like it did last time?"

"I'll find a place," Jack said.

Jack found an alleyway on the outskirts of the French Quarter and parked the truck behind a dumpster.

"Sure about this?" Chief asked.

"It's three blocks to the French Quarter. No one would park this far away."

"Famous last words," Chief said.

"Stow it, landlubber," Jack said. "We got money to make, oysters to eat, and tits to watch. Don't jinx us."

They were soon on their way to Canal Street, the widest thoroughfare on earth. A red streetcar passed as they headed to one of the camera shops. A man with a middle-eastern accent greeted them when they entered. Cameras, radios, and electronics filled the front window. Inside, there was always a deal someone could make.

"How can I help you two gentlemen?:" the salesman asked. "A new single lens reflex camera?"

"We're not buying. We're selling," Jack said.

A smile crossed the man's face with the dark mustache and swarthy complexion.

"What you boys got?" he asked.

Jack pulled the doubloon from his pocket, gave it a spin, and watched as it twirled on the glass cabinet filled with exotic cameras. When it came to a rest on the cabinet, the salesman took it, put it in his mouth, and bit it.

"Fake gold," he said. "I'll give you twenty-five bucks." Jack took the coin and started for the door. "Wait," the man said. "Give you a hundred."

"You wouldn't give me a penny for it if it weren't gold," Jack said.

"It's gold," the man said. "I'd have to get it assayed to determine how much gold."

"Bull shit!" Jack said. "Let's go, Chief."

Again, the man stopped them. "Five hundred dollars."

He grinned when Jack said, "You wouldn't give your mama five hundred dollars unless whatever you were buying was worth a thousand."

"Then tell me how much you want for it," the man said.

"Four thousand dollars," Jack said.

"Excuse me a minute," the man said before disappearing into the back.

He counted out fifteen hundred dollars in hundred dollar bills on the cabinet when he returned.

"Twenty-five hundred dollars or we're walking," Jack said.

"You are an excellent negotiator," the man said with a smile as he counted out five more hundreds. "My last offer."

Chief grabbed the cash. Without giving Jack a chance to reply, he started for the door. Jack didn't take much convincing. Chief handed Jack a thousand dollars back out on Canal Street and put the other thousand in his pocket.

"Let that be a lesson, Chief," Jack said. "I got us a thousand dollars more than the doubloon is worth."

"If you believe that," Chief said. "I have a bridge in Brooklyn to sell you. That man just stuck it up our butts."

"Then why did you take the money?" Jack asked.

"We have two thousand dollars we didn't have yesterday. My grandpa always told me about the Spanish gold hidden on the island. There are more doubloons where that one came from."

"Okay, then," Jack said. "Let's catch the streetcar at St. Charles. "Someone's shucking oysters, and I'm buying all you can eat."

Chapter 3

Jack and Chief waited on the corner for the next streetcar to arrive. When it turned off Canal onto St. Charles and rumbled to a stop, they boarded the antique passenger vehicle.

There's nothing quite as relaxing as sitting in a wooden streetcar seat as it rumbles down St. Charles Avenue. Rush hour had passed, the old streetcar almost deserted as Jack and Chief enjoyed the cool weather and fresh air from the open window. Chief pulled the wire to signal the driver to let them off at Napoleon. Daylight began to wane as they exited the streetcar and headed north.

"We haven't been here in a while," Jack said. "Hope the place isn't out of business."

"If it is," Chief said. "We can head back to the Quarter and eat at the Oyster House."

A breeze fluttered the leaves of the live oaks fronting many of the old houses. The sidewalk was growing dark, though neither man worried about being accosted. They reached the restaurant in ten minutes and entered through the parking lot door.

They found a large room with a wooden plank floor, several patrons waiting for dinner in the main dining room. There were two bars, one for drinking and another for raw oysters.

"Order me an Abita," Jack said. "I'll get us a couple of dozen oysters."

The young black man shucking oysters smiled when he looked up and saw Jack.

"Ain't seen you in a spell. That big Indian with you?"

Jack nodded and shook his hand. "Glad to see you, James. Chief is ordering us beer. Got any oysters in this place?"

The young man grinned. "We got the plumpest, sweetest oysters in all of Louisiana."

"Then you must have known we were coming," Jack said.

"Where you boys been?"

"Recovering from our last visit," Jack said.

"I hear that," James said. "You two about cleaned us out of oysters last time."

"We're going to give it a try again tonight," Jack said.

Pulling a hundred-dollar bill from the pocket of his blue work shirt, Jack passed it across the bar to James.

"For you," he said. "Keep the oysters coming."

James stashed the bill in his shirt pocket. "You boys rob a bank?"

Jack pulled a silver flask out of his back pocket and handed it to James.

"Better than that," he said. "Take a swig of this."

James opened the flask, a smile appearing after he'd taken a drink."

"Man," he said. "That's the smoothest rum I ever tasted."

"1929 Dominican. We found a crate of it on Oyster Island."

"Wouldn't want to sell me a bottle, would you?" James asked.

James grinned again when Jack said, "Son, they don't pay you enough here to afford a bottle of this rum."

"Then maybe you'll let me take another pull."

"Go ahead, just don't drink it all," Jack said. "It's a long way back to Oyster Island."

"You boys have oysters on Oyster Island?" James asked.

"How do you think it got its name?"

"Then why do you and Chief have to come to the city for oysters?"

"The man who owns the island won't allow anyone to touch the beds. Maybe someday."

"Damn!" James said. "You know how much oysters are worth?"

James grinned again when Jack said, "There's way more there than I can afford, at least at the prices you charge."

"I'll bring you and Chief your oysters soon as I get them shucked."

Jack saluted and said, "Thanks."

When he joined Chief at the bar, he found a chilled glass of Abita waiting for him. James tapped Chief's shoulder when he delivered their first batch of oysters.

"How's it going, Chief?" he asked.

"Wonderful," Chief said. "These oysters look great."

"Nothing but the best for my two favorite customers," James said.

Jack mixed horseradish and cocktail sauce, put a fat oyster on a cracker, and then topped it with his concoction before biting into it Chief didn't waste time with condiments, forking an oyster straight into his mouth.

"Uh oh!" he said.

"What?" Jack asked.

"James must have left a piece of shell in this one. I almost broke a tooth."

He fished the object out of his mouth and held it to the light.

"What is it?" Jack asked.

"A pearl," Chief said.

The bartender with thinning hair and bushy mustache wiped a glass with a bar rag.

"Your lucky day," he said. "That's a nice pearl."

"A real beauty," Chief said, dropping it in his shirt pocket.

"Need me to put you on the list for the main dining room?" the bartender asked.

"What about it, Chief?" Jack asked.

"Another couple dozen of these tasty mollusks is all I need," he said.

The bartender nodded and moved away to help another customer.

Many oysters and cold beers later, Jack and Chief exited the restaurant. It was dark, shadows dancing outside the halos of light created by the streetlamps.

"You ready for some titties?" Jack asked.

"Been ready since we left Oyster Island," Chief said.

The streetcar was nearly empty on their return trip to Canal Street. Chief closed his eyes and got fifteen minutes of well-deserved sleep, awaking when the streetcar pulled to a stop. Everyone disembarked at Canal Street.

Jack and Chief walked to the intersection with Bourbon Street. Once on Bourbon, they could see the lights and human activity down the famous venue. The raspy voice of street barkers, live jazz, and many drunk revelers accosted their senses. They were soon standing in front of High Rollers, a Bourbon Street strip club. The barker in the doorway implored them to come in.

"Titties and beer. Best in town," he said. Come in now, and I'll cut the cover charge to only twenty bucks."

The barker grinned when Jack asked, "Twenty bucks for both of us?"

"High Rollers is a strip joint, not a charity," he said. "The twenty bucks comes with one free drink. Come in before the rain starts, and I'll give you each two free drink coupons."

Chief and Jack entered the club, paid the cover charge, and had their hands stamped. Once inside, loud music, the fragrance of perfume, and a gorgeous waitress with a thick thatch of blond hair greeted them.

"I'm Opium," she said. "What are your names?"

"I'm Jack, and this is Chief. Love your name," Jack said. "You look as if you could be addictive.

"Every man's fantasy," she said. "What are you and Chief drinking?"

Opium's pink nightie didn't cover her black panties and mesh stockings entirely. Chief was staring, and Opium didn't mind.

"Pitcher beer and two mugs," Jack said.

"Doesn't the big one ever talk?" she asked.

"Chief's kind of shy, at least until you get him drunk, and then you can't shut him up."

"I'll need a credit card," she said.

Jack handed her the coupons the doorman had given them.

Opium's expression didn't change as she took the coupons.

"I still need a credit card," she said.

"We got cash," he said, handing her a hundred dollars.

Opium stuffed the money into her lacy bra. "Cash doesn't work in High Rollers. We need a credit card, or you'll have to leave."

"What about the drinks we paid for?" Chief asked.

"Wait here," she said. "I'll send the manager

21

over."

A man in a pinstriped suit soon joined them. Though he wasn't smiling, his curled upper lip revealed a gold front tooth.

"You can't stay here unless you got a credit card," he said.

"We got cash," Jack said.

"Don't matter none," The man said.

The man was big, though not nearly as large as Chief, who was also frowning, his arms clasped tightly across his chest. The manager counted out forty dollars and gave it to Jack.

"Rockie's down the street caters to roughnecks, bikers, and college kids. They serve beer and take cash. You and your big buddy will be more comfortable there."

The gold-toothed manager ushered them to the door, waiting until they'd walked out to the street. A light rain had begun falling as they exited High Rollers to Bourbon Street. It hadn't stopped the steady flow of foot traffic. Music poured from one of the bars selling exotic drinks through an open window.

"Guess they didn't want our business," Chief said.

"Then we'll spend our money where they do," Jack said.

"Want a Hurricane?" Chief asked.

"Too sweet for my taste," Jack said. "The truck's not far away. The flask is empty. Let's get our rum. It's in a paper sack, and we can bring it with us."

They found the truck the way they'd left it, the bottle of Dominican Rum under the seat. Drinks from the open bottle elevated their spirits as they headed back to the crowds of Bourbon Street. They soon found their strip joint.

Though not as large and flashy as High Rollers, Rockie's seemed more inviting, slow music emanating from the open door instead of a barker's raspy voice. They waited at the front door for someone to collect the cover charge. The red neon Scorpion in the front window beckoned them to enter. A half-naked waitress with a pitcher of beer in one hand smiled as she grabbed Chief's hand.

"If we hurry," she said, "There are open chairs at the pussy bar."

Two men dressed like roughnecks from an offshore drilling platform beat them to the seats at the elevated stage where a naked young woman was pole dancing to the slow strains of an old Bob Seger song. Like the song's words, the dancer was 'A black-haired beauty with big dark eyes.' Her expression revealed she was happy to be the center of attention.

"Someone beat us to the punch," the waitress said. "How about a table in the corner?"

"That'll work," Jack said.

"What are you drinking?"

Jack answered again, "Pitcher and two cold mugs."

The room was dark, only the stage lights and supernatural glow of rotating spotlights illuminating the room. A fog machine beneath the dance floor shot periodic clouds of mist to the ceiling. The song to which the naked young woman danced blasted out of giant speakers.

Chief nodded when Jack said, "I think we found the right place."

Their waitress soon returned with a pitcher of beer and two chilled mugs.

"I'm Angela," she said. "I'll check back to see if you need anything."

"How about a table dance?" Jack said.

Angela's bouffant blond hair highlighted her great smile and toned body clad only in the skimpiest of blue bikinis.

"I'm a waitress, not a dancer," she said. "I'll send one of the dancers over."

"Sorry," Jack said. "Didn't mean to insult you."

"I wasn't insulted," Angela said.

Angela disappeared into the darkness. Another young woman soon approached Jack and Chief's table.

"Angela told me someone needs a table dance," she said.

"How much do you charge?" Jack asked.

"A hundred bucks," the woman said.

"Damn!" Jack said with a smile. "I should be giving table dances."

"Nobody would hire you," Chief said. "What's your name?"

The young woman sat in the chair between Jack and Chief.

"Odette," she said. "Mind if I sit for a minute? These spike heels are killing me."

"Sit, pretty lady. Are you Cajun?"

"What gave you your first clue?" she asked.

"Your accent," he said.

"You don't like it?"

"You kidding?" Jack said. "I love it."

"Buy me a drink?" Odette asked.

Jack saw Angela and raised his finger. "Angela, please bring this beautiful young woman a drink."

Angela smiled and quickly returned with a tall drink.

"Twenty-five dollars," she said.

Jack did a double-take but quickly handed Angela seventy-five dollars.

"Twenty-five is for you. Bring Odette another when she finishes this one."

Angela kissed Jack's forehead. "Bless you," she said before hurrying off to the bar.

"Angela's working on her Ph.D. in physics at

24

L.S.U.," Odette said.

"With a body like hers, she should be hooking full time," Jack said.

Odette sprang to her feet. "Angela's not a hooker, and neither am I. Keep your drink. I don't sit with assholes, much less dance for them," she said.

Chapter 4

When Chief gave Jack a dirty look, the little man jumped to his feet.

"Wait," he said. "Did I say something wrong?"

"You kidding me?"

"I apologize," Jack said. "I'm an insensitive old bastard and should have thought before I opened my mouth.

"Jack is good as gold but was in the navy for thirty-four years," Chief said. "You have to cut him a little slack."

"What about you? How do you feel about women?"

"One of my granddaughters is a senior at Tulane," Chief said. "She shouldn't have to fight the battles she does. Doesn't mean men and women aren't sexually attracted."

"You have granddaughters?" Odette asked.

"The loves of my life," Chief said. "I have something for you." Chief pulled the pearl from his pocket and handed it to Odette. "Please accept this from Jack and me. It symbolizes purity, incorruptibility, and hidden feminine knowledge."

Odette returned the pearl to Chief. "I accept your apology. Not the pearl. It's bad luck to receive pearls as a gift."

"I was enjoying talking to you," Jack said. "Please stay. I'll do my best not to blurt out any more silliness."

Odette was smiling when she sat. "I'm sorry," she said. "I'm not here to voice my grievances. Want that table dance now?"

"I've lost the mood," Jack said.

Odette was still smiling when she said, "Let me find it for you."

Odette was tiny, probably shorter than five feet. Her blond hair hung in a loose twist that draped almost to her shapely ass. In an instant, she was naked, dancing to the latest song emanating from the giant speakers. Jack winced when she sat in his lap and began grinding against him to the strains of the music.

"Damn!" he said when the song ended. "I'm having a hard time not saying something sexist."

Odette wagged her finger at him. "Don't even think it. My grandma was a Cajun traiteur. Like her, I can read minds."

Odette's erotic dance raised Jack's temperature several degrees, and it took him a moment to remember to give her a hundred bucks.

"What about you, Chief? Ready for a table dance?"

"Don't know if my heart will take a hundred dollars worth," he said. "Can I get a senior discount?"

Odette didn't bother putting her skimpy outfit back on. Men at the surrounding tables were staring when the music started, and she began grinding her shapely ass against Chief's loins. She was sweating when the song finished, and sat in his lap with her arm around his neck. When the next song ended, Odette was still sitting there.

"Better get my g-string back on before I get fired," she said.

Seeing Chief was too bewildered to pay for the dance, Jack gave Odette another hundred for him.

"Doubt that's going to happen," he said.

"I'm up next. I'll be back after my break," Odette said.

Male excitement and the odor of raging pheromones saturated the heavy air in Rockie's as Odette took the stage. Voyeurs, including Jack and Chief, watched her every move.

"That is one hot woman," Jack said.

Chief's big head was shaking. "Rein it in, cowboy. You heard what she said. She's just here for us to look at and not to touch."

Odette finished her song to the wild applause of everyone in the club. Jack and Chief were working on their third pitcher of beer when she returned to their table. Angela smiled when she brought her another drink.

"I didn't forget," she said.

Jack handed Angela fifty bucks. "Twenty-five for you and another drink for Odette when this one runs dry," he said.

"I love the attention. I don't want to take all your money," Odette said.

"There's more where this came from," Jack said. "You like rum?"

"In daiquiris and piña coladas," she said.

Jack handed her the bottle of Dominican rum cloaked in the brown paper bag.

"Take a swig of this?" he said.

"Straight?"

"Trust me," he said.

Odette had to hold the bottle with both hands as she took a drink.

"Oh my," she said. "That is good. What kind of rum is it?"

Jack gave her a peek at the label. "Bottled 1929 in the Dominican Republic," he said.

"It's wonderful," Odette said. "I'm going to get a bottle on my way home."

"Not unless you have a time machine," Jack said. "Chief and I found a crate of this rum on Oyster Island."

"What was it doing there?" she asked.

"Rum runners smuggled booze into the States during prohibition. Coast Guard cutters sank some of their boats. Who knows what happened to the boat carrying the crate this bottle was in."

"How much do you think it's worth?" Odette said.

"You kidding?" Jack said. "An unopened bottle of nearly century-old Dominican rum has to be worth a couple of thousand dollars."

"Bet you're shooting too low," Odette said. "You think there's more where this came from?"

"Rum runners packed their holds with booze," Chief said. "The Coast Guard ships chasing them were too large to enter shallow water. If they couldn't catch the rum runner, they used cannons to blow them to bits."

"And you think the crate of rum you found came from a sunken rum runner?" Odette asked.

Chief gave Jack a dirty look when he said, "A sunken rum runner laden with a fortune in Dominican rum not far from Oyster Island."

"Oyster Island?" Odette said. "Never heard of it."

"On the Louisiana coast," Jack said. "About fifty miles southeast of here."

"I think it's time for us to go," Chief said.

Odette got out of her chair and sat in Chief's lap. "Wait, it's time for is another table dance," she said. "This one's on me."

Chief was shaking his head. "We need to get

29

on the road."

Odette waved to someone across the crowded bar. Another young woman soon joined them.

"This is Cheyenne, my best friend. You haven't lived until you've had a table dance from two hot blonds."

Cheyenne's hair was platinum blond, her eyes blue as an April sky. She and Odette stripped before Chief could protest, and they began giving him a double table dance. Chief lost track of time as the bodies of the two women moved in sync to the slow rock ballad coming from the giant speakers. When the song ended, Odette and Cheyenne sat naked on Chief's legs.

When the music began again, Odette and Cheyenne held hands and ascended the stage where their erotic, lesbian-smacking performance momentarily quieted the rowdy crowd.

"You opened your big mouth this time, didn't you?" Chief said.

"I don't want to hear it," Jack said. "You did your share of shooting off your mouth."

"Maybe," Chief said.

"Maybe? I didn't hear you protesting when those two girls were rubbing their naked bodies all over you."

"What was I supposed to do?" Chief said.

Jack cleared his throat. "You didn't have to look so happy about it. What if she does know about the rum? What's she going to do about it?" he asked.

"Guess that's the sixty-four dollar question," Chief said. "Can't change things now."

"When the girls return, let's get them drunk on the rest of our rum and try to change the subject," Jack said. "Maybe they'll forget about the rum."

"We have about as much chance of getting two strippers drunk as we do sprouting wings and flying back to Oyster Island," Chief said.

"You got a better idea?" Jack asked.

Chief crossed his legs and didn't bother answering. After a break, Odette and Cheyenne returned, holding hands, to the table.

Odette grinned when Jack asked, "Are you two . . . ?"

"Best friends," Odette said. "We both like men, if that's what you mean. What you saw is our act. Did it turn you on?"

"I'll say," Jack said.

Cheyenne pulled up a chair beside Jack. He flinched when she put her hand on his knee.

"You have to try their rum," Odette said.

Cheyenne's reaction to tasting the rum was much the same as Odette's had been.

"I can't believe how good it tastes," she said.

Seeing Jack's arms clasped tightly around his chest, Cheyenne sat in his lap and put her arms around his neck.

"You need to share your rum with Odette and me," she said.

"Drink as much as you want," Jack said.

"That's not what I mean," she said.

Cheyenne only smiled when Chief asked, "What do you mean?"

Cheyenne and Odette's eyes grew large. Jack was over the edge and responded to Chief's dirty looks by ordering more beer and setups. When Jack reached in his pocket to pay for the latest rounds, he realized their funds were running dry. Not knowing what else to do, he showed them the piece of eight.

"Is that real?" Odette asked.

"It's real," Jack said. "Take what we owe you out of this. We're out of dough and have to go.

"You found the old coin at Oyster Island?" Odette asked.

Chief nodded. "You find gold coins from time

to time all over the coast. I don't think it means anything in particular."

Odette took the piece of eight. "Don't leave just yet. You can drink the rest of the night. I'll take care of your tab."

The alcohol he'd drank, the scantily-clad young woman in his lap, and the relief that they had enough money to pay their tab resulted in an instant change in Jack's demeanor.

"Tell me again how to get to the island?" Odette said.

Neither Jack nor Chief answered her question.

"So, we're square on our tab?" Chief asked.

"Drink up," Odette said. "I'll take care of everything from this point on."

"It's a long way back to Oyster Island," Chief said.

"What's your hurry?" Cheyenne asked. "Have another pitcher of beer. Odette and I are treating."

"One more pitcher won't hurt anything," Jack said.

Cheyenne's arms draped Jack's shoulders, the silly look on his face pegging him as either drunk, psychotic, or maybe both. Chief got to his feet and grabbed his arm.

Angela appeared through the crowd carrying two pitchers of beer and fresh mugs. Without being asked, she filled one of the mugs and handed it to Chief. When he seemed reluctant to drink it, Odette climbed into his lap and held the glass to his lips.

Jack was slurring his words when he said, "Chief, tell Odette and Cheyenne about the Rougarou."

"Good idea," Chief said.

"What's a Rougarou?" Cheyenne asked.

"Sort of like a werewolf," Odette said.

32

"For real?" Cheyenne said.

Jack's head bobbed. "Chief shot him point-blank with his double-barrel shotgun. He ran away. The blast didn't kill him," he said.

"You have to be kidding," Cheyenne said.

"He's not," Odette said. "They haunt the swamps at night."

"Where do they come from?" Cheyenne asked.

"They're shapeshifters, people during the day, and monsters at night."

"How do you know so much about Rougarous?" Jack asked.

Talk of the Rougarou had Odette gesturing with her arms. "I told you my grandma is a traiteur. She knows all about such things," she said.

"What's a traiteur?" Cheyenne asked.

"A spiritual healer," Odette said, "though some people call them Cajun witches."

"You're scaring me," Cheyenne said.

"Odette, you're up," a voice called from the bar.

"We'll be back," Odette said.

The moment they were out of sight, Chief got to his feet. Jack was too drunk to resist as Chief dragged him out of the bar.

"What the hell are you doing?" Jack asked. "We were just about to get lucky."

"We're lucky to get the hell out of there before those two bloodsuckers get their fangs into our necks," Chief said. "My guess is we haven't heard the last of them."

"Impossible. They don't have a clue where Oyster Island is," Jack said.

"You don't remember giving directions to Odette?"

"Generic directions."

"She's not stupid," Chief said. "She can easily

find Oyster Island on the Internet."

"I'm not worried about it," Jack said.

"Why did you give them the piece of eight? It has to be worth five or six hundred dollars."

Jack began to squirm. "We're out of money. I didn't want her calling the cops and having us thrown in jail."

"Not to mention we forgot the bottle of rum," Chief said.

"Maybe they won't remember anything tomorrow," Jack said.

"Don't know about them, but you sure won't," Chief said. "Give me the truck keys."

"The hell you say. I'm good to go," Jack said.

"We won't make it out of town with you driving."

"You drank as much as I did," Jack said.

"I'm bigger than you are," Chief said. "Give me the keys."

They were still arguing when they reached the truck. After relieving themselves behind the dumpster, Jack opened the door and rested his head against the steering wheel.

His eyes had already half-closed when he mumbled, "Sleeping in the truck is safer than driving home right now. The dogs will be fine till we get there."

Chapter 5

J ack and Chief awoke to the incessant honking of a garbage truck.

"Move that old piece of shit. We have trash to haul, and you're in our way," the driver said.

Jack gave him a hand wave as he searched for the key in his pocket.

"Shit," he said. "Can't find the damn key." Chief handed it to him. "What are you doing with it?"

"You wanted to drive back to Oyster Island last night. I didn't think it was a good idea."

"You kidding?" Jack said. "We'd be in bed right now waiting for the coffee to perk."

"Or in the parish hotel," Chief said. "Stop somewhere, and let's get breakfast."

"We got no money," Jack said. "Remember?"

Chief began rummaging through the console. "I found enough change for a cup of coffee. Stop at a convenience store. We can get the coffee and go to the bathroom."

"One cup of coffee?" Jack said.

"Stop bitching and find a store," Chief said. "Half a cup of coffee is better than none at all."

They soon shared coffee in a paper cup and headed home from New Orleans.

35

"Tastes like bayou mud," Jack said. "How do you feel?"

"Like hammered shit," Chief said. "You?"

"Pretty much the same."

"Things can only get better," Chief said.

"Don't jinx us," Jack said. "I can't take much more of this happy horseshit."

"I hear that. At least we have plenty of gas," Chief said. "Don't we?"

"We'll be lucky to coast in on fumes," Jack said.

"Why didn't you fill up when we had money?" Chief asked.

"That's what I intended to do. It didn't work out that way."

"You know what they say about the road to hell?" Chief said.

"No, but I'm going to let you out on the road to Oyster Island if you don't shut the hell up," Jack said.

There are no hills in south Louisiana to coast down, so Jack conserved gas by driving slow and feathering the throttle. He and Chief were relieved when they reached the short bridge to Oyster Island. Jack's house was eerily quiet when they entered the front door.

"Where are the dogs?" Chief asked.

"Probably in the backyard," Jack said.

They had a surprise when they went into the backyard. One section of the six-foot stockade fence lay on the ground, the dogs nowhere around.

"What the hell?" Jack said.

Chief grabbed Jack's arm. "Hold it," he said. "Let me see what the tracks say before you go traipsing around out there."

No grass grew in Jack's backyard. There was only sand. Chief eased out the backdoor of the house and began surveying the tracks. He had soon walked to the wrecked portion of the fence.

"The Rougarou was trying to get in the house," he said.

"What about Oscar and Coco?" Jack asked.

"The dogs were inside, probably asleep. They didn't come outside until later. Their tracks lead through the hole in the fence."

"Damn it!" Jack said.

"Get the ATV. I'll fix this portion of the fence and meet you out front," Chief said.

Chief lifted the section of the fence back in place and braced it with driftwood. He was staring at the sand when Jack drove up behind him in the ATV. Holding up his hand, he signaled Jack to stop the vehicle.

"Get in," Jack said.

"Can't see the tracks as well that way," Chief said. I'll walk ahead. Drive slow and follow me."

Chief's pace accelerated toward the wooden walkway leading to the Majestic. When they reached it, Chief signaled Jack with a finger slice across his neck for him to turn off the ATV and join him.

"Is he in the Majestic?" Jack asked.

Chief's long gray hair swayed when he shook his head.

"He went down the ramp. Don't know how long he was there before returning to the sand and heading toward my teepee."

"Then get in. That creature may be killing Coco and Oscar as we speak."

Chief was barely in the ATV when Jack powered away toward the distant hilly part of the island.

"What the hell do you intend to do if we catch him? Strangle him with our bare hands?"

Jack patted his belt. "I brought my service .45 caliber pistol. This baby will knock the biggest man off his feet with one shot."

37

"He's a monster, not a man," Chief said. "My double-barrel only stunned him."

"We got to try," Jack said.

Jack parked the ATV at the foot of the hill. Chief was already out of the vehicle and running up the trail. He was staring in the flap of his teepee when Jack, his big pistol drawn, arrived.

Oscar was lying on his side, blood from a wound caked and clotted. Coco's tail was wagging slowly, and he was licking Oscar's face.

"Oh my God, no!" Jack said as he knelt beside his fallen dog.

Chief was petting Coco with one hand, his other on Oscar's neck.

"He's alive," he said. Finding an Indian blanket, Chief handed it to Jack. "Wrap him in this. We need to get him to a vet."

"He'll die before we get him there," Jack said. "I have drugs and vet supplies at my house. If we make it that far, I'll stitch him up."

Chief left the tent, returning with a bowl of water.

"Grandma's magic well water," he said.

Oscar's tongue moved when Chief held the bowl to his mouth. His eyes opened, and he slowly lapped the water.

"Thank God for your grandma," Jack said as he scooped up Oscar in the colorful blanket.

Jack disappeared down the trail with the bulldog in his arms, Chief's heart aching as he rubbed Coco's head.

"I need a bath, buddy, and to pray for your friend," he said.

As the little dog followed Chief out the flap of the teepee, he seemed to understand. They walked up a trail leading to a spot near the top of the hill. When they reached a pristine pool of water complete with a tiny waterfall, Chief stripped off his clothes, tested the water with his toe, and then entered the rock-bottom pool. When he was beneath the waterfall, he submerged his head. Coco lay in the sand, waiting for Chief to emerge from the blue pool of water. Chief was in no hurry.

The little dog seemed to understand when Chief said, "This water is magical. It's giving me the strength I so desperately need. Did you chase away the wolfman?"

Coco's tail began wagging, and he barked.

"You're a warrior," Chief said.

Chief grabbed Coco and dunked him in the water. When he sat Coco on the bank, the little dog shook himself dry and rolled in the sand. Chief didn't have a towel, water dripping from his body as he hurried down the trail to his teepee.

The chicken coop was undamaged, his free-range chickens scouring the hill for bugs. They all came running when he called them and sprinkled handfuls of grain on the bare ground. Mable, his favorite hen, jumped into his arms.

After seeing all his animals were safe, Chief entered the teepee and dressed in clean clothes. He knew he had to return to Jack's and was afraid of what he would find. Coco followed when he started down the hill.

"Coco, you stay," he said.

Coco was having none of it. Chief finally gave up and allowed the little dog to go with him on the walk back to Jack's. The sky was blue, smoke coming from the chimney of Jack's little house as they approached it. Coco was first into the house, and Chief could tell by his wagging tail everything was okay. Chief drew a deep breath before entering.

Oscar was lying in his bed, a large bandage on his back. He and Coco were soon exchanging face licks.

"I stitched the gash on his back and gave him

a pain killer. We should all be as healthy as that dog."

"I can't tell you how worried I was," Chief said.

"Me either," Jack said. "How about some breakfast?"

"Thought you'd never ask," Chief said.

The aroma of bacon and eggs filled the kitchen as Chief sat at the plank table. Coco had climbed into the doggie bed beside Oscar, his tail wagging as if he knew in what extreme peril his best friend had been. Chief split a slice of bacon with them when he thought Jack wasn't looking.

"I saw that," Jack said. "Doesn't matter. There's plenty left for us."

Chief and Jack were soon drinking strong coffee and enjoying steaming plates of bacon and eggs and Jack's homemade buttermilk biscuits.

"That trash truck driver this morning put me in a bad mood," Jack said.

"Just doing his job," Chief said. "I imagine it was a shock to his system finding two old drunks blocking his dumpster."

"To hell with him if he can't take a joke," Jack said. "Thank God, we got out of the strip bar in one piece."

"I don't think we're out of the woods yet," Chief said. "Odette seemed like one savvy customer."

"I agree," Jack said. "She somehow managed to take every penny we had."

"I enjoyed it," Chief said.

"Guess you did. It'll be a long time before I get the image of those two naked girls sitting in your lap out of my mind."

"That's the bad thing about booze," Chief said. "It tastes good going down, but it messes with your memories. Everything that happened last night feels like a dream."

"Trust me," Jack said. "It wasn't a dream. Those two strippers were rubbing themselves all over you."

"I can barely remember, and it doesn't seem real," Chief said. "The one thing I do remember is you told Odette there's a fortune in Dominican rum, not to mention gold doubloons on the island."

"I promise you, we'll never see her again," Jack said.

"I believe you," Chief said. "But I believe you're lying."

"No use worrying about it now?" Jack said. "How about a little hair of the dog?"

"Why not?" Chief said. "You intending to crack open another bottle?"

"Yes," Jack said.

"It's too expensive to drink," Chief said.

"One more bottle won't bankrupt us," Jack said. "Odette was right. There's a rum runner out there in the bay somewhere with a hold full of Dominican Rum."

"How are we going to find it. We don't even have a boat."

"There's the old trawler in the bay," Jack said. "When Mr. Castellano's man comes to take over the Majestic, we'll have him lend it to us."

"Why would he let us use the boat?" Chief said.

"Why not? Won't hurt to ask him."

"I have no clue how to steer a boat that big," Chief said.

"I was in the navy for thirty-four years. I do."

"That's down the line," Chief said. "We have bigger problems to worry about."

"The rougarou?"

"Your fence didn't stop him last night and won't stop him next time he tries to get into the house," Chief said.

41

"What should we do?"

"Kill it before it kills us and everything else on this island," Chief said.

"How do you intend to kill it? Your shotgun barely fazed him, and you said yourself, my service pistol won't do the trick."

"That's the problem," Chief said. "Rougarous are immortal."

"Nothing's immortal," Jack said.

Chief nodded. "If there's a way to kill the beast, we need to know it."

"Maybe we should consult one of Odette's Cajun witches," Jack said. "She seemed to think they know about rougarous."

"It was native Indians who taught traiteurs all they know about the spirit world," Chief said. "We can do this ourselves."

"How's that?" Jack asked.

"Consult my ancestors and the Great Spirit," Chief said.

Jack scoffed. "Call them on your cell phone? You don't even have a phone."

"There's a way," Chief said.

"Then maybe you'd better explain," Jack said.

"Sweat lodge," Chief said.

Chapter 6

Jack poured himself another cup of coffee from the pot on the stove. "What makes you think you can communicate with the dead?"

"You doubt it?" Chief asked.

"I'm not a religious man," Jack said. "I didn't think you were."

"Have you ever known me to go to church?"

Jack shook his head. "Nope."

"Just because I don't belong to an organized religion doesn't mean I'm not spiritual," Chief said.

"Being spiritual and speaking with the dead are two different things. I'm not buying it."

"My grandparents raised me, and neither of them ever attended a day of school. Doesn't matter because they knew things not found in textbooks."

"Like what?" Jack asked.

"Like how to communicate with their dead ancestors. I once saw it done."

Jack tried hard not to crack a smile as he sipped his coffee. "Okay, Chief, tell your story."

"You don't sound enthusiastic," Chief said. "If you're unwilling to hear me out, I'll do it myself."

"Get your dauber out of the dirt and tell me,"

Jack said. "I'm listening."

"Are you going to keep an open mind?" Chief asked.

"Unless you say something that's complete bullshit, like when you told me you killed a bear with your bare hands."

"I was entertaining you. I didn't expect you to believe me," Chief said.

"Then how do I know you're not trying to entertain me now?"

"I was drunk. I'm sober now. Hungover, maybe. What I'm about to tell you is the truth," Chief said.

"Then hit me with it."

"As Odette said, rougarous have been haunting the swamps forever. Indians, Cajuns, and other people who live in the swamps have managed to coexist with them. I don't know much about rougarous, though I'm betting my ancestors did. They'll tell us how to handle the beast."

"And if they don't?" Jack said.

"Then we're back to square one," Chief said. "Nothing ventured, nothing gained."

"How long is this going to take?"

"If we start now, we'll have our answer by this time tomorrow."

"What if the rougarou returns while we're in the sweat lodge?" Jack asked.

"It won't."

Jack's eyes squinted. "How can you be sure?"

"Like the tide in the bay, shapeshifters respond to the phases of the moon. Ever hear of the werewolf diet?"

"Hell no!" Jack said. "What's that?"

"All creatures are affected by moon phases. Fluids in your body move like the high and low tides out there in the bay. If you fast during a full moon, your body rids itself of toxins faster, hence the werewolf diet."

"Cute," Jack said. "What's it got to do with not having to worry about being attacked while we're in the sweat lodge?"

"Rougarous are shapeshifters, active during a full moon. That happened two days ago. The creature won't bother us tonight."

"Sure about that?" Jack asked.

"Only thing I'm sure about is you're starting to piss me off," Chief said. "You going to help me, or not?"

"What about Oscar?"

"Coco will stay with him. They'll be fine," Chief said.

The sky had grown dark as they headed across the island in the ATV. Yet another storm moving in from the Gulf. Jack parked beneath the branches of a live oak. The top was up, and he made sure the plastic flaps were closed.

Chief fed his chickens when they reached the teepee and then grabbed an armload of blankets and handed them to Jack. After collecting various things he thought they'd need, he started up the hill to the pool of water he called the Magic Fountain.

Chief constructed a frame for the sweat lodge using willow saplings. Before covering the structure with the blankets, he built a firepit and began rummaging in the bushes. He returned to the pit with an armload of rocks.

"Sacred rocks," he said. "Been in hiding since the last time Grandpa and I used the sweat lodge."

"Can you tell me about it?"

"It was after my parents died. I was only ten and so filled with grief I could barely function. Grandpa decided to summon my mom and dad and let me talk to them."

"You talked to your deceased parents?" Jack

45

asked. Chief nodded. "If you don't mind me asking, how did they die?"

"The same way most of my tribe died: infection."

"What infection?" Jack asked.

"Don't know," Chief said. "My parents and grandparents were the last of the Atakapas. Grandpa moved us to this island to avoid the white man's diseases that had infected and killed my people. My parents were the last victims. They are buried, like my grandparents at the highest point of this island."

"I'm so sorry," Jack said. "How did you become educated?"

"The vision of my mom and dad. They told Grandpa to send me to the white man's school and learn the white man's ways."

"You didn't get infected?"

"You kidding me?" Chief said. "I had mumps, measles, chickenpox. You name it."

"How did you keep from giving it to your grandparents?" Jack asked.

"Jimbo Kershaw and his wife Mable," Chief said. "A Cajun couple who lived beside the palmetto swamp on the far side of the island. They never had kids of their own. They took me in, sent me to school, and cared for me when I got sick."

"Are they . . . ?"

"Died about ten years back," Chief said. "Jimbo was a trapper; he and Mable the only two white people on earth my grandma and grandpa trusted."

Chief almost smiled when Jack said, "Your favorite chicken's name is Mable."

"People go to lengths to memorialize those they loved. I'm no different."

Jack let the matter drop as Chief arranged the sacred rocks in the center of the sweat lodge

46

and started a fire to heat them.

Chief and Jack gathered wood for the fire and piled it outside the entrance to the sweat lodge. An oaken bucket filled with water from the Magic Fountain and the wooden ladle from which Chief's grandma drank water straight from the well sat beside the fire. Finally, Chief gave Jack a breechcloth telling him to strip down and put it on. The last thing he did was wrap the blankets around the sweat lodge.

The sky was dark and growing heavy with impending rain when Jack said, "Now what?"

"Crawl in," Chief said.

There was no room to stand in the tiny structure, and Jack crawled on his hands and knees. Chief followed. The temperature inside the sweat lodge had already grown hot, and there was no blanket to sit on. Sweat began dripping down Jack's arms.

"It's dirty," he said. "Couldn't we at least sit on a blanket?"

"This is a time for introspection, not comfort," Chief said. "If we intend to see visions, we must remain thoughtful. That means no talking. If you want to chant or pray, that's okay. Otherwise, remain silent."

"What if it gets too hot?" Jack said.

"Not if, but when," Chief said. "It's going to get so hot in here you'll start thinking your skin's about to fall off. If you can't handle it, leave the sweat lodge, drink water, and take a dip in the Magic Fountain. We'll take periodic breaks. Are you ready?"

Jack nodded as Chief dipped water from the bucket and ladled it on the hot stones. Swirling steam filled the sweat lodge as Chief began to chant.

Chief was right. The air was soon so hot Jack could barely catch a breath. Sweat dripped from

47

his body. Chief continued chanting, occasionally dousing the hot stones with water. Jack was about to flee the sweat lodge when Chief grabbed his arm and tugged. Jack followed him out the flap.

Light rain falling slowly from the darkened sky felt good on their arms and backs. Chief had brought the wooden bucket with him. After filling it with water from the Magic Fountain, he dumped it over Jack's head and repeated it on his. Jack quickly drank two ladles of cold water before he began cooling down.

Chief shook his head when he asked, "Did you have a vision yet?"

"We've just begun," Chief said. "Let's get back in there."

Jack followed Chief into the sweat lodge. The little blanket-covered structure had grown so hot he almost turned around. He didn't. The sweat lodge was so painfully uncomfortable that he closed his eyes, focusing on pleasant thoughts. They didn't come.

All Jack could hear was Chief's incessant chanting and the sizzle of hot stones when he poured more water on them. He was unaware how long they'd been in the sweat lodge when Chief tugged on his arm again, signaling time for a break. The sky was black, rain pelting their heads, arms, and backs.

"I don't know about this, Chief," Jack said, "We could die in there, and wild animals eat our bodies."

"It's okay," Chief said. "Sit in the Magic Fountain awhile, then return to my teepee, put your clothes on and go home."

"What about you?" Jack asked.

"I'm going to finish this," Chief said.

"Not if it kills you, you won't."

"I've gone too far to turn back," Chief said.

"Crazy talk," Jack said. "You got it too damn hot in there. We need to open a flap and cool it down."

"Pain is part of the process," Chief said.

"Death isn't," Jack said. "If your granddad were here, he'd tell you the same thing."

"I'm almost there," Chief said. "A sweat lodge isn't supposed to be comfortable."

"Even saunas have thermometers," Jack said. "We're way past the danger zone."

"It was this hot when I sat with Grandpa so many years ago. I'm going back in."

"Dammit to hell, Chief!" Jack said. "Your head is as hard as a brick."

Chief didn't respond as he crawled into the sweat lodge. Jack followed him. Chief continued to chant, breathing nearly impossible as the heat became almost unbearable.

No matter how hard he tried, Jack was incapable of getting a full lungful of air. He was on the verge of panic, a feeling he hadn't experienced in years. Though he'd suppressed the memory, it began seeping back into his psyche.

Jack couldn't remember how his mother and father had looked. A head-on collision had sent their old Ford careening off an embankment, the impact throwing him from the car. His mom and dad perished in the fiery crash. He was barely thirteen when his aunt and uncle had taken him in to keep him from becoming a ward of the state.

Uncle Jack, his namesake, was in a wheelchair and couldn't work. He and Aunt Faye had one son. Jack's cousin Pete was seventeen and working after school until ten at night to help support his mom and dad. When Pete turned eighteen, Jack stole his birth certificate from the family bible, hitchhiked to Boston, and joined the Navy.

Though Jack had never grown much bigger

than he now was, he'd been almost as large when he was fourteen. He remembered cruising the Mekong River in a gunboat and firing his deck-mounted machine gun at muzzle flashes from the jungle surrounding the river.

He was on his way back to the states when the Navy discovered he wasn't yet fifteen. Though he'd sent most of his meager Navy pay to his aunt and uncle on Cape Ann, he'd returned there only to tell them he'd signed on as a crew member on a tanker about to set sail for Greece.

Jack had forgotten his mom's brown eyes. He didn't remember his dad's steady right hand, which he used to hammer nails or rest on his shoulder when he was frightened. Jack saw his mom's beautiful smile and felt the comforting touch of his dad's hand on his shoulder. His mom and dad were in the teepee with them, the vision filling him with happiness he'd never experienced.

"You're not alone," the spirit of Jack's mom said.

"Though danger surrounds you," the spirit of his dad said. "You will prevail."

Jack's vision ended when he heard the thump as Chief's large body tumbled across his legs. He didn't know if Chief was dead or alive as he pulled him from the sweat lodge. Chief didn't respond when Jack dumped the bucket of water on his head. Not knowing what else to do, Jack dragged him into the Magic Fountain and submerged his head beneath the little artesian waterfall.

Jack could feel no pulse when he put his finger on Chief's neck. He came to and at first didn't know where he was. Jack helped him out of the pool, concerned as the big man sat in the sand, contorting his jaws to pop his ears. He was about to try mouth-to-mouth when Chief's dark eyes popped open.

"I think I died in there," Chief finally said.

"Wherever you went, they didn't want you," Jack said.

The rain had ceased, a golden moon popping in and out of the cottony clouds. Chief finally looked at Jack as if seeing him for the first time.

"I failed," Chief finally said. "I did everything like we were supposed to, and nothing happened."

Jack was grinning when he said, "Maybe not to you. It worked for me, and I can't stop thinking about it."

Chapter 7

hief's demeanor changed in an instant. He was almost smiling after ducking his head beneath the Magic Fountain and then popping up for air. Almost. The rain had returned, falling harder as he climbed out of the pool of water.

"Let's go to the teepee and get dry. Then you can tell me about your vision," he said.

The trail had become slippery as Jack followed Chief down the hill. The teepee was large and comfortable, the fire pit providing immediate warmth as they entered. Chief tossed jack a towel. Once they were dry and dressed, Chief began brewing a pot of coffee on the open fire.

The Indian rugs covering the floor of the teepee were thick and comfortable as Jack and Chief sat around the fire, colorful blankets draping their shoulders.

Chief's long hair was still damp when he said, "I'm disappointed I didn't have a vision."

"You were trying too hard," Jack said. "When I finally gave up trying to get comfortable and realizing nothing about the experience was normal, a light I didn't know I had popped on in my brain."

"What did you see?" Chief asked.

"My mom and dad. They told me what to do about the rougarou."

"You're from Massachusetts," Chief said. "How would your mom and dad know about rougarous?"

"Don't know, but they did. The answer is so obvious I'm surprised we didn't think of it."

"Then tell me," Chief said.

"Dogs," Jack said.

"What about them?"

"The rougarou is scared of dogs. That's why it ran away when Coco chased him. Not because of your shotgun."

"No way," Chief said.

"Coco and Oscar are too small to hurt the rougarou though they sure scared him."

"We don't have any big dogs," Chief said.

"There's an animal shelter in Chalmette," Jack said. "I'll bet they have plenty of big dogs, most of them probably there for a while because people intent on adopting tend to choose small breeds. Tomorrow, we'll head over there and rescue some."

"Where are we going to keep them?" Chief asked.

"You keep some of them at your place. I'll keep the rest at mine," Jack said.

"I don't have a pen big enough."

"That's the beauty of it. We won't keep the dogs in pens. They'll have the run of the island."

"We can't have dogs terrorizing the island," Chief said.

"There's no one here to terrorize," Jack said. "We'll provide them plenty of food to eat and shelter from the weather. They'll stick close to home. When the rougarou returns, the creature will get the surprise of his life."

"What if they're mean?" Chief asked.

53

"Dogs are only mean if their owners teach them that way," Jack said. "Trust me. My plan will work."

"If the answer came to you in a vision, then it has to be right," Chief said.

Jack poked his head through the flap of the teepee.

"It's what I think," he said. "It has stopped raining. I'm going home. Come by tomorrow, and we'll visit the animal shelter in Chalmette."

Jack was waiting at the front door of his little house when Chief arrived the following morning. The way he was smiling and bouncing around, Chief worried something was wrong with him.

"Why are you so happy?" he asked.

"I haven't felt this good in years," Jack said. "Maybe there's something to that sweat lodge of yours."

"It'll suck the toxins out of you," Chief said. "I'm so dehydrated I've been drinking water all morning."

"Maybe you need a spot of rum."

"Maybe so," Chief said.

"Come in. I'll get you a mug."

When Chief walked in the door, Coco jumped out of Oscar's doggie bed. His tail was wagging when the big man lifted him off the floor and let him lick his face.

"Miss me?" he said.

From Coco's excitement, he didn't have to ask.

"Hungry?" Jack asked.

"Starved," Chief said.

"How about an avocado, cream cheese, and tomato omelet?"

Jack handed him a steaming mug and pointed to the plank table.

"Sounds wonderful," Chief said.

"I added coffee to the rum," Jack said. "Hope you don't mind."

"Just what I needed. How's Oscar?"

"Doing better. Got out of his bed this morning, drank some water, and ate his dog food. After a quick trip to the backyard, he crawled back in bed."

"That's how I felt this morning," Chief said.

Jack put the omelet on the plank table in front of Chief.

"Don't know what's wrong with you. I haven't felt this good in twenty years. I'm looking forward to doing the sweat lodge again, only this time I'm controlling the heat."

"The experience brought back old memories, some of them not so pleasant," Chief said.

"You never told me what happened to your wife," Jack said.

Chief cracked a rare smile. "Emily and I had a beautiful daughter together. Roxie's the only thing we ever had in common. When Emily filed for divorce, I celebrated."

"Is she still alive?" Jack asked.

"Married a corporate lawyer. They live in the Garden District, belong to the country club, drive an Audi and spend more on entertaining and Sunday brunch than I make in a year."

"You sound jealous," Jack said.

"Emily's an heiress and didn't need to marry into wealth. We lived in a million-dollar house in the Garden District. I hated every minute of it."

"How long were you married?" Jack asked.

"Eighteen months."

"Damn!" Jack said. "I have toenails older than that. Do you regret the divorce?"

"The only thing I regret is not spending more time with Roxie while she was growing up. Emily

55

poisoned my daughter's opinion of me, and we've never been close."

"You told Odette you have granddaughters," Jack said.

"Jo, Meg, Amy, and Beth. Roxie named them after the sisters in *Little Women*."

"You see them much?" Jack asked.

"They were never allowed to visit me," Chief said. "They barely know I exist."

"Now that they're older, why don't you reach out to them?" Jack asked.

Chief shook his head. "It might burden them down."

"But they're Atakapas," Jack said. "Don't you think they'd like to know about their heritage?"

"I doubt they have a clue they have Indian blood," Chief said. "I'm not going to be the one to tell them. What about you? Have you ever been married?"

"We were talking about you," Jack said.

"And it's making me uncomfortable. Let's talk about you for a while."

"I get the message," Jack said. "Eat your omelet, and I'll shut my big fat mouth."

Coco wasn't happy about missing another trip in Jack's truck but was dutiful in taking care of his buddy Oscar. He and the bulldog were lying together in the doggie bed when Jack and Chief headed out the door.

Located in the chain of islands east of St. Bernard Parish, the road leading from Oyster Island was built and maintained by the few inhabitants who lived mostly in seclusion on the islands. The country road across the bridge was muddy from the rain, making traction difficult. There were no service stations along the route. If you had a flat or another mishap, you were on your own.

Jack's truck was full of gas and in no danger of running dry. Though traction was lacking, it reached the parish blacktop without getting stuck. They arrived at the animal shelter in Chalmette, a large one-story building that would have covered a football field. The sound of barking dogs greeted them as they walked through the front door.

Stormy weather had limited the number of people visiting the shelter, with no one waiting in line. An attractive gray-haired woman greeted them with a smile, dark eyes, and high cheekbones, strongly suggesting she was of American Indian heritage. Her turquoise earrings and squash blossom necklace helped seal the impression.

"How can I help you, gentlemen?" she asked.

"We'd like to look at your dogs," Jack said.

"Any particular breed you're looking for?" the woman asked.

Her smile grew larger when Jack said, "Big dogs, no particular breed."

The woman pointed. "The big dogs are through that door," she said. "There are workers who can assist you."

"Thanks," Jack said as he started up the concrete walkway.

The barking grew louder as they entered a large, open room filled with pens and cages. Workers feeding the dogs and taking care of the cages wore hearing protection. As the noise grew louder, Jack and Chief could hear why. It became quickly apparent that most big dogs were pit bulls or mixed breeds.

Jack grabbed the elbow of a young man who worked in the shelter and waited until he removed his sound-canceling headphones.

"How many dogs are we allowed to adopt?"

"How many do you want?"

"Four, maybe five," Jack said.

"I'll get Millie," the young man said. "She'll have to help you if you're getting more than one dog."

Millie, her arms tightly crossed and smile gone, joined them. "We have a difficult time finding homes for our large dogs though I'd be remiss not to ask why you need so many," she said.

"We live on Oyster Island east of here, and we have a problem," Jack said.

"What problem?" Millie asked.

"A rougarou is prowling the island," Jack said.

"Pardon me, a what?"

Jack glanced at Chief. "Will you explain why we need the dogs?"

Chief extended his hand and waited until Millie shook it.

"I'm Grogan La Tortue, an American Indian. My partner is Jack Wiesinski. Mr. Wiesinski and I have a government grant to train large shelter animals to become therapy and police dogs and teach them other beneficial services. The island is large, and the animals will be cared for and loved. After we train the first batch, we'll return for more."

Millie's frown began to disappear, and her arms uncrossed. "How do I know what you say is true?"

"We left the official papers on the island. We can just run up to New Orleans if that's a problem. They know us there."

"That won't be necessary," Millie said. "I'll help you pick out the dogs."

"We notice you have lots of pits," Jack said.

"There's a stigma associated with the breed because historically, bad people bred them for fighting and aggression. Despite their reputation,

58

they are gentle and make excellent pets," Millie said.

Most of the dogs in the cages they passed were active, barking and wagging their tails when Jack, Chief, and Millie stopped to look at them. They walked past one cage where a large black German Shepherd lay in a stupor and was unresponsive when they stood in front of the cage.

"What's the story on this dog?" Chief asked.

"We call him Old Joe. He's been here longer than any dog we have."

"Why is that?" Chief asked. "He's beautiful."

"He's black," Millie said. "People have a prejudice against large black dogs. He also has a reputation."

"Such as?" Chief asked.

"A refinery purchased Old Joe for use as a watchdog, chaining him until someone reported them for abuse. That's why he's here at the shelter."

"Breaks my heart," Chief said.

"A regular dog chain wasn't strong enough to hold him. The chain they used on him was heavy and not meant for dogs."

Chief whistled to him. "Hey, Joe."

The big dog didn't move. "Old Joe has become resigned to his fate," Millie said. "It breaks my heart, too."

They'd soon picked out six dogs, two pits, two Rottweiler's, and two large mixed breeds. Chief stopped when they passed Old Joe's cage.

"I want Old Joe," he said.

Jack shook his head. "I don't think it's a good idea."

Chief glanced at Jack, his stern gaze causing him to turn his eyes to the floor.

"He'll get my attention," Chief said.

"Let's go to my desk and fill out the paperwork," Millie said. "To what Indian tribe do you belong?" she asked.

"Atakapa," he said.

"Impossible," she said. "The tribe no longer exists."

"No one but me," he said. "Are you Indian?"

"Choctaw," she said.

Millie smiled and nodded when Chief said, "Good tribe."

It took almost an hour to complete the paperwork for the dogs.

"Since you are doing such wonderful service for the community, I'm waiving the fees. Do you have a way to transport all the dogs you rescued?"

"We'll take as many as we can now and come back for the rest," Chief said, "unless you have a truck large enough to deliver them." Jack and Millie watched as he pulled a tattered checkbook from his back pocket and wrote out a check for one thousand dollars. "Will this cover the expense?"

Millie smiled and made eye contact with Chief when she took the check. "I'll accompany the driver when he delivers them to your island. I'd love to inspect your facilities."

Jack wasn't smiling when Chief said, "Great, I look forward to seeing you again."

Millie buzzed the intercom. "Bring Old Joe to my office," she said. "He just got adopted."

Chapter 8

The young man who appeared at Millie's door with Old Joe on a leash wasn't alone. Every shelter employee was there, and they erupted into applause when he handed the leash to Chief. Millie joined in the applause when Chief put his arms around the big dog's neck and hugged him.

Realizing he was leaving the animal shelter forever, Old Joe strutted to Jack's pickup truck. Old Joe leaped into the passenger seat when Chief opened the front door. Chief shut the door and climbed into the backseat of the crew cab.

"Guess we know what the pecking order is around here," Jack said.

Chief gave Old Joe a head rub. "Enjoy it, big fellow. You deserve it." When Chief looked up, he saw Jack was staring at him. "What?" he said.

"That pack of lies spewing from your lips," Jack said. "I'll never trust another word you say as long as I live."

"Hey, I had to do something when you froze up and started whining about rougarous. If it hadn't been for me, we wouldn't have gotten our dogs."

"You think they'll get delivered when your

thousand-dollar check bounces?"

"It won't bounce," Chief said.

"Oh?" Jack said. "You planning to have me wait in the truck while you knock over a bank?"

"Don't need to," Chief said. "I brought this." Chief held up an unopened bottle of their Dominican rum. "It's time we found out what this hooch is worth."

"You mean we try to sell it at the same place we sold the doubloon?"

"Why not?" Chief said. "We aren't far from New Orleans. Let's go back to the camera shop on Canal Street and see what they'll give us for it."

Jack shook his head as he pulled out of the parking lot and headed up St. Bernard Highway toward New Orleans. Old Joe was looking through the window when Jack rolled it down for him.

"He won't jump out, will he?" Chief asked.

"You kidding? He loves this truck. We may have to use a pry bar to get him out when we reach Oyster Island."

Old Joe barked as if he understood what Jack was saying.

"Maybe," Chief said.

"What's the deal with the shelter lady?" Jack asked.

"What the hell do you mean?" Chief asked.

"Your flirting was so apparent I'm surprised she didn't slap you."

"She wasn't wearing a wedding ring, and she didn't protest," Chief said.

Jack shook his fist at a passing car that had barely missed crunching his truck's rear fender.

"Damn New Orleans' drivers!" He said.

"Watch your road rage," Chief said." "We don't need a ticket."

Jack shook off the near-miss and returned his attention to Chief and Millie.

"You stepped on it by asking her to visit the

island. Now, what are we going to do?" he asked.

"We'll have to build something to give her the impression I wasn't lying," Chief said.

"Wouldn't it have been so much simpler not to ask her to the island?"

"I like her," Chief said. "I want to see her again. You got a problem with that?"

"All right," Jack said. "I'll get off your back. At least for now."

"When we reach Canal Street, where do you plan to park?" Chief asked.

"I don't," Jack said. "Parking in New Orleans is too damn expensive, and we can't leave Joe alone in the truck."

"You plan to find a parking meter?"

"Either that or I'll let you drive around the block while I go in," Jack said.

"This was my idea. What's the matter with me going in?" Chief said.

"Because I'm the better negotiator."

"You kidding? You left a thousand dollars or more on the table when you sold our doubloon."

"I know rum better than I know gold," Jack said. "I'll get us the best possible price."

Jack smiled when Chief asked, "Do I have your Louisiana guarantee?"

Jack didn't bother answering as he pulled to a stop in front of the same Canal Street electronics shop where they had sold the doubloon. Chief climbed behind the wheel when Jack exited.

"Unless I see the cops, I'll wait here," Chief said. "Otherwise, I'll drive around the block and pick you up."

The same salesman who had bought their gold smiled when he saw Jack enter the shop.

"Back with more gold?" he asked.

"Something sweeter than metal," Jack said.

"What you got?" the swarthy man asked.

"A bottle of rum," Jack said.

"We don't buy rum. There's a liquor store down the street."

"What I have can't be bought at any liquor store," Jack said. "If you're not interested in looking, I'll go elsewhere."

The salesman uncrossed his arms. "Show me what you got," he said.

"You like rum?" Jack asked.

"I don't drink," the man said.

Jack opened his paper bag and sat the bottle of rum on the counter.

"151 proof rum, Whistling Winds Distillery, Dominican Republic, bottled 1929."

"So?"

"By the way, we've never met. I'm Jack."

Jack extended his hand, and the man shook it. "Robert. Like I said. So?"

"Whistling Winds, the famous Dominican Republic distillery, is defunct. They haven't produced rum in over seventy years. Rum runners brought in this bottle during Prohibition. The bottle, the label, and the rum are in mint condition."

"You think it's a fake?" Robert asked.

"Chief and I found a case of it in the surf." Jack pulled the silver flask from his back pocket. "Try it, and then tell me it's not the best rum you've ever tasted."

Robert took a drink, swirled the rum in his mouth, and then drank more.

"It's good," he admitted.

"I thought you didn't drink," Jack said.

"I don't. This is business."

Robert smiled when Jack said, "I can tell by the way you look it's the best rum you've ever tasted."

"How do I know it's the same rum as in the bottle you have?"

"You don't unless you open it," Jack said. "Doing that would destroy the value of the intact bottle."

"How much do you want for it?" Robert asked.

"A collectible like this could bring ten grand or more at auction."

"I'm not giving you ten grand," Robert said. "How much will you take for it?"

"Five thousand dollars and not a penny less," Jack said.

"Twenty-five hundred dollars," Robert said.

"You're going to cut a fat hog even at five thousand dollars," Jack said. "And there's more where this came from."

"How many bottles do you have?" Robert asked.

"A crate load minus two bottles."

"Tell me again where you found the crate?" Robert asked.

Jack shook his head. "I didn't say."

"Throw in the flask, and I'll give you four thousand dollars for the bottle, but . . ."

"But what?" Jack asked.

"I want all the bottles in the crate."

"Four thousand each?" Jack asked.

Robert nodded and then disappeared into the back. He returned with a roll of hundreds. After removing the rubber band from the roll, he counted forty bills. Jack handed him the flask, the bottle of Dominican rum and started for the door.

"Wait," Robert said. "You got a card or some way for me to contact you?"

"I'm Jack Wiesinski, the lighthouse keeper on Oyster Island."

"Where's Oyster Island?" Robert asked.

"On the Gulf, not far from here. You can check it out on the Internet."

"I'll be in touch," Robert said as Jack hurried out the door.

Chief was pulling up to the curb as Jack left the camera shop. He opened the door to get out, but Jack crawled into the backseat.

"You drive and get the hell out of here before Robert changes his mind."

"Who the hell is Robert?"

"The man who bought the doubloon from us."

"How much did you get?" Chief asked.

"Four thousand bucks. About a cool grand more than I expected to get," Jack said.

"You kidding me?" Chief said. "That's wonderful."

"I thought so," Jack said.

"Damn!" Chief said. "If he gave you four, it's probably worth at least eight."

"I was thinking the same thing," Jack said. "The deal went way too slick."

"No problem," Chief said. "Even if you left money on the table, we still have the rest of the bottles in the crate."

"Maybe not. I had to give our friend Robert first right of refusal at the same price on the rest of the crate."

"How's he ever going to find us?" When Jack didn't answer, Chief said, "You didn't tell him where we live, did you?"

"Doesn't matter," Jack said. "We'll never see him again."

"Shit!" Chief said. "Now, we're going to have to find a place to hide the rum."

"Robert's an honest man," Jack said.

"You think?" Chief said. "Let me tell you again about the bridge in Brooklyn I'm selling."

"You're no better," Jack said. "You invited the shelter lady to visit the island."

"My guess is Millie doesn't pack heat," Chief said.

Chief pulled over. "You drive. I need a drink from the flask."

"Sorry," Jack said. "Robert took it as part of the deal."

"There's plenty more where that came from," Chief said. "We can break open another bottle and celebrate when we get back to the island. Right now, stop at my bank in Chalmette so I can cover my check. Don't want to upset Miss Millie."

It was still daylight when they crossed the bridge back to Oyster Island. Clear weather had held all day, a golden glow lighting the horizon over the Gulf of Mexico. Chief opened the front door of the house for Old Joe.

"This island is your new home, big boy," he said. "What do you think?"

It took a minute before the big dog decided to jump out of the truck. When he did, he ran in a circle. Then he took off in a run toward the beach. When he got there, he ran through the surf, frolicking like a puppy. Finally, he returned to where Chief and Jack were waiting. When he licked Chief's hand, the big man knelt and hugged his neck.

"You hungry?" Jack asked.

"You kidding? We haven't eaten since this morning."

"Good," Jack said. "I left a pot of chowder simmering on the stove. You break open a bottle of rum. I'll get the chowder."

Coco barked when Old Joe came in the door to Jack's house.

"You have a new big brother," Chief said. "Bet that old rougarou will think twice before he comes around again."

Oscar was doing better, his butt and little tail wagging as the two dogs quickly made friends. After Coco and Old Joe had sniffed each other, the chihuahua's tail wagged, and he licked Old

Joe's nose. Sensing Oscar was injured, the beautiful animal went to his doggie bed.

"Give them some food and check their water," Jack said. "They haven't eaten all day either." Coco was such a frequent visitor he had his food bowl. Jack handed Chief a big bowl. "Old Joe can use this until we get him one of his own."

Before long, Jack, Chief, and the dogs were eating and drinking.

"I never ate chowder until I met you," Chief said. "I'll have to admit I love it."

"Not much of a compliment coming from you," Jack said.

"What's that supposed to mean?" Chief asked.

"Just that you'd eat the rear end of a horse."

"One dish you've never cooked," Chief said.

"And never will," Jack said. "Nothing but the best for me and my newly-rich buddy."

It was dark, the bottle of rum half gone, when a sound outside the house got their attention. It was a police siren. Jack and Chief peered out the window at the front of the house, where a police cruiser had pulled up beside Jack's truck. The light on top of the police car flashed as the siren continued to blare. A bullhorn protruded from the driver's window. The person's voice was loud and echoed across the island.

"Come out with your hands up," the voice said. "You're under arrest."

Chapter 9

Jack and Chief were reaching for the sky as they walked out the door, the intense glare of a spotlight blinding them. The man with the bullhorn continued barking orders.

"Up against the wall and spread 'em."

Chief and Jack leaned against the house and spread their legs. The door of the police cruiser opened, and someone got out.

"What are we being arrested for, officer?" Jack asked.

"No questions," the man said. "Gained a few pounds, haven't you?"

The voice sounded familiar to Chief. The officer was laughing when Chief wheeled around to face him.

"Jean Pierre Saucier. You asshole! You scared me half to death."

Jack looked relieved as he turned to face the police officer wearing a large Stetson and a big pistol in a holster around his waist.

Jean Pierre's grin was infectious. "Sorry, Chief, I couldn't resist giving you a little hell."

"You'd be laughing out the side of your mouth if I'd had a heart attack," Chief said.

"Come on, now," Jean Pierre said.

"Jack Wiesinski, this is Jean Pierre Saucier. He's a St. Bernard Parish deputy sheriff and a real prick sometimes."

Jack and Jean Pierre shook hands. "You put the fear of God in me," Jack said.

Jean Pierre was still grinning when he said, "Sorry about that,"

Jean Pierre Saucier had dark hair and eyes and the good looks of a French movie star. With the spotlight extinguished, Jack could see St. Bernard Parish stenciled on the police car, Jean Pierre's gold badge, Stetson, and khaki uniform marking him as a police officer.

The heads of all three dogs were sticking out the door when a beautiful chocolate lab jumped from the front seat of the cruiser. Coco's tail wagged as he hurried out of the house to rub noses with the dog.

"I'm off duty, so I brought Lucky with me," Jean Pierre said. "I'm here for a reason."

"Such as?" Chief asked.

"The department had a call from Millie Folsom, the administrator of the Chalmette Animal Shelter. She said you boys came in today and adopted a bunch of big dogs. She was worried you wanted them for dogfighting. She asked us to check you out."

J.P.'s words disturbed Chief. "She didn't say that, did she?"

"You and I know you're not a dogfighter. Millie didn't. After you drove away, the thought crossed her mind. It bothered her so much she called us to check it out."

"I hope you set her straight," Chief said.

"I told her I'd never known you to be involved in anything illegal. When I asked her why you wanted the dogs, she said, you have a grant to train police and therapy animals."

"I can explain," Chief said. "Millie isn't married, is she?"

"Why?" J.P. asked. "You got the hots for her?"

"You kidding?" Jack said. "He hasn't stopped drooling since the first time he saw her."

"I'm just interested because she's Indian. Maybe we have more things in common."

"You're out of luck there, Chief. I don't believe she's looking for a husband," J.P. said.

"And I'm not looking for a wife," Chief said. "Though it would be nice to have someone to take to dinner or go to the movies with."

"What was the last movie you saw?" Jack asked.

"I can't remember," Chief said.

"Maybe because you've never been to the movies," Jack said.

Chief crossed his arms and said, "Whatever."

"You'll be seeing her again tomorrow," J.P. said. "After I convinced her you aren't hosting dogfights on the island, she lined up a transport truck. She's coming along to inspect the facilities."

"Just peachy," Jack said.

"Why didn't you just tell her the truth?" J.P. asked.

"When Millie put Jack on the spot," Chief said. "He all but pissed his pants. I had to think of something before she kicked us out of the shelter."

"Chief made up the story on the fly because Miss Folsom didn't believe the real reason we need the dogs," Jack said.

"Which is?" J.P. asked.

Jack didn't answer the question, asking one of his own instead.

"Are you a drinking man?"

"Does an alligator shit in the bayou?" J.P. said. "I'm off duty, and tomorrow's my day off."

71

J.P.'s infectious smile grew larger when Jack added, "I have a pot of chowder simmering on the stove."

"This is sounding better all the time," J.P. said.

Jack started for the door. "Then follow me. Chief and I have an open bottle of the finest rum you'll ever taste. We'll tell you about the dogs once you eat and have some rum."

"Sounds like a bribe, and I love it," J.P. said.

J.P. was soon sitting at the plank table digging into a bowl of steaming chowder.

"How's it taste?" Jack asked.

"Best chowder I've ever eaten, and you were right about this rum. It's so smooth it would be a desecration to mix it with anything. What liquor store did you buy it at?"

"Didn't come from a liquor store," Jack said. "Chief found it under the bridge during low tide. We have a crate of it, less three bottles."

"Dominican rum," Chief said. "We think the crate came from a rum runner the feds sank during Prohibition."

"You mean it tastes this good after being in the water for. . ."

Jack finished J.P.'s sentence. "More than ninety years," he said.

"And the bottles are in one piece?" J.P. asked.

"There was a waterproof covering. It did its job."

Chief showed him one of the unopened bottles. "These babies must be worth good money," J.P. said.

"We sold a bottle yesterday for four grand," Jack said.

"Who gave you that much?" J.P. asked.

"The owner of one of those camera shops on Canal," Jack said.

J.P. whistled. "Hate to tell you. If he gave you four, it's worth at least ten."

Jack gave him a dirty look when Chief said, "He told the man he'd sell all the bottles for four grand each."

"Did you sign a contract?" J.P. asked.

"No contract," Chief said. "Who knows who he's connected with?"

"How are they going to find you?" J.P. asked.

"Mr. Big Mouth gave him directions," Chief said.

Jack felt better when J.P. said, "There's no indication they have any mob connections. You'll be fine. Is that the reason you thought you needed a bunch of big dogs?"

"Nope, we had a visit from a rougarou."

"You kidding? It's been a few years since I've heard of a rougarou sighting."

"You believe rougarous are real?" Jack asked.

"I've seen them with my own eyes," J.P. said.

"Our visit was more than a sighting," Chief said. "When he ripped a hole in my teepee, I let him have it at point-blank range with both barrels of my shotgun. The creature returned the next night. Oscar and Coco chased it away."

"I had to stitch the lacerations on Oscar's back," Jack said.

"Why do you think the rougarou is scared of dogs?" J.P. asked.

"We sat in the sweat lodge and consulted our ancestors. According to Jack's mom and dad, the rougarou is afraid of dogs."

J.P. gave them both a look. "Jack's mom and dad? What did your ancestors say?"

"Don't ask," Chief said.

"When I tried to explain to the shelter lady why we needed the big dogs, she looked at me as if I were crazy," Jack said. "Chief concocted the story about the grant and training program on the spot."

A clap of thunder shook the house. J.P. ignored it. "Such a grant isn't that farfetched," he said.

Jack was suddenly interested in what J.P. had to say. Their bottle of rum was almost empty.

"Chief, I think we should break open another bottle," he said.

"I'm all for it," Chief said.

The dogs were asleep, Coco and Oscar in Oscar's doggie bed, Lucky and Old Joe on a colorful rug Jack had purchased in some foreign port of call. J.P. and Jack had silly grins on their faces as Chief opened another bottle and filled their mugs with expensive rum.

"Now," Jack said. "Tell us about this grant."

"There's a shortage of well-trained police dogs all over the country," J.P. said. "It costs about twelve grand to train a dog. Police departments gobble them up for upwards of twenty-five grand."

"Damn!" Jack said. "I would never have thought."

"Service dogs sell for fifteen to thirty grand. Dogs trained to perform specific services go for as high as fifty thousand dollars," J.P. said.

"That's crazy!" Chief said.

"Crazy but true," J.P. said. "The Louisiana Law Enforcement Association gives grants of up to a hundred grand to qualified training facilities."

"Jack and I don't know anything about training dogs," Chief said.

"I do," J.P. said. "I've been to three seminars in the past eighteen months. I don't have a place big enough to pull it off. A place on Oyster Island would be perfect."

"When are you going to have time to train dogs?" Chief asked.

"I have a month of accrued vacation coming," J.P. said. "If I can spend some time on the island, we could apply for the grant and get started."

"There are plenty of rooms in the Majestic," Jack said. "Problem is, Mr. Castellano is hell-bent on renovating the old casino and bringing tourists back to the island."

"Frankie Castellano?" J.P. said.

"New Orleans' biggest mob boss," Jack said. "He owns the whole island except for what Chief does."

"How much do you own?" J.P. asked.

"According to my grandpa, the entire island," Chief said.

"Can you prove it?" J.P. asked.

"I've never checked into it because I was afraid I'd be proven wrong and kicked off the island," Chief said.

"Wouldn't want that to happen," J.P. said.

"Mr. Castellano is only interested in the old casino, the beach, and Oyster Bay," Jack said.

"You know that for a fact?" J.P. asked.

"Even if he isn't, the lighthouse doesn't belong to Castellano," Chief said. "It's Louisiana property."

"Ten or more acres worth," Jack said.

"The state would never let us use it," J.P. said.

"I'm the lighthouse keeper," Jack said. "I can do anything I want with it. Let's get that grant and start training dogs."

"I have a travel trailer and don't need a room at the Majestic. What about Castellano?" J.P. said.

"He knows I have two jobs," Jack said. "Castellano may be a mobster, but what he does on this island is all legal. He's not a bad dude, and I enjoy working for him."

"How are we going to split this?" J.P. asked.

75

Jack gave Chief a dirty look when he said, "You take sixty percent. Jack and I get twenty percent each."

"There'll be plenty of work to do for all of us. I'm happy with an even three-way split," J.P. said. "A third each."

"Why not?" Jack said. "If we keep drinking our high-dollar rum, we're going to need something else to fall back on."

Another clap of thunder shook the house. Jack opened the front door and gazed out at rain beginning to fall in torrents.

"Hope you rolled up your windows," Chief said.

"You aren't going to make it back to Chalmette tonight," Jack said. "I'll give you a pillow and some sheets, and you can sleep on the couch. I have a pallet for Chief, and he doesn't mind sleeping on it."

"Thanks for your hospitality, Jack," J.P. said. "I'm not ready to go to bed as long as we have rum left."

"Partners, then?" Jack asked.

The three men shook on it.

The wind whipped the curtains, rain blowing through the open windows when Jack slammed them shut. The noise and lightning didn't wake the dogs.

"The mark of a potential police dog," J.P. said. "They aren't afraid of loud noises."

"My little Coco is way too small," Chief said.

"What's the big German Shepherd's name?" J.P. said. "He looks like a candidate."

"Old Joe," Chief said. "We got him at the animal shelter."

"Let me try something," J.P. said.

Old Joe's eyes were instantly open when J.P. said, "Joe, come here." Joe went to J.P. and waited for another command, Jack and Chief observing

76

as he sat, shook hands, laid down, and stood, all on command. J.P.'s holster was hanging from the back of a chair. "Joe, fetch my pistol."

Joe went straight to the holster and brought it to J.P.

"My God!" Jack said.

"Building, blind search," J.P. said. They watched as the big dog began searching the interior of Jack's house. Joe stopped dead when J.P. said, "Stand still. Good boy, come and sit."

Joe stopped his search and sat in front of J.P.

"He understands every word you say," Jack said.

"You kidding?" J.P. said. "Old Joe here is a fully-trained police dog who knows every trick in the book. I can't imagine what he's experienced or how he ended up at the Chalmette Animal Shelter."

"He is one smart animal," Jack said.

"A local refinery was using him as a guard dog," Chief said. "They kept him heavily chained."

"That's criminal," J.P. said. "I'm glad Chief ended up with him."

Old Joe barked when Chief said, "Doesn't matter how he got there. He's mine now, and he's never going back."

Chapter 10

Jack liked to wake up early and rarely slept past six in the morning. He found he was the last to get out of bed when he awoke. Chief, Coco, and Old Joe were gone, Oscar and Lucky nowhere around. J.P. was sitting at the plank table, drinking coffee and working on his laptop. His smile appeared when he saw Jack.

"Thought you were going to sleep all day," he said.

"Where's Chief?"

"Went home already. Wanted to clean up and change clothes before Millie gets here. I'm working on our online grant application."

"You boys are making me feel bad," Jack said.

"Don't do that," J.P. said. "I enjoyed the hell out of myself last night. Thanks for the hospitality."

"You're welcome," Jack said. "Hungry? I'll fix breakfast."

"Love it," J.P. said. "There was coffee in the pot on the stove. I got a cup and warmed it in the microwave." Hope you don't mind.

"Glad you did," Jack said. "I'll make us a fresh pot."

The aroma of scrambled eggs and bacon filled

the kitchen. Hearing Jack, Oscar and Lucky came running through the doggie door. Jack fed them and made sure they had plenty of water. Seeing J.P.'s expression was intense as he worked the computer keyboard, Jack went about his kitchen business and didn't further interrupt him.

"Done," J.P. said after hitting the send button. "Now, all we have to do is to wait. Your bacon and eggs smell mighty good," he said.

Jack poured J.P. a cup of fresh coffee. "When I got out of the Navy, I joined the Merchant Marines. One of my many jobs was ship cook.

"You're good enough to cook for any restaurant in New Orleans," J.P. said.

"Thanks," Jack said. "I know I'm a good cook, though compliments never grow old."

"How did you end up on Oyster Island?"

"After retiring from the Merchant Marines, I applied for the job of lighthouse keeper and got it," Jack said. "Turns out there weren't many applicants because the island is so secluded."

"You seem to like it," J.P. said.

"I'm a hermit by nature. The solitude suits me just fine. Chief and the dogs are all the company I need."

"What will you do when Castellano reopens the Majestic?" J.P. asked.

"I haven't thought that far in advance. The hardest part of this gig is staying in one port," Jack said. "Maybe I'll move on."

"How did you meet Frankie Castellano?" J.P. asked.

"The former lighthouse keeper retired and moved to California. He was also the caretaker for the Majestic and the property that goes with it. It was natural Mr. Castellano would offer me the job.

"Sounds like you do pretty well for yourself," J.P. said.

79

"With my pension, lighthouse keeper stipend, and salary from Mr. Castellano, I manage to keep food on the table."

"Not just food; great food!" J.P. said.

The door hinges creaked, Chief and his dogs interrupting J.P. and Jack's conversation. Both Jack and J.P. did a double-take when they saw his fresh brown chinos and light blue cotton shirt matching the headband around his combed hair.

"Wowee!" J.P. said. "Who are you trying to impress? Wait, don't tell me."

Chief ignored their grins. "Thought I smelled breakfast. Am I too late?"

Jack returned to his stove. "Never too late around here," Jack said. "Sit down and rest your bones."

"Thought you'd never ask," Chief said.

Jack soon put a plate of bacon and eggs on the plank table in front of him.

"J.P. and I were talking about Miss Millie's impending visit," he said.

"Oh?" Chief said. "What about it?"

"Where do you intend to keep the dogs when Millie gets here with them?" J.P. asked.

"I'm keeping some with me. Chief will take care of the others," Jack said.

"Millie's going to frown on that," J.P. said.

"Why?" Jack asked.

"People with too many pets tend to ignore some of them and not give them the care they need," J.P. said.

"Trust me when I tell you, Chief and I will treat them like kings," Jack said.

"I know you will. The perception is your backyard isn't very big. There are no doghouses or shelters for the animals to get out of the weather."

"Chief and I intend to build a shelter for them."

J.P.'s smile had disappeared. "That's not the way Miss Millie is going to look at it."

"What do you mean?" Jack asked.

"Most people adopting already have the facilities for their new pet," J.P. said.

"What can I do?" Jack asked.

"Not we, us," J.P. said. "We're partners now and all in on this together."

"Suggestions?" Jack asked.

"Smoke and mirrors," J.P. said. "When Miss Millie gets here, let me do the talking."

A truck from the animal shelter arrived just before noon, the driver an older man named Red. Red's hair and handlebar mustache had gone gray. His stoic expression never changed as they put the four new dogs in Jack's backyard.

"What are you doing here, Officer Saucier?" Millie asked.

"As I told you on the phone yesterday, I've known Chief for years. Since I hadn't seen him in a while, I decided to drive down and find out in person what he's up to."

"Anyone hungry?" Jack asked. "I have lunch ready."

Miss Millie seemed distressed when Red said, "I have another load to deliver and need to get back to town."

"I was hoping to spend some time talking with Messieurs Wiesinski and La Tortue about their plans."

"I'm going back to town later," J.P. said. "You're welcome to ride with me. "Jack is a great cook, Red. You don't know what you're missing."

"Wish I could, but we're shorthanded."

"I made chicken salad for lunch," Jack said. "I have a loaf of day-old French. I'll make you a sandwich to go."

Red nodded without smiling. "Thanks," he said. "I appreciate it."

81

Red disappeared across the bridge, enjoying chicken salad on French. Millie gazed around Jack's little house as he seated her at the plank table.

"Your house is so . . ."

"Shipshape?" Jack said, finishing her sentence. "After years in the Merchant Marines, it's inbred in me."

"Thank you, Officer Saucier. Mr. Redd didn't tell me he couldn't stay for an hour or so. Guess I should have asked."

"I'm off duty. It's just J.P. This is Jack and Grogan. Mind if we all use first names?"

"Of course. I'm Millie."

"Unless you want something stronger, I have ice tea," Jack said.

"Tea is fine, and the chicken salad looks lovely," Millie said. In deference to Millie, Jack, J.P., and Chief were also drinking tea. "Your chicken salad tastes as good as it looks," Millie added.

"Glad you like it," Jack said.

Millie had only half-finished her salad. She wasn't smiling.

"I hate to be blunt," she said. "You don't seem to have kennels or any other facilities here. How do you intend to shelter the dogs? Where are you going to train them?"

Jack started to speak when he noticed the slight shake of J.P.'s head.

Millie turned her gaze to J.P. when he said, "Let me answer for you."

"Please do," she said.

"I've attended three dog training seminars in the past eighteen months and was immediately interested when I heard Jack and Chief were planning to open a facility. Like you, I was disappointed when I arrived and learned they'd gotten the cart ahead of the horse by adopting the dogs.

"Mr. Red couldn't have gone far," Millie said. "Perhaps I should call and have him return to pick up the dogs."

"Please don't do that," J.P. said. "When I set Jack and Chief straight, they asked me to assist in the project."

Millie had pushed away from the table, her arms crossed.

"That doesn't answer my question about the facilities," she said.

Though Jack and Chief's butts had puckered, J.P. never stopped smiling.

"I've been planning to open a training facility for more than two years. The opportunity to locate the facility on the island was more than I could resist."

"Do you have time to work two jobs?" Millie asked.

"I have a month's vacation coming up. If everything works out, I'll retire from the force."

"It seems to be lots of happenstance here," Millie said.

"Or kismet," J.P. said. "I have detailed plans in my car. If you'll excuse me while I get them, I'll discuss them with you."

Jack cleared the table while they waited for J.P. to return. That he'd spent many hours contemplating the opening of a dog training facility was apparent as he rolled out his plans on the table. Millie, Jack, and Chief watched for almost an hour, their attention rapt as J.P. explained his plan.

"We have more than ten acres with which to work. With the grant from the Louisiana Law Enforcement Association, we'll be well funded and able to begin construction this coming weekend."

Millie seemed pleased with the plans but had more questions.

"Is your experience training dogs limited to the seminars you attended?"

"No, ma'am," J.P. said. "Would you like a demonstration?"

"Of course," Millie said.

J.P. had a unique whistle attached to a chain around his neck. They heard nothing when he blew it. Old Joe did and came running through the doggie door. J.P. put him through his paces. Millie was smiling when J.P. ended the demonstration, and Old Joe lay on the floor beside Chief.

"You didn't teach him all that in one day," Millie said.

"No, ma'am, I didn't. Like humans, not all dogs have the same level of intelligence or innate ability to learn. Old Joe is one of the smartest dogs I've ever seen, and I'm sure he understands every word we say. Part of being a competent trainer is the ability to recognize talent."

"I am impressed," Millie said. "The dogs still deserve a comfortable and safe place to stay until you complete the facilities."

Jack held up his hand before J.P. could respond.

"We're going to double the size of my backyard tomorrow," he said. "We have all the materials needed to do it in my work shed. The dogs will stay inside with me until they have a proper kennel."

Millie's dour expression morphed into a smile. "Okay, you've sold me," she said. She glanced at Chief for the first time. When they made eye contact, she asked, "Grogan, do you live here with Jack?"

"My teepee is on the hill toward the backside of the island," Chief said.

"You live in a teepee?"

She smiled when he deadpanned, "Doesn't

everyone?"

"I'd love to see it," she said.

"If you can talk Jack into firing up the ATV, I'll give you and J.P. the scenic tour," Chief said.

They were soon on their way across the island in the ATV.

"It's beautiful," Millie said, "And so hilly for Louisiana."

"This island sits atop a salt dome," Chief said. "An oil company geologist told me it had lifted the island. It's probably the reason it has weathered so many tropical storms so well."

"What is that large building?" Millie asked.

"The Majestic. During Prohibition, it was the biggest casino north of Havana."

"How big is it?" Millie asked.

"Three stories of casino, restaurants, and hotel rooms. It sits over water and is accessible only by the plank walkway. Seventy years ago, yachts and motor craft filled the bay surrounding the Majestic."

"So gorgeous," Millie said.

"With a little maintenance and a fresh coat of paint, it would be the beautiful lady it once was," Chief said.

"The island is perfect for the dogs," J.P. said. "They'll have plenty of room to run when I exercise them on the beach."

Jack drove past the Majestic to Chief's property.

When Jack parked at the foot of the hill, Chief said, "We'll have to walk from here."

Millie was beaming when they reached the top of the hill and the clearing with Chief's teepee. She turned to gaze out at the island.

"What a great view. It's like a picture postcard with the Majestic and the crashing waves of the Gulf of Mexico in the distance," she said.

The chickens had heard them come up the

hill. Mable, Chief's hen, came running and jumped into his arms. He stroked her head and carried her across the clearing to the well.

"Your teepee is so large," Millie said. "It's like how I would imagine an American Indian encampment a century ago."

"Little has changed since I grew up here with my grandparents."

"I just love it," Millie said.

Chief drew a bucket of water from the well and handed Millie the ladle.

"Have a drink," he said. "Grandma always said the water is magic and will cure what ails you."

Millie took a sip and then handed the ladle to J.P.

"I've never tasted better water in my life," she said. "It's truly magical."

"There's a rock-bottom pool at the top of that path," Chief said. "I call it the Magic Fountain because it's a spiritual experience every time you take a dip in it."

Chapter 11

When Jack parked the ATV in front of the house, Millie looked at her watch.

"Gentlemen," she said. "It's been lovely. I really must get back to Chalmette. Are you ready, J.P.?"

"Yes, ma'am," he said. "I'll get Lucky."

When J.P. disappeared into the house, Millie said, "Your chicken salad was the best I've ever tasted."

"Why thank you," Jack said.

Millie turned her attention to Chief. "Do you get to Chalmette much, Grogan?" she asked.

"Not as often as I'd like," he said.

"I'd love to take you to dinner and discuss our Indian heritage," she said.

"It would be my pleasure," he said.

"Tomorrow is Friday, the beginning of the weekend. How about tomorrow?"

Jack nodded when Chief glanced at him. "What time?" he asked.

"There's a restaurant outside of town on the banks of Lost Lagoon. The view at sunset is wonderful. About seven?"

"Jack will have to bring me. I don't have a car," Chief said.

87

"Can you drop Grogan off at the animal shelter about seven?" she asked Jack.

"You bet," he said.

"Grogan," Millie said. "This will be my treat."

J.P., Lucky in the backseat, pulled around the front in his police cruiser. After escorting Millie into the passenger seat, he winked at Jack and Chief.

Cupping his mouth so that Millie wouldn't see, he said, "I think we hit a home run. I'll be back in a couple of days to help expand your backyard."

J.P. opened the car's front door to get in, thought better of it, and returned to Jack and Chief.

"Forget something?" Chief asked.

J.P. handed him the dog whistle. "Keep it," he said. "It may come in handy, and I have another in Chalmette."

Jack was grinning as the police car drove across the bridge.

"What?" Chief said.

"From the sound of things, you're the one who's getting lucky," Jack said.

"What the hell are you talking about?" Chief said.

"You dog. Miss Millie's taking you to a romantic sunset dinner, picking up the tab, and knows you don't have a car."

"So?" Chief said.

"You don't have a place to spend the night. Sounds to me like she plans to take you home with her."

"What about you?" Chief asked.

"I'm not waiting alone in Chalmette," Jack said. "You'll probably still be holding hands at midnight."

"What if it doesn't work out the way you say?" Chief said.

"I don't know what to tell you, Chief," Jack said. "You're a grown man. Since Millie made a point of not asking me to go with you, you're going to have to figure it out for yourself."

"Got any rum left?" Chief asked as Jack started for the door to his house.

"Come in," Jack said. "We may as well crack open a new bottle and celebrate."

The sky over the Gulf was beginning to grow dark again, rain falling in the front yard. The dogs came through the doggie door, all seven of them.

"I'm not so sure about this dog training facility," Jack said.

"Then what is it we're celebrating?"

"Possibilities."

"Of what?" Chief asked.

"There's probably a sunken rum runner, its hold filled with crates of rum, somewhere out there between the beach and the barrier islands. We need to find it."

"You have a plan?" Chief asked.

"The currents haven't changed much since the rum runner sank," Jack said. "They probably moved the hulk along the bottom until a natural barrier stopped it. What we need are the nautical charts of the area."

"You already have them," Chief said.

"No, I don't," Jack said.

"Want to bet?" Chief said. "There's an office in the lighthouse. Your predecessor, old man Thompson, showed me once. There are detailed charts and maps for Oyster Island, the bay, and the barrier islands. Let's check it out."

"Unless we want a mutiny on our hands, we better feed this hungry pack of dogs first," Jack said.

Coco was the only small dog. It didn't seem to matter as all the canines were on their best behavior.

89

"We're lucky," Chief said. "Old Joe is the alpha, the other dogs taking his lead."

"The rougarou's going to catch hell next time he shows up," Jack said.

"Let's hope so. Those dogs are going to eat us out of house and home," Chief said.

"Good thing they sell dog food in fifty-pound bags," Jack said. "We'll fill up the bed of the truck when we go into Chalmette Saturday."

The dogs were soon fed and asleep on the area rug, Chief glancing at Jack's galley.

"I got leftover chowder," he said. "Want me to heat it?"

Chief pulled up a chair at the plank table. "Thought you'd never ask. It's still raining too hard outside to go to the lighthouse. Maybe we should switch to cheap hooch instead of this four thousand dollar a bottle brand."

"It goes down so easy," Jack said. "Let's make this the last bottle we drink."

"Famous last words," Chief said.

They finished their chowder and sat at the plank table for nearly an hour, waiting for the rain to abate.

"Maybe we should just make a run for it," Chief finally said.

"You kidding? The wind's about to blow off the roof, the rain coming down sideways," Jack said. "Let's have another bowl of chowder."

Jack was putting away the dishes when Chief opened the front door and glanced out.

"It's still sprinkling. If we're going tonight, we better go now," he said.

A keychain rattled when Jack retrieved it from a nail in the wall. It took Jack a minute to unlock it. His big flashlight cut a broad swath through the darkness as they reached the door to the lighthouse.

"When was the last time you opened the door

to this place?" Chief asked.

"I have a switch in the house where I control the light. I haven't been inside the lighthouse since I took over."

Chief had to duck through the door. "Why is that?"

"This old structure gives me the creeps."

Chief was pulling cobwebs out of his hair. "I'll say. It needs a good cleaning."

"Have at it anytime the feeling moves you," Jack said.

"You're the one who gets paid to take care of it, not me."

"I wouldn't be coming in here now by myself," Jack said.

"Are you afraid of ghosts?"

"I don't relish meeting one in person if that's what you mean," Jack said. "Especially on a night like this."

"You think there's a ghost that haunts the lighthouse?"

"More than one, according to Zeke Thompson."

"He saw them?" Chief asked.

"Said he did," Jack said. "A man and a woman."

"Who were they?"

"Hell, I don't know. You believe in ghosts?"

"Damn right I do," Chief said.

"Then what the hell are we doing here? We can get the charts tomorrow."

Jack didn't wait for an answer, stepping back from the stairs and starting for the open front door of the lighthouse.

"Wait a minute. You're a Navy vet and scared of a ghost?" Chief asked. "You must have seen all sorts of scary shit out there on the ocean."

"Here's the flashlight," Jack said. "You go first."

The circular stairway made of wood steps and metal rails creaked when Chief started up. The stairs swayed due to the combined weight of the two men.

"The person who built this stairway didn't design it for a big man," he said.

"People weren't as big two hundred years ago as we are now," Jack said.

"This lighthouse is two hundred years old?"

"Or more," Jack said. "Where are the charts?"

"Second floor," Chief said.

Chief and Jack stepped off the stairs on the second floor. The space was cramped and claustrophobic, the sound of thunder echoing against the walls. Another sound riveted their attention: the unmistakable rattle of chains.

"What the hell was that?" Jack asked.

"I don't think we want to know," Chief said. "Let's find the charts and then get the hell out of here."

"Right behind you," Jack said.

An antique desk, a few old chairs, and a flat wooden file cabinet were all the furniture occupying the room. Chief shined the light on the file cabinet and pulled on the top drawer. It opened with a groan.

Cobwebs and dirt daubers' nests were everywhere, an inch of sand and bat guano covering the floor.

"I see now why you don't come in here very often."

"We should be wearing hats," Jack said.

Chief shined the light into the rafters and saw the reason for Jack's remark. Hundreds of bats were hanging from the old wooden beams. Wind and rain whistled through an open window revealing the way the bats came in and out."

"Damn!" Chief said. "It's not a fit night out for man nor bats. At least they had sense enough to stay home."

"Then grab the charts, and let's get the hell out of here. I may be bat shit crazy, but it stinks in here, and I don't cotton to being covered in guano."

"There are three drawers all filled with charts," Chief said. "We'll have to make a second and maybe even a third trip to get them all."

"Then let's get what we can and go."

Chief scooped up a handful of dusty old charts and handed them to Jack. He was opening the second drawer when they heard the sound of chains again. This time, an unearthly wail accompanied it. Chief shined the flashlight on the far wall.

"What the hell?" he said.

The old plaster surface began to bubble and crack, the outline of a body starting to protrude. The grotesque creature popping out of the wall looked like a cancerous demon Jack had seen in old horror comic books and his worst nightmare.

"Good God All Mighty!" he said.

Another demon was popping out of the wall behind them. The second monster looked even more horrid than the first, all bones, loose flesh, and distended eyeballs. Chief fished in his shirt pocket, put the whistle to his lips, blew it, and began to pray.

Chief continued to blow the whistle as the howls and growls of many dogs came running from the house. Jack and Chief could hear them coming up the circular stairway though they didn't know if they would reach them before the demons did.

Chief was tall though dwarfed in comparison to the two demons. He had Jack's arm and was preparing to pull him to the stairway when the pack of dogs, led by Old Joe, reached the second floor.

"Attack," Chief said.

All seven dogs, even Coco, did just that, tearing at the flailing arms of the demons and biting at their legs. The demons backed away from the attack and disappeared into the wall, the dogs running in circles trying to find them.

Old Joe stopped circling the room and sat when Chief said, "Stop." The other dogs did the same.

"Let's get out of here," Jack said.

"Not till we get all the charts," Chief said. "This is the first and last time I'm ever entering this building again."

Jack and Chief hurried down the creaky old stairs with their arms loaded with antique charts and maps. The dogs stayed put, waiting for the demons to reappear, until Chief blew the whistle. Jack kicked the door shut when the last dog exited from the lighthouse.

"Let's get these into the house. I'll come back and padlock the door."

Jack dropped his armload of charts and maps on a table. Chief did the same. When Jack returned from padlocking the lighthouse, the dogs were asleep on the rug as if nothing had happened. Chief was waiting for Jack with a mug of rum.

"Glad I left the door cracked," Jack said.

"Me too," Chief said. "I did some thinking while you were gone."

"About what?" Jack asked.

"About breaking our rule."

"What rule?" Jack said.

"Going back to the cheap hooch and not opening any more bottles of Dominican rum. After what we just saw, I may drink a whole bottle all by myself tonight before I'm able to get to sleep."

Chapter 12

Jack and Chief opened another bottle of Dominican rum as the storm grew stronger. The dogs were all asleep, Jack and Chief resting in a pair of old recliners.

"Whoever built this house knew what they were doing," Jack said. "I can only imagine how many storms it has survived."

"Same with the lighthouse," Chief said. "It's rock solid."

"Makes me wonder how long the ghosts have lived there. What do you think we ought to do about them?"

"There's a traiteur in Chalmette who could help us," Chief said.

"You mean like Odette's grandmother?"

"Some people call traiteurs witches though Paula calls herself a sensitive," Chief said. "She can talk to ghosts and convince them to move on to a different plane of existence."

Jack frowned. "Get out of here," he said. "Is she an Indian?"

"Indians aren't the only people who confer with spirits."

"I believe you, but I believe you're lying," Jack said.

95

"After seeing those two demons, getting rid of them isn't something I would lie about," Chief said.

"How do you know this woman?" Jack asked.

"She's Cajun. Thanks to Jimbo and Mable Kershaw, I know lots of Cajuns. They are good people."

Lightning flashed through the window, thunder shaking the roof of the house.

"You may as well make yourself comfortable," Jack said. "It's too wet to walk back to your teepee and too stormy to break out the ATV."

"I have to go home sometime," Chief said. "Remember my date with Miss Millie tomorrow night?"

"I'd almost forgotten," Jack said. "We'll go early enough to visit the grocery store, lay in some supplies, and maybe talk with the sensitive about exorcising the ghosts."

"And don't forget the dog food," Chief said.

"Those big dogs wouldn't let us forget for long," Jack said.

"What about building materials?"

"There are tools, nails, plywood, cement, and you name it in storage in a building near the Majestic. Mr. Castellano told me to use anything I needed. You may be in Miss Millie's love nest through the weekend."

"You think?" Chief asked.

"You kidding me?" Jack said. "That woman has the hots for you."

"Maybe she wants to keep me as her sex slave."

Jack laughed. "Drink some more rum and dream on," he said.

Sometime during the early morning hours, the storm abated. Jack had gone to bed, leaving Chief sprawled on the recliner, an old Afghan draped over him. Sun shining through the window and the aroma of bacon and eggs cooking in a skillet awoke him the following day.

"Thought you were going to sleep till noon," Jack said.

Chief stretched his back until it popped. "Are you ever going to buy new furniture?"

"You'd bitch about a sharp stick in the eye," Jack said. "Make yourself useful and feed the dogs."

The dogs had eaten and gone into the backyard when Chief sat at the plank table, waiting for his bacon and eggs. After breakfast, Chief started for the door.

"I'm going to the teepee, get cleaned up, and change clothes. What time do you want to leave for Chalmette?"

"No hurry. We have all day," Jack said. "Want a ride in the ATV?"

"I'll walk," Chief said.

As Jack had suggested, Chief took his time. He found his cat Buttercup resting on the pallet inside his teepee. She purred when he picked her up and stroked her.

"Where in the world have you been? I was worried sick. I thought the rougarou got you."

Chief petted her some more, sat her back on the pallet, and gave her a handful of cat treats. When he went outside, his hen Mable jumped into his arms. Feeling guilty about his chickens, he fed and watered them. As he strolled up the path from his teepee, he decided not to worry about leaving Coco and Old Joe at Jack's.

It was after three when he returned to Jack's dressed in his best chinos, sky blue cotton shirt with matching headband and handmade moccasins. He'd even braided his long gray hair. Jack glanced up from the broth he was cooking when Chief walked in the door.

Whistling, he said, "Look at you. All you need is an eagle feather in your headband."

"Do I look okay?" Chief asked.

"Like a million bucks. Hope you don't get your clean duds dirty loading groceries and dog food."

"I'll be careful."

"Explain to Old Joe he's in charge while we're gone," Jack said.

"You think he's that smart?" Chief asked.

"J.P. says he understands every word we say. I believe him. I made beef broth to pour on their hard food."

Chief petted Old Joe's head, the dogs wagging their tails as they ate.

"Jack and I are going into town. You're in charge while we're gone. Can you handle it?" Chief said.

Old Joe barked twice.

"Guess that means yes," Jack said. "Let's go."

They were soon on the road to Chalmette, Jack doing his best to avoid the newest potholes caused by many days of rain.

"Mr. Castellano's going to have to get a bulldozer out here if he expects any customers for the Majestic."

Jack didn't comment when Chief said, "Then let's don't tell him."

After reaching Chalmette, they spent the next couple of hours buying groceries and animal food and packing it in the truck bed. Jack brought ice chests and dry ice to keep the frozen food frozen.

"What'll we do now?" Jack asked. "We have almost two hours before Miss Millie is expecting you."

"Visit Paula Boutet, the traiteur, and ask her about helping us with the ghosts," Chief said.

"Where does she live?" Jack asked.

"She and her husband have a little acreage on the edge of town."

"She won't be expecting us," Jack said.

"Trust me when I tell you, Paula will be waiting at the door," Chief said.

"You're scaring me," Jack said.

"She's the real deal. She'll help us."

Paula's old house on the edge of town sat in the middle of a manicured two-acre lot. The gorgeous giant oaks, shrubs, and multi-colored flowers highlighted the house's fresh white paint and blue shutters. There were also wind chimes hanging everywhere. Like Chief had said, Paula was at the front door.

"Been expecting you," she said with a smile. "Come in this house."

Paula was much younger than Jack had anticipated, probably in her early thirties. She had a winning smile, a full head of dark hair, and tan and toned arms from working in the yard.

"Where's Jimmy?" Chief asked.

"Fishing on the bayou," Paula said. "Don't know what I'm going to do with that man."

"Love him is all you can do," Chief said. "You're never going to change him."

"That's a fact," she said, smiling at Jack. "I'm Paula."

"Jack. Chief said you'd be expecting us."

"Chief has powers he doesn't even know about," she said. "He's been broadcasting he was coming since last night. Come in the kitchen. I have a fresh pot of coffee on the stove, and you can tell me what your problem is."

Jack gave Chief a quizzical glance when Paula turned for the kitchen. Chief sat at the table, and Jack joined him.

"Jack's the lighthouse keeper on Oyster Island. He's only been in the lighthouse once since he took the job. Last night, we were there looking for some old maps."

"And you saw ghosts?" Paula asked.

"More like demons," Jack said. "Scared the holy hell out of me."

Paula laughed. "They were just ghosts and wouldn't have harmed you. They adopted the personas of demons to frighten you away. The truth is they were as scared of you as you were of them."

"I doubt that," Jack said.

Jack shook his head when Paula asked, "Have you ever seen them outside the lighthouse?"

"Last night was the first and only time I ever saw them," Jack said. "Old Man Thompson said it was a couple."

"Probably the lighthouse keepers, maybe from a hundred years ago," Paula said.

"What happened to them?" Chief asked.

"A hurricane?" Paula said. "However they died. I'm guessing it was unexpected."

"What can we do?" Jack asked.

"Whatever killed them was traumatic and left their lives unresolved. We need to help them pass through the veil separating this life and the hereafter."

"Can you do that?" Jack asked.

"It would help to know what happened to them," Paula said. "I'll find out what I can online and at the Chalmette library. I may even have to reach out to local historians."

"Then you'll help us?" Jack asked.

"Of course, I will," Paula said. "I have a calling. It's what I do. Another cup of coffee?"

"You bet," Jack said. "The best coffee I ever tasted. What's your secret?"

"Eggshells and a pinch of salt in the coffee grounds," Paula said. "Most people never notice."

Paula smiled when Jack said, "I promise I'll never reveal your secret."

"Pretty damn good," Chief said.

"Now," she said. "Tell me why you're all dressed up."

"Chief has a date with Millie Folsom, the supervisor of the Chalmette animal shelter."

"She's a kind and wonderful woman and has a problem with men," Paula said.

"Is she . . . ?"

Paula laughed and said, "She's not a lesbian if that's what you mean."

"Then what's her problem with men?" Chief asked.

"Millie comes from a prominent St. Bernard Parish family. She was jilted at the altar in front of hundreds of guests by the man she loved."

"Sounds like someone who needs to have his ass kicked," Jack said.

"Quinton, her fiancée, also comes from a prominent local family. After jilting Millie, he married the homecoming queen. They had three children, all blond, blue-eyed and beautiful. He inherited his father's meatpacking plant and never apologized to Millie. That was twenty years ago, and she's never married."

Paula nodded when Chief said, "Quinton Stockton? I believe it. I've never heard much good about the man?"

"If Millie has a problem with men, why did she ask Chief out on a date?" Jack asked.

"To humiliate him, I'm afraid," Paula said. "She's done it before and has a reputation here in Chalmette."

Chief glanced at Paula, then at Jack, and then back to Paula.

"This doesn't sound good," Chief said. "We're going to Lost Lagoon. I don't have a car and can't just leave if she flips out on me. I'm going back to the island with Jack."

"Don't do that," Paula said. "Though Millie doesn't know it, she needs your help to let go of her past."

"What am I supposed to do?" Chief asked.

"You have to help her confront her demons. Ghosts aren't the only lost souls who have suffered an unexpected loss."

"I don't have a clue how to do that?" Chief said.

Paula opened a cabinet, returning with an unlabeled herb jar. She put a small dollop into Chief's coffee.

"This is what you need," she said.

"What is it?" Chief asked.

"A concoction of herbs, plants, and roots. All natural," Paula said.

She smiled when he asked, "What does it do?"

"It's a Cajun mood enhancer. It'll make you happy and dissolve away all your worries."

"Sounds like Prozac," Jack said.

"Far better," Paula said. "And everything in it came from my garden, the forest or the bayou."

Chief drained the coffee. "How long does it take it to start working?"

"Not long," Paula said. "You'll soon have a feeling of warmth and well-being."

"Shouldn't we be giving the same concoction to Millie?" Jack asked.

Paula frowned and shook her head. "It's not right to give someone something so powerful without their knowledge."

"Not even if it's going to do them a world of good?" Jack said.

"My potion will help Chief to assist Millie in overcoming her fear of rejection. It's so much more than simply a feel-good elixir. It's soul medicine, I guarantee."

Someone calling from outside the door caught their attention.

"Paula, come see what I caught."

"It's Jimmy," Paula said, heading for the front door. She soon stuck her head back into the kitchen. "You won't believe the size of the catfish Jimmy caught. Come see."

Jack lagged as Chief followed Paula out the door. Grabbing the potion bottle she'd left on the table, he opened the flask of rum and dumped a liberal dose into it, shaking it to dissolve the concoction. After looking to see if anyone had seen what he had done, he hurried to have a look at Jimmy's giant catfish.

Chapter 13

Millie was waiting at the door of the animal shelter when Jack's truck pulled up to the curb. Jack grabbed Chief's arm when he opened the door.

"You forget something?" he said. "Take this."

Though Chief wasn't grinning, he was coming as close to it as Jack had ever seen.

"I don't need any rum," Chief said. "I've never felt more wonderful in my life."

"Stop thinking about yourself," Jack said. "Miss Millie may want a taste."

Chief put the flask in his back pocket as he stepped out of the truck. He was almost smiling as he walked up the sidewalk to where Millie awaited. Since the last time he'd seen her, something about her had changed.

Chief had forgotten about Paula's potion and what was causing his buoyant mood. Gone also were the feather earrings and squash blossom necklace Millie had worn during her visit to the island. Instead, diamond studs sparkled from her earlobes, a gold necklace with a dangling heart around her neck.

Millie had curled her gray hair and was wearing a stylish red summer dress that buttoned up from the hem. Expensive flats highlighted her height as she was five-eight or nine, carrying a big straw purse. She also had a white summer jacket sitting on her shoulders. Chief wondered for a moment if he had dressed appropriately.

Millie flashed Chief a smile when he said, "You're gorgeous."

"Don't start," she said.

Chief heard a whistle when Millie used her car key to open the door of a silver Lexus. He had to duck his head to get into the sporty vehicle.

"You look so . . ."

"Indian?" Chief said, finishing her sentence. "You said you wanted to discuss our Indian heritage."

"I guess it's okay," Millie said.

Though Chief's mood had heightened, it didn't stop him from noticing the condescending tone of her voice.

"What?" he said.

"You look as if you're going to a costume party," Millie said.

"I don't own a suit and tie," he said.

"It's okay," she said.

Signaling something was amiss, the edge to Millie's voice would usually have set off Chief's warning bells. Not tonight.

"I'm excited," he said. "I love beautiful sunsets."

"Then you're in for a treat," she said. "People come from all over the parish to see the sunset from the restaurant's deck overlooking Lost Lagoon."

"I can't wait," Chief said.

Boudreaux's Claws and Craws sat alone outside of town on the banks of Lost Lagoon. Cars and pickups already occupied the parking lot paved with bleached and broken shells. Not yet dark, the place was already jumping.

Raucous Cajun music poured from the large wooden building which sported a deck overlooking Lost Lagoon. The sun was already sinking in the west, the deck crowded with diners drinking beer, wine, and mixed drinks and enjoying the view from the overlook while still light enough to see.

Everyone on the deck seemed to know Millie. They spoke and exchanged pleasantries as a waiter led them to a table near the end of the deck. The location afforded them the best possible view of the sunset. It didn't pass Chief's notice that Millie hadn't introduced him to anyone. His mood bright and cheery, the revelation didn't bother him.

"Heather will take your drink order," the man said. "She'll be right with you."

Chief waited until the man disappeared into the restaurant.

"You must rate. This is the best table on the deck."

"I know the owner," Millie said.

Millie smiled when Chief said, "I think you know everyone here."

"Chalmette is a small town. I've lived here all my life."

"Do you ride horses?" he asked.

"Why yes. How did you know?"

Millie's complexion didn't allow her to blush. If it had, she would have when he said, "You have gorgeous legs."

"I didn't realize how high I'd unbuttoned my skirt," she said.

"I did," Chief said.

Chief's comment made Millie uncomfortable, and she would have said something if a pretty waitress dressed in cutoff jeans, cowboy hat, and colorful Claws and Craws tee shirt, knotted just below her breasts, hadn't arrived to take their order. After handing them menus, she glanced up for the first time, placed her hands on her hips, and smiled. The young woman had tied her dark hair in a ponytail. Equally dark eyes flashed in the dim light reflecting from the Japanese lanterns swaying in the bayou breeze blowing across the deck. In a flash, she was in Chief's lap and put her arms around his neck.

"Chief, I ain't seen you in going on forever. Where you been?"

"Don't get into town much. Miss Millie, this is Heather. Her daddy owns the place."

"Nice to meet you, ma'am," Heather said. "I've known Chief since I was a baby, and he's one of the nicest persons on God's Green Earth."

"My pleasure," Millie said. "I know your father."

Heather didn't bother getting out of Chief's lap to shake Millie's hand. Instead, she cupped his face with her palms and kissed him on the mouth.

"Sorry, Miss Millie," Heather said with a smile. "Chief's so big and strong I love feeling his muscles. What are you drinking?"

"Chardonnay," she said.

"Abita," Chief said. "Draw if you have it."

"I know what else you like," Heather said. "I'll bring you two dozen oysters." She grinned and put her hand over her face. "That didn't come out just right, now did it?"

When Heather was gone, Millie asked, "Is she your girlfriend?"

"Heaven's no," Chief said. "She's young enough to be my granddaughter."

"It's okay if she is," Millie said. "This isn't even a real date."

"Maybe not to you. It is to me," Chief said.

Heather returned with drinks and oysters before the conversation with Chief and Millie could continue. A damp breeze had whipped up, the Japanese lanterns swaying on the deck and the wind chimes singing as the sun disappeared beneath the horizon to everyone's applause.

"Are you mad at me for some reason?" Chief asked.

"Why do you ask?" Millie said.

"You're treating me like your eccentric cousin."

"I wasn't expecting you to pick me up looking like an extra from an old cowboy and Indians movie," she said.

"Am I embarrassing you?"

"You could have dressed more appropriately," Millie said.

"I'm not a movie extra. I'm a real live Indian, the last Atakapa and proud of it."

"Let's not make a scene," Millie said.

"You're an Indian, full-blood unless I miss my guess. Are you ashamed of your heritage?"

Millie wasn't looking at him when she said, "I don't like rubbing it into people's faces. Please, let's change the subject."

Chief nodded and tapped Millie's wine glass.

"Cheers," he said.

"I never developed a taste for beer," she said.

"You like rum?"

"In a Hurricane from Pat O'Brien's, maybe," Millie said. "Why?"

"Ever tasted hundred-year-old Dominican rum?" Chief asked.

"I don't believe I'd like straight rum no matter where it's from or how long it's aged."

Chief put the flask on the table. "Please," he said. "Take a sip."

"I've never drunk out of a flask, even when I was a freshman in college."

"Oh, where did you go?" Chief asked.

"University of New Orleans."

"Me too," he said. "Love that place."

"You went to UNO?" she asked.

"For six years," he said.

"Did you graduate?"

"Master's degree in American history," he said. "You?"

"You have a Master's degree?" she said.

"I was going to teach. Life got in my way."

"I wish I had studied history," Millie said. "I have an MBA, and it's dry and lifeless. Why did you study history?"

"You kidding? I never considered anything else."

"But why?"

"New Orleans and Louisiana are steeped in interesting history that only continues. I've just always enjoyed swimming in it."

"You haven't used your degree," Millie said.

"I use it every day," he said.

Millie could hear the change in the tone of Chief's voice and decided not to press it.

"Please hand me the flask," she said. "I'll put a little on my tongue."

Chief was almost smiling as Millie touched the flask to her lips. It was her turn to smile when she took a sip.

"This is so smooth. I can't believe how good it tastes," she said.

"Drink some more," he said when she tried to hand the flask back to him.

Millie took another drink and then another, her neck turning red as she glanced up at Chief with a big smile on her face. She seemed to notice the oysters on the table for the first time.

"I've never eaten oysters," she said.

"You kidding me? You grew up in Chalmette, and you've never eaten oysters?"

She laughed when she said, "They look disgusting."

"Well, they aren't," Chief said. "Let me fix one for you."

"Fix as many as you like," Millie said. "I'm not eating an oyster."

Using one of the chilled stainless steel ramekins, Chief mixed cocktail sauce and horseradish. With a cocktail fork, he plucked a plump oyster from its shell, dunked it in the sauce, plopped it on a cracker, and then held it to Millie's lips until she ate it.

"What do you think?" he asked.

Millie was smiling as she licked the sauce off her lips."

"Please make one more for me?" she said.

"Coming up," he said.

Millie had soon eaten six oysters and had yet to return the flask of rum to Chief. When Heather returned, Millie handed it to her.

"Please, take a drink of Grogan's rum. You won't believe how good it is."

Heather, not having to be asked twice, put the flask to her lips.

"Whoa!" she said. "That is so good and goes down so easy."

"I know," Millie said. "I'm eating oysters, drinking straight rum, and liking it. I don't know what's come over me."

"Chief has that effect on women," Heather said. "Are we eating anything besides oysters?"

"Bowl of gumbo for me," Chief said.

"I'll have the same," Millie said.

Heather drank more rum when she brought their gumbo and another swig when she returned to check their drinks.

"This is so good," she said.

Chief had forgotten about Paula's potion, and neither he nor Millie knew why they were feeling the way they were. Cajun fiddle music poured from hidden speakers, the flickering of hundreds of lightning bugs putting on a light show by the Lost Lagoon.

"I can't remember having such a wonderful experience," Millie said. "So sorry about giving you a hard time with your clothes. It now seems so trivial to me. Weren't you ever embarrassed by being an Indian?"

"Never thought about it," Chief said. "It's who I am."

"I wish I could be that way. My father spent his entire life denying he was Indian."

"But why?" Chief asked.

"He was a self-made man and never wanted to be on a roll or the dole."

"What about your tribe?" Chief said.

"We never participated in tribal events," Millie said.

"I'm the last full-blood Atakapa," Chief said. "Now my tribe is Jack, my dogs, cat, and chickens."

"That's so sad," Millie said. "You long for a tribe. I have one, and I've always turned my back on them."

"You've done wonderful things for the homeless animals in your community. You should be proud."

"Very proud, though sad I can't do more," Millie said.

"You're helping Jack, J.P., and me," Chief said. "We'll make a difference."

"I hope so," she said.

"A tribe is nothing more than a group of like-minded people. You're part of our tribe now," Chief said.

Happy diners consuming beer, whiskey, and other after-dinner drinks crowded the deck when someone flung open the double doors leading into the main restaurant. Raucous Cajun music poured out the doors as Heather pranced onto the deck, smiling, sweating, and dancing to the delight of the crowd.

Heather's dance grew ever more erotic as she weaved her way through the crowd, sitting in men's and even a few women's laps. After tossing her cowboy hat to someone, she untied the knot in her western shirt, unbuttoned it, and grinned when she exposed her naked breasts.

When Heather used the wadded blouse to mop the sweat off her glistening tits, the crowd issued a communal gasp. She tossed it to an older man whose equally gray-haired wife, her mouth opened wide, stared with the rest of the people on the deck at the half-naked young woman.

Chapter 14

C hief didn't have to watch Heather's dance for long to realize she needed a helping hand to resolve the situation. Leaving his chair, he pointed to the summer jacket draped around Millie's shoulders.

"May I?" he asked.

Millie handed him the jacket. "Of course," she said.

Chief waded into the crowd, covering Heather with the jacket. After escorting her into the restaurant, the people on the deck gave him a standing ovation. Millie was one of them.

"That was a wonderful thing you did," she said.

"I've known Heather since she was a little girl. Some people will be talking," Chief said.

"I doubt anyone will remember her performance tomorrow," Millie said. "Most of the people on the deck are inebriated as Heather is."

"You're right," Chief said. "No use worrying about it."

Heather didn't return to their table. Instead, the young man who seated them when they arrived brought them fresh drinks and Millie's jacket.

"My dad wants to thank you for rescuing Heather. He's comped your tab and all your drinks."

"Thank him for us," Chief said.

"I will," the young man said. "I'm Matt. Heather's my sister."

After the excitement, people paid their tabs and left the deck, Millie and Chief the only two remaining.

"Have any more rum?" Millie asked.

"Heather finished the last of it," Chief said. "We'll have to make do with wine and beer."

"After your rum, wine doesn't rate anymore. Are you ready to leave?" Millie asked.

"Anytime you are, though I could stay here with you forever," he said.

"You got me to thinking about my Indian heritage," Millie said.

"Good. We all need a port in the storm," Chief said.

"When we finished eating, I was going to drop you off at Detective Saucier's house," Millie said.

Millie shook her head when Chief said, "Does that mean you're going to take me home with you?"

"I've already spent too many nights alone in that house. I want to spend this one with you in your teepee."

"Are you sure?" Chief asked.

"I've never been so sure about anything in my life. Can you handle it?"

"Hope so," he said. "At any rate, I'm going to love trying."

They waited in front of the building for the valet to bring Millie's car. When he did, he handed the keys to Chief.

"The road to Oyster Island is dark, washed-out, and treacherous this time of night," he said. "Want me to drive?"

"You don't trust a woman driver?" Millie asked.

"More than I trust myself to pilot that little car of yours."

"Then give me the key and get in," she said.

Persistent clouds covered the moon and stars, only the headlights of Millie's Lexus illuminating the narrow road they traversed. Chief breathed a sigh of relief when they crossed the Oyster Island bridge and started across the sand to his property. The moon poked through the clouds, illuminating their path as they walked up the hill to the teepee.

"Have you ever soaked in a Magic Fountain?" Chief asked.

"Do you have a bathing suit for me?"

Realizing she was serious, Chief said, "There's no one to see us except the moon and stars, and they're mostly behind the clouds."

Chief blinked when she said, "I've never been naked with a man."

"Never?" he said.

"Never."

"Does that mean . . . ?"

"If you're asking if I'm a virgin, the answer is yes," Millie said.

Chief lowered his head and put his hand over his face.

"I think I need more rum," he said. "I have an unopened bottle inside."

Millie followed Chief into the teepee lighted only by the dying embers glowing in the firepit. When he switched on a battery-operated lantern, Millie's mouth opened wide.

"I can't believe this is real," she said. "It's like a time machine has transported us to a magical place in the distant past. I never imagined how regal and colorful the inside of a teepee could be."

"You should be here when it rains," Chief

said. "It's like a little slice of heaven."

Buttercup was lying on Chief's pallet when Millie saw her. Grabbing up the calico cat, she clutched her in her arms.

"I didn't know you liked cats," she said.

"Love cats," Chief said. "Buttercup's my baby."

"She's adorable," Millie said.

"You have a cat?"

Millie shook her head. "No cat, no dog, not even a parakeet," she said.

"You run an animal shelter and don't have a pet?" Chief said.

"I've never been able to commit," she said.

Chief motioned to the colorful Indian rug on the pallet. "Please, sit. I think we both need more rum." She nodded when he said, "You live alone?"

Chief plopped down on the pallet beside Millie, opened the rum, and drank straight from the bottle.

"You don't need to get me drunk," Millie said. "I haven't changed my mind about sleeping with you."

Chief took another drink of the rum. "It isn't you that I'm worried about."

"Something the matter?" Millie asked.

"I've never made love to a virgin," Chief said.

"I've never made love, and that makes us even."

Millie took the rum. Like Chief, she drank straight from the bottle, giggling when the amber liquid dribbled down her cheek and then her neck.

"This is all a bit overwhelming to me. I can only imagine how it is for you. You sure about this?" Chief said.

"I'm sure," Millie said. "I was kidding about the bathing suit," she said. "I want you to see me naked."

"Then take off your blouse," he said.

Millie had left her summer jacket in the car. Realizing Chief was watching her every move, she slowly unbuttoned the blouse as deftly as a professional striptease artist.

"Now what?" she said.

"Take it off and your bra," Chief said.

Millie's performance continued. After removing her blouse and laying it on the rug beside her, she unlatched her black lacy bra, milking every last dramatic moment as she dropped the straps off her shoulders. The bra ended in her lap, and she didn't bother moving it.

"Well?" she said as he stared at her.

"In all my years, I've never had a premature ejaculation," he said. "If we don't go through with this soon, that's all about to end."

"You're lying," she said with a smile.

"Let's get our clothes off and head up the trail to the Magic Fountain. You've heated me, and I need something to cool me down."

"I don't want you cooled down, and don't dare change your mind," Millie said. "You're staring at my breasts as if you want to eat me alive. If we don't do this, right here, right now, I'll be crushed. I'm as hot and bothered as you are, and your Magic Fountain can wait."

Chief and Millie were both soon naked in the lantern's dim light. Chief's muscles tightened when Millie said, "Stop."

"What?" Chief said.

"I've never been this close to a naked man, and your body is beautiful," Millie said. "Turn around slowly so I can see every inch of you."

Chief could feel Millie's stare as he did a slow three-sixty.

"Now, I'm nervous," Chief said.

"Take me in your arms and carry me to your bed," she said.

"I don't have a bed," Chief said. "I sleep on the pallet. It can be a little hard if you aren't used to it. Want me to turn out the lantern?"

"No way," she said. "I told you I'm a virgin. I want to drink in every glorious second of my first sensual experience."

Despite Millie's wishes, the lantern flickered and went out when thunder rumbled in the distance. The rain began, slowly at first and then in a cacophony of nature's drumbeats on the tympanic membrane that was the teepee. As they lay huddled in each other's arms beneath a colorful Native American throw, neither Millie nor Chief knew how much time had passed. Finally, Chief tossed the cover aside and pulled Millie to her feet.

"The Magic Fountain. Are you ready?"

"I've never been more ready in my life," she said.

Chief had two old blue towels that said Pontchartrain Beach. After handing one to Millie, he wrapped the other one around his waist. Chief took Millie's hand and pulled her through the flap of the teepee. Lightning was still flashing out over the Gulf, thunder still rumbling.

"We better hurry," Chief said. "This little break in the weather won't last forever."

"I don't have shoes," Millie said.

"You won't need them," Chief said. "It's a dirt path up the hill. Tonight, it'll be a little muddy."

"Then lead the way," Millie said.

The storm continued over the Gulf, providing a distant light show as they climbed the path to the Magic Fountain. Millie smiled when she saw the tiny waterfall in the reflected light.

"Now I know what makes it a fountain," she said.

Chief dipped his foot into the water. "It's warm," he said.

He continued holding Millie's hand as he tossed the towel to the sandy bank of the pool and waded into the water. Millie dropped her Pontchartrain Beach towel on the pool's bank and followed him.

With water up to her neck, Millie said, "This is wonderful."

"I told you," he said.

"You were wonderful," Millie said. "The brave knight in shining armor I've always dreamed about."

"Millie," Chief said. "I have to confess to something."

Fearing their magnificent moment was about to end, she said, "What?"

"I was so nervous I had doubts about being able to perform."

Millie laughed. "If your performance was impaired, I can't imagine you at full throttle," Millie said. "Must be the rum."

"You have a body like a French showgirl," Chief said. "You heated me pretty fast, and I forgot about my insecurities."

Millie kissed him. "I can't imagine you've ever been insecure," she said.

"Trust me when I tell you I have. I feel I have a psychic link with you."

"Don't get attached," Millie said. "I told you I have a problem with commitment."

"You said you'd never been with a man."

"That's true."

"I've never been with a woman like you," Chief said. "Don't you feel the same about me?"

"You are big, strong, and knowledgeable. Your body is so muscular. I love touching you."

"But?" Chief said.

"Now that I have touched you, you've opened my mind to everything possible in my life. So let's make love again, right here in the pool."

"We could drown," Chief said.

"I don't think so."

They were soon immersed in a sexual trance and up to their necks in warm water. Time flew by until they ended up beneath the waterfall. Water up their noses ended their lovemaking and left them both laughing. They sprawled on the sandy bank of the pool, staring at the light show in the sky.

"You have a great body," Chief said. "How do you stay in such amazing shape?"

"I run," she said. "Since I was a girl. I love it. Do you run?"

"Nope," Chief said. "I'm tall enough to play basketball and big enough for football, but my passion was always baseball. The only running I ever did was the bases when I hit a home run."

Millie said, "I'll bet you got lots of home runs."

"I feel so good right now; it's like I just hit a grand slam," Chief said.

Millie kissed him on the mouth. "Thank you for relieving me of the burden of virginity."

"My pleasure," he said. "The storm is starting to kick up again. Let's get out of here before we get struck by lightning."

Chief and Millie retrieved their towels and hurried to the teepee.

Morning light was shining through the flap when Chief opened his eyes. Millie was gone.

Chapter 15

The aroma of bacon and eggs greeted Chief when he opened the door to Jack's house.

"What the hell are you doing here?" Jack asked when he saw Chief. "I thought you were in Chalmette."

"Miss Millie wanted to spend the night in my teepee," Chief said.

"Where is she?" Jack asked.

"She left while I was asleep," Chief said.

"Then give me a high five," Jack said. "Mission accomplished."

"Maybe," Chief said.

"Maybe? You just told me you and Miss Millie spent the night in your teepee. Am I missing something?"

"There's little doubt in my mind Miss Millie had an epiphany," Chief said.

"And?"

"I think I was more of a catalyst than a love interest," Chief said.

"Are you saying you didn't make love to her?" Jack asked.

"I didn't have to," Chief said. "She made love to me. I was just an unwitting participant."

"Maybe you'd better explain," Jack said.

121

"Miss Millie was acting out some wild fantasy. She had a plan of her own. I lay back and let it happen."

"You didn't enjoy it?" Jack asked.

"I didn't say that," Chief said.

Jack was full of questions. "So, where does your relationship stand?"

"I think it's over," Chief said.

"Over?" Jack said. "You just told me it was a wild night of sexual fantasy."

"You're welcome to make up any story you like," Chief said.

"I'm not making shit up," Jack said. "It's what you just told me."

"No, I didn't," Chief said. "Clean out your ears."

"You're one weird dude," Jack said.

"No crazier than you are," Chief said. "Believe whatever you want. My Indian intuition is screaming at me right now."

"Yeah, what's it saying?" Jack asked.

"It's another day in paradise, and I still have no girlfriend. I got to thinking; there's not a single female on this entire island."

"You're wrong about that, Chief," Jack said. "There's Mable and Buttercup."

Chief came close to smiling. "Guess you're right. I stand corrected."

"How about some breakfast?" Jack said.

"Thought you'd never ask," Chief said. "What day is it?"

"Saturday," Jack said. "J.P. is supposed to come to help us enlarge my backyard."

Jack and Chief had barely sat down at the plank table when someone drove up out front. It was J.P. and Lucky. Behind J.P.'s black Dodge truck was a shiny Airstream trailer. When J.P. opened the truck door, Lucky came running, meeting Coco at the front of the house. Both of

122

their tails were wagging. Oscar soon joined them.

"Hope you don't mind I brought my travel trailer," J.P. said.

Jack glanced at the iconic silver trailer made of shiny aluminum.

"What a beauty," Jack said. "Must have set you back a bunch."

"Thirty-four years old, and still in great shape," J.P. said. "Even so, it wasn't cheap, though nothing compared to what a new one costs."

"All the comforts of home," Jack said.

"Got that right," J.P. said. "I'm only available for the weekend. We can get our project on the road while I have a few days to help."

"Great," Jack said. "Even the dogs are happy about it."

"I swear those mutts love each other," J.P. said.

"No doubt," Jack said. "You had breakfast yet?"

"No, and whatever you're cooking smells like a little slice of heaven," J.P. said.

Jack shook his head and grabbed another plate. J.P. was smiling as he took a sip of Jack's coffee.

"What the hell?" he said. "This is the best tasting coffee I've ever had. You learn a new trick, old dog?"

"Salt and eggshells," Jack said. "Who would have thought?"

"Don't apologize," J.P. said. "You'd make someone a great wife."

"Kiss my ass," Jack said.

"Just kidding," J.P. said as he glanced at Chief. "What the hell did you do to Miss Millie?"

"Nothing," Chief said. "Why do you ask?"

"Turned in her resignation at the animal shelter, put her house on the market, and left this morning for Santa Fe, New Mexico."

"You shitting me?" Jack said.

"No way," J.P. said. "Chief was supposed to spend last night with me. When he didn't show up, I got worried. What the hell happened?"

J.P. and Chief's attention turned to Jack when he said, "Guess I'm to blame."

"What?" they both asked at once.

"Chief and I had an encounter with two demons in the old lighthouse," Jack said. "Chief knows a traiteur in Chalmette."

"Paula Boutet?" J.P. asked.

"You know Paula?" Jack asked.

"All my damn life," J.P. said. "On the way to a football game, we made out on the band bus. Paula's big brother Andrew kicked my ass. "Found out later she was sweet on Jimmy, her husband now and Andrew's best buddy."

"You played in the band?" Jack asked.

"Alto sax," J.P. said. "You play?"

"Me too," Jack said.

"Hell, Jack," J.P. said. "We'll have to get drunk and break out the old instruments sometimes."

"I haven't touched mine in more than fifty years."

J.P. was grinning. "How old are you?"

"Old enough to be your daddy," Jack said.

"What did you and Paula cook up that caused Miss Millie to pack up and leave Chalmette?"

"Yeah," Chief said. "What part did you play?"

"Paula was telling us how Miss Millie could be abusive to would-be suitors. She mixed up what she called Cajun Prozac for Chief so he could withstand whatever might come his way. When they weren't watching, I laced Chief's flask with the concoction."

Though Jack and J.P. were laughing, Chief had pushed his plate aside, a dark frown on his face. J.P. was the first to notice.

"You okay?" he asked.

"I've never met another woman like Miss Millie," Chief said. "I'm not a teenager, though I had a crush on her. Now, you tell me she's gone, and at least part of the fault is Jack's."

"Hell, Chief, you already knew it when you walked in the door this morning," Jack said. "Indian intuition is what you told me."

"Maybe," Chief said. "I didn't expect to get slapped in the face with it this quickly."

"Not all men have wives and kids," J.P. said. "The only significant woman I've ever had in my life was my mama, and you don't hear me whining."

"J.P.'s right," Jack said. "At least you got lucky last night. I haven't been with a woman since the last time I was in Singapore."

"How many years ago was that?" J.P. said.

"Don't ask," Jack said.

"I'd feel better if I had a shot of Dominican rum," Chief said. "Let's open another bottle."

"I second that emotion," J.P. said.

"Then let's make this the last bottle," Jack said. "We can't afford to keep drinking our profits."

"Maybe we should just drink some more of Paula's Cajun Prozac," Chief said.

"You knew about Paula's potion," Jack said. "She told both of us."

"You didn't tell me about spiking Miss Millie's too," Chief said.

"Stop it," Jack said. "At least everything worked out for the best."

"Who says so?" Chief asked.

"You said yourself Miss Millie had an epiphany," Jack said. "I'm guessing whatever happened last night changed her life for the better."

"Maybe," Chief said. "Doesn't matter because she's still gone."

"Things always have a way of working out for the best," Jack said.

"Sounds to me like all three of us could use a trip to Bernadine's for a little attitude adjustment," J.P. said.

"What's Bernadine's?" Jack asked.

"Best little whorehouse in St. Bernard Parish," J.P. said.

"You're the police," Jack said. "You aren't supposed to be frequenting whorehouses."

"Hell, Jack, you can't police everything," J.P. said.

J.P. grinned when Jack asked, "You get a discount?"

"Always," J.P. said. "I can't speak for you and Chief, though."

"You two have fun," Chief said. "I had enough sexual activity last night to last me a while."

"You may change your mind after we have our dog training facility off and running," J.P. said.

"You're right," Jack said. "That's something to celebrate."

After opening another bottle of Dominican rum, Jack, J.P., and Chief drove the ATV across the island to the storage warehouse near the marina. The inside of the old structure was musty, humid, and warm and filled with furniture, automobiles, boat parts, and lots of lumber, bricks, flagstone, and other building materials. Jack's big flashlight cut a hazy swath through the gloom.

"Good God almighty," J.P. said. "What a goldmine. You sure we can use what's in here?"

"Mr. Castellano told me to take what I need."

The three men soon filled the ATV's trailer with

126

building materials and started back to Jack's. After three trips, they sat in the shade of the lighthouse, relaxing and drinking rum.

"Something came across the wire at the office," J.P. said. "It may be a clue to your rougarou."

"Tell us," Jack said.

"A trapper visited the emergency room a few nights ago. The E.R. doctor spent a couple of hours popping buckshot out of his skin. The report said it looked like someone shot the man from almost point-blank range. Sound familiar?"

"What was his name, and where did he come from?" Jack asked.

"Said his name was Antoine. He paid cash for the medical treatment."

"I know lots of Cajun's," Chief said. "What was Antoine's last name?"

"He didn't give it," J.P. said.

"What did he look like?" Chief asked.

"Mid-forties, dark hair and lots of tattoos," J.P. said.

"Surely the E.R. got all of the man's medical records," Jack said.

"Trapper's don't have insurance," Chief said.

"Or credit cards," J.P. said. They come in all the time with snakebites and alligator mishaps and pay in cash. It's common in south Louisiana, and the doctors always treat them."

"When did this happen?" Jack asked.

"The day after the last full moon," J.P. said.

"That's about the time the rougarou visited the island," Jack said.

"I dealt with an outbreak a few years back over on Goose Island," J.P. said. "There's a monastery there, and all the monks were infected."

"Infected? What the hell are you talking about?" Jack said.

127

"A researcher lives in the Garden District of New Orleans. He attributes this shape-shifting from man to wolf to a virus akin to rabies," J.P. said. "We used a medicine administered by pneumatic pistols to cure the monks. I still have a pistol."

"What about the medicine?" Jack asked.

"The researcher never published his findings," Jack said. "I don't know if he's even still alive."

"Maybe we should take a trip to the Garden District to find out," Jack said.

"And sell the rest of our rum on Canal before we drink it all," Chief said.

"Exactly what I was thinking," Jack said.

"Sounds like a plan," J.P. said. "Speaking of plans, we'd better get back to work."

The sky had begun to darken when the three men erected the last fence panel to expand Jack's backyard. They'd also constructed a comfortable and well-ventilated kennel for the dogs to sleep and shelter from the elements.

"That's enough for the day," J.P. said. "I'm heading to my trailer to take a shower and clean up for Bernadine's."

"Think I'm going to pass," Jack said. "I'm worn out."

"No way!" J.P. said. "You're coming with me. You'll feel better after a shower and putting on some clean clothes."

"I'll go with you," Jack said. "I'm too tired for any more physical activity."

"You'll change your mind when you see Miss Bernadine's crew of gorgeous women," J.P. said.

"Maybe," Jack said. "What about you, Chief?"

"I have to feed my cat and chickens. After that, I will soak in the Magic Fountain and drink more rum. What's on the agenda for tomorrow?"

"Get back at it," J.P. said. "I have to return to my paying job on Monday.

"Need a ride home?" Jack asked.

"I'll walk," Chief said. "Coco and Old Joe will keep me company."

Once the sun was down, the island's temperature cooled rapidly into the seventies. Chief fed Coco, Old Joe, Buttercup, and the chickens. The dogs and cat were soon sleeping on Chief's pallet. After stripping, he headed up the path to the Magic Fountain.

The Magic Fountain's cool water had natural restorative powers. The water, rum, and solitude combined to relaxing Chief; his eyes closed when distant thunder over the Gulf awoke him. The island's vista, visible only from the highest point on the hill, stretched before him. Chief's eagle eyes spotted something in the distance.

Someone was camping on the beach, a fire illuminating a small tent. After returning to the teepee and checking on the sleeping animals, Chief donned moccasins and a loincloth before starting down the hill to investigate.

Chapter 16

Chief had a secret he'd never shared with anyone. He knew things other people didn't know. He could see in the dark, sense danger a mile away, and wasn't afraid of anything.

A full-blooded Atakapa, Chief was more than his name. He was a chief, a natural leader in total harmony with the creator and one with the earth.

Moreover, he was a warrior who could kill an enemy in battle or be the protector of the most vulnerable creatures.

Though Chief had never used all his powers, he knew they were there if and when the situation ever arose. So as he strolled across the island, he understood something was wrong, someone was in need.

Chief didn't need the Internet. Instead, his mind and body connected directly to the plasma of life emanating from everything around him. As he approached the campsite, he became aware of someone behind him and raised his arms.

"I give up. Don't shoot," he said.

A voice he recognized spoke. "Chief, is that you?"

"It's me, Odette. What the hell are you doing

here?"

Odette dropped the speargun she was holding and ran to embrace Chief.

"Oh my God, I was praying someone would come," she said.

Odette, the Cajun stripper, had latched her arms around Chief's near-naked body. She was covered head to toe in a black wetsuit, her blond braid draping down over the back.

"Something attacked you?" Chief asked.

"Your damn rougarou. The monster would have torn me to shreds if it hadn't been for Mudbug."

"Mudbug?"

Hearing her name, a tiny dog appeared from the little pop-up tent. She wagged her tail and licked Chief's face when the big Indian lifted her off the ground.

"This tiny little dog chased away a rougarou?" Chief asked.

"She held the creature at bay until I put a spear through its chest."

"You shot the rougarou?"

"That's when I started getting scared," Odette said. "The beast glared at me, pulled out the spear, and tossed it into the sand."

"Then what happened?" Chief asked.

"Damned creature must have heard you coming up the beach. I think it's gone. What now?"

"You can't stay out here. Too dangerous. Jack has an extra bedroom. Break camp and let's head over there," Chief said.

"I'm going nowhere," Odette said.

"And why not?" Chief asked.

"I can take care of myself. If the beast returns, I'll put another spear in his chest."

"The creature is supernatural," Chief said. "You can't kill it. Come with me."

"Right now, this little tent is my home. It's mine to protect, and that's what I intend to do," Odette said.

Chief reached for his flask before realizing he was half-naked and didn't have the flask.

"I need a drink," he said.

"Let's sit by the fire," Odette said. "I've got nothing alcoholic to drink, but I got pot."

Chief came close to grinning. "Last time I smoked pot, I ended up in jail."

"There are no cops within fifty miles," Odette said.

"Wrong about that," Chief said. "Jack and I are partners now with a St. Bernard Parish cop named Jean Pierre Saucier."

"Partners in what?" she asked.

"Jack and I figured out the rougarou is scared of dogs. We got some big ones from the Chalmette animal shelter. Unfortunately, they didn't want to give us as many as we needed, so I made up a story."

Lightning, punctuated by booming thunder, danced across the horizon over the Gulf. Odette gathered some driftwood to stoke the fire in front of her tent. Then, when the little fire began to crackle, she returned to the blanket beside Chief.

"What story?" she asked.

"I told the lady who ran the shelter we had a grant to train police and service dogs. She bit and let us adopt several dogs."

"You lied to her?" Odette said.

"I didn't intend to hurt anyone," Chief said. "The lie suited my needs."

"So you're telling me you're not a perfect person?" Odette said.

"Far from it," Chief said. "J.P. turned my lie into a reality."

"Jean Pierre Saucier?" Odette said.

"Yes," Chief said. "He'd been to several

seminars and was working on the concept. We decided to partner with him when we heard about how much service and police dogs sell for. I don't see a car. So how did you get here?"

"Hitchhiked," Odette said. "I found Mudbug in a sack someone had thrown in the ditch."

"Someone tried to kill that precious little pup?" Chief said.

"People's cruelty never ceases to amaze me," Odette said. "I'm just so thankful I was able to save her before she smothered or drowned."

"Amen to that," Chief said. "Now tell me what the hell you're doing here? There are no jobs on the island."

Odette opened her palm and showed Chief the piece of eight he and Jack had given her during their excursion to the Bourbon Street strip club.

"Looking for more of these," she said.

"You quit your job to look for doubloons?" Chief asked.

"Stripping boosted my ego and helped alleviate lots of body image problems I've struggled with my entire life. The pay was great, but I'd had it up to my neck with drunks groping my tits and grabbing my ass. I was going to hitchhike to Venice and get a job cooking on an offshore rig."

"Venice is south of here, in the opposite direction," Chief said.

Odette nodded. "After I found Mudbug, I stopped by the side of the road to clean her up and got to thinking."

"About what?" Chief asked.

"Even if I weren't naked, I'd probably have been the only woman on a jack-up drilling platform along with scores of horny men. Then I remembered how nice and well-mannered you and Jack were, even though you were both wasted."

"So you decided to come to the island instead

of going to Venice?" Chief said.

"Something like that," Odette said.

"How did you find your way here? Oyster Island isn't on the beaten path," Chief asked.

Odette showed him her cell phone. "I asked the voice in the box for directions. She guided me directly here."

"What about all your clothes and belongings?" Chief said.

Odette smiled. "I'm a minimalist. I brought all my worldly goods with me in my backpack."

"Must be a big one," Chief said.

"I may be small, but I'm strong," Odette said.

"Headstrong, at least," Chief said.

When Odette zipped her wetsuit to her waist, Chief realized she had no bathing suit underneath. She peeled the rubber down to her waist.

"What's the problem?" Odette said when she saw Chief's pained expression. "My tits are pretty standard. And besides, you've seen them before."

"Not the same," Chief said.

"What's different?"

"I'm sober, and we aren't in a strip club where the public condones nudity."

Odette laughed. "You're so full of shit! Tits are just tits. You're practically naked, yourself. That loincloth you are wearing is more suggestive than if you were naked. It turns me on. I can't help it; it's just human nature."

"But I'm not naked," Chief said.

"I can see the outline of your dick beneath the loincloth," Odette said.

"Maybe you better give me a blanket," Chief said.

"Shut the hell up," Odette said. "You want some pot or not?"

"You got no alcohol?"

"I told you I don't," Odette said, lighting up a

joint.

Thunder shook the island as Odette took a long draw on the joint and then handed it to Chief. Chief put it to his lips, thought about it a moment, and then took a puff.

"We had ladies' night every Tuesday at the club," Odette said. "The women who packed the place were anything but ladies." Odette laughed and shook her head. "You aren't supposed to touch. That never stopped anyone. The male dancers had great bodies. Most were gay and could care less how hot the audience got."

"You're getting me hot talking about it," Chief said.

Chief covered his crotch with his arms when Odette said, "I can tell. You have a body better than all of the dancers in our club. You'd have been a star."

"I couldn't have handled it," Chief said.

"Probably not," Odette said. "I'd pay good money to be in the audience if you ever did."

Chief took another puff of the pot. "This is good stuff, though not as good as my rum."

"You boys and your alcohol," Odette said. "Something I'll never understand."

"You said your grandmother was a traiteur," Chief said. "Jack and I visited a traiteur in Chalmette. Her name is Paula Boutet. Heard of her?"

Odette shook her head. "Why did you need to consult a traiteur?"

"Ghosts," Chief said. "There are two in the old lighthouse. Paula is going to exorcise them for us."

"When?" Odette asked.

"Tomorrow," Chief said.

"I told you I could read minds," Odette said. "I wasn't kidding. Can I help?"

"You aren't afraid of ghosts?" Chief asked.

"I'm not afraid of anything," she said

Light rain began sprinkling their shoulders, Mudbug asleep in her arms. She took the little dog to her tent, returning without her. Odette shivered and wrapped an old orange and brown Afghan around her shoulders.

"It's okay with me if it's okay with Paula," Chief said. "Have you ever seen a ghost?"

"There's not a Cajun alive who hasn't seen a ghost," Odette said. "I was barely five years old when I saw my first. I'd broken my arm, and my grandmother visited me in my dreams."

"What did she say?" Chief asked.

"She put her hand on my forehead and told me how pretty I was. Then, she wiped away a tear and told me things don't always go the way we want them to."

"Maybe it was just a dream," Chief said.

Odette took a puff of the pot. "Maybe this is just a dream. Do any of us know?"

"I'm an Indian, but a well-read Indian," Chief said. "Socrates said, 'The only thing I know for sure is that I know nothing for sure.'"

"You're a wise man," Odette said.

"Time for bed. I'm returning to my teepee," Chief said. "Will you be okay?"

"I'm scared the rougarou will return," Odette said.

Chief had the silent dog whistle on the chain and handed it to Odette.

"Wear this around your neck. If the rougarou returns, blow this. Big dogs will come to chase the monster away."

"Where's Jack?" Odette said.

"He and J.P. went to Bernadine's Whorehouse," Chief said.

"Jack went to a whorehouse?"

Chief said, "Men get urges. I think it's probably natural."

Odette was frowning. "Why do men think they have to pay for pussy?"

"I'll take the fifth on that one," Chief said.

"You need your big ass kicked, you know it?" Odette said.

"Hey," Chief said. "Women aren't perfect."

"A big amen to that," Odette said. "But we are human."

"I'm leaving," Chief said. "I have rum at my teepee. If the rougarou returns, blow the whistle. The dogs will bail you out."

Lightning continued dancing out over the Gulf as Chief and Odette exchanged a hug, and Chief started away into the darkness. He stopped when Odette spoke.

"Chief, I don't know who this John Paul Saucier is. If he's a cop, I don't trust him."

Chief turned. "There are few people I'd trust more than J.P."

"I've never known a cop you could trust," Odette said.

"Maybe not," Chief said. "Goodnight, Miss Odette."

"Goodnight, Chief," Odette said with a wave.

The rain had intensified, peppering Chief's bare shoulder's as he headed back to his teepee. The dogs and cat were asleep on his pallet, spread out such there was no room for him. Scooping up Coco and Buttercup, he moved them to the opposite side of the pallet and crawled in beside them. Neither of them awoke.

Old Joe opened his eyes long enough to lick Chief's hand before returning to sleep.

Chapter 17

J ack was waiting when J.P. arrived at the front door decked out in his police uniform, complete with polished boots, badge, and Stetson hat.

"You can't go like that. They'll think it's a bust," Jack said.

"You kidding me? The girls will love it. They'll be so hot."

"You can't show up at a whorehouse in a police uniform," Jack said.

"The girls know I'm not there to bust them," J.P. said. "The uniform adds to the fantasy."

"This is reality, not fantasy," Jack said.

"Hell, Jack," J.P. said. "Everyone needs a little fantasy now and then. Go put on your navy uniform."

"I haven't worn a uniform in years," Jack said.

"Don't you still have your dress uniform in the closet somewhere?"

"I'm not going to a whorehouse in a white dress uniform," Jack said.

"Yes, you are. Go put it on," J.P. said.

"You're nuts," Jack said.

"Just do it. Trust me when I tell you there is

no better aphrodisiac."

Jack was grumbling as he disappeared into his bedroom, returning dressed in a white coat, pants, and hat, colorful military awards pinned over his heart.

"I feel like an idiot," he said.

"Your uniform looks brand new," J.P. said.

"Because I only wore it once," Jack said.

"Those are navy medals," J.P. said. "I thought you were in the Merchant Marines."

"The Navy discharged me when they found out I'd lied about my age," Jack said.

"How old were you?"

"Fifteen," Jack said.

"You joined the Navy when you were fifteen? How did you get away with that?"

"Don't ask," Jack said.

"You were in Vietnam?"

"On a gunboat patrolling the Mekong," Jack said.

"Good God Almighty!" J.P. said. "See any combat?"

"Don't ask," Jack said.

"I understand," J.P. said. "I was in Iraq."

"This is crazy. I don't want to look like an old fool," Jack said. "I'm putting my jeans back on."

J.P. grabbed his elbow and nudged him toward the door. "No, you're not. Let's go."

Jack continued to grumble as he climbed into J.P.'s big truck.

"Where is the place?"

"Up the road," J.P. said. "Relax and have a shot of rum."

J.P. finally left the unimproved road leading from the island and headed to St. Bernard's main rural intersection. Semis occupied the big parking lot behind the gas pumps, retail store, and fast-food joint.

"This place is a goldmine," he said. "The

drivers can get a shower, buy books, C.D.s, fast food, groceries, gamble on the slots, and visit the girls in the back. Wish I had a piece of the action."

"Slots?" Jack said. "They aren't legal at truck stops."

"Everything you can pay for under the table is legal in Louisiana," J.P. said.

"You're a cop," Jack said. "Aren't you supposed to uphold the law?"

J.P. laughed. "You gotta be from Massachusetts. There's always been gambling and prostitution in rural Louisiana. Where do you think the congressmen come to get laid?"

"We aren't going to get busted?" Jack asked.

"I'm the law in these parts," J.P. said. "I'm not busting anybody, and no one is busting me. Unless I cross the wrong politician, that is."

"I don't want to spend the night in jail," Jack said.

"Shut the hell up, or I'm going to bust you right now and run you into Chalmette," J.P. said.

"You wouldn't," Jack said.

"No, and nobody else is either," J.P. said.

J.P. parked the truck behind the neon-lighted super-station. Jack stood behind him as he banged on the big door in the back.

"It's J.P., Bernadine," he said. "Let us in. I'm horny as hell."

The door opened after someone had peeked through the eyehole. It was a woman dressed in a short red skirt, an older woman with the body of a thirty-year-old. J.P. was smiling as he picked her up, twirled her around, and then, after returning her feet to the floor, gave her a big hug.

"You asshole, J.P., I thought it was the cops."

"It is the cops, Bernadine. Get your clothes off right now, or I'm going to run you in."

Bernadine's dour expression had morphed

into a smile.

"Girls," she called. "Your favorite wayward St. Bernard cop is here."

Three scantily-clad young women, all descending on J.P., quickly appeared from somewhere in the back.

"Where have you been, J.P.?" a blond cutie dressed in a pink see-through teddy asked."

"Leave him alone," the brunette in a blue teddy said. "You had him last time. It's my turn."

"The hell, you say," The pretty red-head in a yellow teddy said. "He's mine tonight."

The three women squealed when J.P. said, "You girls control yourselves, or I'll get my handcuffs out."

"You promised you'd choose me next time you came in," the blond woman said.

"You're all so pretty. I can't make up my mind. How about a foursome?"

J.P. had a giant grin on his face as the girls dragged him toward a door. Before disappearing behind it, he tossed his Stetson to Bernadine.

"We won't see them for a while," she said.

Except for a few wrinkles identifying her as an older woman, Bernadine could have passed as one of her working girls. She had brown hair, ruby lips and smiled when she gave Jack a wink.

"Hope you're not expensive," Jack said. "Three girls must cost quite a penny."

Bernadine's throaty laugh surprised him. "The cost of doing business," she said. "We keep the cops happy, and they don't bust us."

"You're worried that J.P. would bust you?" Jack asked.

"That's the way the game works," Bernadine said, extending her hand. "I'm Bernadine. To whom do I have the pleasure of speaking?"

"Just Jack," he said.

"Love your uniform," Bernadine said. "You

look a bit too old to be in the military."

"J.P. made me wear it. Said it affected women."

"It does. I haven't turned a trick in twenty years. That solid white uniform of yours has heated me for the first time in a decade."

"Those girls that went with J.P. are too young for me. I could be comfortable with you, though?"

Bernadine's throaty laugh froze him in his tracks. "I'm the madam," she said. "I own the place and don't do tricks anymore."

"You like rum?" Jack asked.

"Who doesn't?"

"Take a sip of this," he said, handing her his flask.

"Does it have an aphrodisiac in it?" she asked.

"Taste it and decide for yourself."

Bernadine opened the flask and took a sip, "Oh, my God, this is wonderful. Are you married?"

"Not guilty," Jack said. "I'm the lighthouse keeper over on Oyster Island."

"Never been there," Bernadine said. "Is that where the Majestic Casino was?"

"Not was, is. It's old and still magnificent," Jack said.

"People keep telling me tales about the Majestic," Bernadine said. "They had many beautiful ladies of the night there."

"Courtesans famous the world over for their looks, though not a single one could match your beauty," Jack said.

Bernadine smiled and unfolded her arms. "You are trying to get into my pants, sweet talker."

"You say I have a chance?"

"Flesh and blood ages though I still have fantasies," Bernadine said.

"I have a few fantasies of my own," Jack said.

"Who else lives on the island?"

"No one but Chief and me," Jack said.

"Chief?"

"The last of the Atakapas," Jack said.

"Want me to get one of the girls for you?" Bernadine asked.

"I want you," Jack said.

"I'm not available," she said.

"Why not?" he asked.

"I told you, I'm the madam, and I own the place. We have plenty of girls who would be happy to accommodate you."

"I haven't been with a woman in twenty years," he said. "I want an older woman. I want you."

"You don't have enough money for me, honey," she said.

"Wait a minute," he said.

Jack went to the truck and returned with an unopened bottle of Dominican rum.

"What about this?" he asked.

"You want me to make love to you for a bottle of rum?"

"Not just any bottle of rum," he said. "This one's worth at least four thousand dollars."

"No bottle of rum is worth that much," she said.

"This one is. It's almost one-hundred years old."

"You'd pay four-thousand dollars to have sex with me?" Bernadine asked.

"Even more if I had the money," he said. "You're beautiful."

Bernadine grinned. "No one has told me I'm beautiful in twenty years. You're lying through your teeth."

"I'm not lying. You're gorgeous. I'm giving you a bottle of rum worth four thousand dollars.

Make love to me."

The lobby bartender listened to the conversation as he polished a glass. Bernadine took the bottle of rum from Jack and handed it to him.

"Otto, open this bottle and tell me what you think it's worth."

The balding little man took the bottle, opened it, poured a shot, and put the glass to his lips.

"This is the best rum I've ever tasted in my life," he said.

"Is it worth four-thousand dollars?" she asked.

"Every penny of it," he said.

Bernadine left the bottle on the bar, grabbed Jack's hand, and led him through the closed door. He followed her down the narrow hallway to an apartment in the corner of the building. Though bigger and newer, it reminded him of his house on Oyster Island.

"Take off your jacket," Bernadine said. "It can't be comfortable in this weather."

Jack peeled off the long-sleeved jacket. "Thought you'd never ask," he said, hanging it and his hat on a hatrack in the corner.

"Okay," Bernadine said. "What's your fantasy?"

"Tell you the truth, I haven't had a fantasy in years."

"Not good. Everyone needs a fantasy."

"What's yours?" Jack asked.

Bernadine grinned. "I've had part of my biggest fantasy fulfilled already tonight."

"Which is?"

"Someone paying me four grand to have sex with them," she said.

"What's the other part?"

"It's personal," Bernadine said.

"We all have secrets," Jack said. "Some too

dark to talk about."

"What secret do you have?" Bernadine asked.

Jack smiled. "I'm vain. I was a cook in the Merchant Marines. Though I don't usually brag, I think I'm the best cook in the world."

"You're kidding me," Bernadine said.

"Want me to cook you something?"

"I know you aren't going to believe this. That's the other part of my fantasy," she said.

"Being able to cook?"

"Having a man cook for me."

"Hell, you can satisfy that fantasy at almost any restaurant in New Orleans."

"Someone who cooks for me because they want to, not because I pay them to do it," Bernadine said.

Jack's grin disappeared when he opened the refrigerator. From there, he moved to the pantry.

"You don't cook much, do you?" he asked.

"Soup, T.V. dinners, and sandwiches are what I live on," Bernadine said.

"Like eggs benedict?" he asked.

"I adore eggs benedict and champagne," she said. "I have all the ingredients though I've never attempted it."

"Why not?" Jack asked.

"Guess I was waiting for you to come along."

An old recliner sat in front of Bernadine's wall-sized television. He took her hand and led her to the comfortable chair, adjusted it, removed her shoes, and gave her feet a soothing massage. Not done, he massaged her neck.

"Eggs benedict is easy. My from-scratch Hollandaise sauce is tricky," Jack said. "Relax, take a nap or watch T.V. until I finish. I promise you won't be disappointed."

Along with the wonderful aroma wafting from the kitchen, the foot and neck massage acted as a relaxing sedative Bernadine hadn't anticipated.

Her eyes opened when Jack gave her shoulder a gentle shake.

"You ready?"

"Smells like heaven," Bernadine said.

Jack had found a candle in one of the kitchen cabinets. The orchid-scented candle popped and flickered in the center of the table as Bernadine took her first bite of the eggs benedict.

"Hope you don't mind. I opened the bottle of Dom you had chilling in the fridge," Jack said.

"It's been waiting for just this moment. Your meal is perfect. I've never tasted better eggs benedict," she said.

"And you never will," Jack said. "I'm the only person in the world who knows the ingredients in my Hollandaise sauce."

"And you're not telling?" she asked.

She laughed when he said, "If you twist my arm, or maybe something else."

They held hands and cuddled on the couch like teenagers when they finished eating. Jack finally got to his feet.

"J.P. will be waiting," he said. "I'd better go."

"You can't go. We haven't made love yet," Bernadine said.

Jack kissed her forehead and said, "Yes, we have."

Chapter 18

The morning sun was peeking up from the Gulf of Mexico as Chief arrived at Jack's little house, the aroma of brewing coffee and freshly-baked biscuits already emanating from the open door. Old Joe, Lucky, and Coco wasted no time in hurrying into the house. J.P. was emerging from his Airstream.

"How did it go last night?" Chief asked.

"Great for me," J.P. said. "You'll have to find out from Jack about his experience."

"He didn't tell you?" Chief asked.

"When I asked him last night on the way back to the island, he smiled like the Cheshire cat and wouldn't tell me anything."

They walked in on Jack whistling a catchy tune as he set the table, flour and coffee stains on his white apron. He flinched when Chief poked him in the ribs.

"Got something you want to tell us?" Chief asked.

Jack didn't take the bait. "Like what?"

"Like how was your visit to Bernadine's?"

"Do you always meddle in other people's business?"

"Just yours," Chief said. "If you have a story

147

to tell, then let's hear it."

"Who says I have a story?"

"Why are you so defensive?"

Chief's question didn't go well with Jack as he started clearing the food from the bench table.

"Don't take mine," J.P. said. "It wasn't me harassing you."

Chief glared at J.P. "I'm not harassing anyone," he said. "You went to a whorehouse last night. I'm curious how it went. Sorry if I touched a nerve."

"I had a wonderful time," Jack said. "I cooked for Miss Bernadine, and we watched T.V."

"You cooked for the owner?" Chief asked.

"What else got cooked?" J.P. said.

"Nothing," Jack said. "We simply got to know each other."

"You did more than that," J.P. said. "You gave her a bottle of Dominican Rum for her services. I had to wait almost an hour with Otto at the bar. We put a dent in Miss Bernadine's bottle."

Chief gave Jack a dirty look. "You paid for sex with a bottle of rum that's half mine?"

"Get your panties out of a wad," Jack said. "There was no screwing involved. We have seven bottles of rum left, three are mine, and four are yours. I don't spend other people's money. Even if I did, we're partners, and partners are supposed to help each other and not stab them in the back."

An unexpected voice at the door interrupted the dispute. It was Paula Boutet and her husband.

"Hello," she said. "It's Jimmy and me. Are we disturbing something?"

"Paula," Chief said. "I'd almost forgotten you were coming today."

"If it's a bad time," she said. "We can reschedule."

Jack rushed to the open door, grabbed Paula and Jimmy's hands, and pulled them into the house.

"I've cooked breakfast," he said. "Have you eaten?"

"We ate before we left the house. Doesn't matter. Jimmy's always hungry," Paula said.

Paula's smile faded when she noticed J.P. for the first time.

"J.P.," she said. "What are you doing here?"

"Jack, Chief, and I are partners in a dog-training facility. We're building kennels, pens, and training structures."

Jimmy didn't seem to notice his wife's discomfort as he shook J.P.'s hand.

"How you doing, J.P.?" he asked.

"I'm good, Jimmy. I never had a chance to talk to you about Paula and me."

Jimmy's grin was infectious. "That was ten years ago when we were all still in high school. Don't worry about it. Me and Paula are happily married. What's your deal with the dogs?"

"We're going to train police and service dogs," J.P. said.

"No kidding? Any chance I could be part of the group?"

J.P. and Chief glanced at Jack. "We have three partners," he said. "I'm not sure we need four."

"Guess Paula didn't tell you about my side business."

J.P., Jack, and Chief glanced first at Paula and then back to Jimmy.

"What side business?" Jack asked.

"I have a website where I market specialty dogs all over the world: hunting dogs, police dogs, service dogs. No dog changes hands in the world without checking my website first. I can get us the best price for your graduates, plus I'm a hell of a carpenter. Take me as a partner. I promise I'll carry my weight."

"If you already sell dogs, what advantage is it for you to work with us?" Jack asked.

"Though I market dogs," Jimmy said, "I've never worked directly with them. I want to become a trainer because I believe it can only help grow my business."

"A four-way split of the profits cuts things thin," Jack said.

"You don't realize how much I can bring to the table," Jimmy said. "A four-way split of a million dollars is better than a three-way split of a hundred thousand."

J.P. glanced at Jack and Chief. "Sounds good to me," he said.

"Hell," Jack said. "Marketing is the name of the game. Count me in."

"When do you start?" Chief asked.

"I'm ready right now. Tell me what you want me to build," Jimmy said.

"Let's eat first," J.P. said. "We can't let Jack throw away his wonderful chow."

The spat concerning Bernadine momentarily forgotten, Jack began returning the biscuits and eggs to the plank table. Paula was smiling as she helped him serve. All conversation stopped when an attractive young woman dressed in only a black bikini stood in the doorway, a small dog in her arms. Jack was the first to notice.

"Odette, is that you?"

"It's me. Chief didn't tell you I was on the island?

Chief could only shrug when Jack and J.P. gave him a look.

"Don't you think you should have shared your information with your partners?" Jack asked.

"I was going to tell you. Other things got in the way," Chief said.

"Did you tell them about the rougarou?" Odette asked.

Jack gave Chief another look. "The rougarou returned to the island last night?" he said.

"Scared the hell out of Mudbug and me," Odette said.

Jack was no longer smiling. "Chief?" he said.

"I was going to tell you," Chief said.

"What about the rougarou?" Jack asked.

"It attacked Mudbug and me last night. I put a spear through its chest. The creature yanked it out and tossed it on the sand."

Jack shook a kitchen knife at Chief. "Remind me again why I continue to feed you?"

"Maybe I should have kept my big mouth shut about Bernadine's," Chief said.

"Might have been a good idea," Jack said. "Odette, this is Paula and Jimmy Boutet, and Jean Pierre Saucier."

"Pleased to meet all of you," Odette said. "Chief tells me you're a traiteur. So was my grandmother."

"Then you must have special powers," Paula said.

"Chief says ghosts haunt the old lighthouse, and you are here to chase them away."

Paula smiled. "My goal is to help them pass peaceably from this dimension into the next."

"I've been interested in this sort of thing my entire life. Would you mind very much if I helped you?"

"I don't mind at all," Paula said.

"Something smells wonderful," Odette said.

"Good," Jack said because I have a place set for you at the table."

"Your little dog is precious. Her name is Mudbug?" Paula asked.

"I hitchhiked here from New Orleans and found Mudbug in a ditch. Someone had put her in a garbage bag and tossed her out of the car. There was a hole in the bag, or she would have smothered."

"That is so awful," Paula said. "Some people have no soul. If you let me, I'll hold Mudbug while you eat."

Odette was smiling when she handed the tiny dog to Paula. When Paula put the squirming dog on the floor, she ran out the doggy door.

"Oh, my!" Paula said.

J.P. had made sure he sat beside Odette. "She'll be fine," he said. "The other dogs won't hurt her."

"Sure about that?" Odette asked.

"You have my Louisiana guarantee," he said.

"Are you the cop?" Odette asked.

"Yes, ma'am, I am."

"I don't usually trust the police," Odette said.

"You can trust me, ma'am," J.P. said.

"You don't have to call me ma'am," she said. "Odette works just fine."

"My mama taught me to be respectful of all women," J.P. said.

"Your mama must be Cajun," Odette said.

"One hundred percent," J.P. said.

"Why is it I have a feeling you're pulling my leg?" Odette asked.

Jack and Chief groaned when J.P. said, "That's something I would never do."

Odette gave Chief a look. "What am I missing?"

"When J.P. starts pouring on the charm, run away as fast as you can," Chief said.

"I thought we were friends," J.P. said.

"When you get to heaven," Jack said, "God's going to turn you away for lying."

J.P. didn't miss a beat. "God knows I'm Cajun. He gives us a special dispensation."

Odette couldn't help but laugh as she worked

on her eggs and biscuits.

"I like you," she said. "Even if you are a cop."

"You shot a rougarou last night?" J.P. asked.

"Hit him square in the chest," Odette said. "Didn't even bother him."

"Because he's supernatural," Jimmy said. "I seen one in the swamp once."

"J.P. seems to think there's another explanation," Jack said.

"My mama always told me they were supernatural," J.P. said. "Turns out there's a scientific reason."

"I've never heard that," Paula said.

"Rougarous are humans infected with a rabies-like virus. They become monsters when phases of the moon trigger the disease."

"That sounds so crazy," Odette said.

"But true," J.P. said. "Fortunately, there's a cure."

"A cure for a disease no one has ever heard of?" Odette said.

"There was an outbreak a few years back on Goose Island. A researcher in the Garden District developed a medicine to cure the disease. We cleaned it up by administering the medicine to the rougarous."

Jack snickered. "Rougarous can't be too monstrous if they let you give them a shot in the arm."

"We used pneumatic guns," J.P. said. "Only problem is you have to get pretty close before you pull the trigger."

"Count me out," Jack said.

"Do you have a suspect in mind?" Odette said.

"A doctor recently treated a Cajun trapper for buckshot wounds. The trapper disappeared back into the swamp before anyone could question him. My best guess is he's our rougarou."

"Then give me one of the guns with the medicine," Odette said. "Won't be long before that monster returns to avenge the spear I stuck in his chest."

"I still have the gun, but nothing to fill them with," J.P. said.

"Can you get more?" Odette asked.

"Maybe. Jack, Chief, and I are going to visit the Garden District to see if the researcher is still alive."

"Can I go with you?" Odette asked.

"We were going to do a few other things while we were there," Chief said.

Odette grinned. "Like visit the strip club?"

"Maybe," Chief said.

"You can take me," Odette said. "I enjoy watching naked girls dance. Especially when I can drink and don't have to work."

Jimmy was smiling, Paula looking horrified. "Don't you dare ever set foot in a strip joint, Jimmy Boutet. If I'm not enough woman for you, I'll file the divorce papers tomorrow."

J.P., Odette, Jack, and Chief looked the other way when Jimmy said, "Honey Babe, I'd never lust after any woman except you."

After clearing the breakfast dishes, Jack, Jimmy, J.P., and Chief exited the kitchen to work on the dog training facilities. Paula was sitting on the couch, a crazy look on her face. She beckoned Odette to join her. After taking her in her arms, she began to cry.

"What's the matter?" Odette said.

"You're a traiteur. I sensed it when you walked in the door."

"My grandmother was a traiteur," Odette said. "She never told me anything about it."

"It's not something you learn. You are born with the ability."

"What ability?"

"To see the future and the past; to commune with the dead and everything in between," Paula said.

"Are you . . . ?

"A witch? I am, and so are you. It's something I've never told anyone, not even my husband."

"What does it mean?" Odette asked.

"Only females are traiteurs, you and I sisters. If you're born to practice necromancy, you'll never be the same again. It's a damned curse you can never escape. Prepare for knowledge you never thought you'd have and a devil's curse that has already seized your soul."

Chapter 19

An unexpected storm brought an early end to the construction, the men returning to Jack's before they were ready to stop for the day. Paula helped Odette prepare lunch with ingredients found in Jack's larder. With appetites whetted from their physical exercise, they tore into the gumbo and French bread waiting for them on the plank table.

"Best gumbo I ever tasted," Jack said. "Good work, Paula."

"I didn't make it," Paula said. "Odette did. I had a taste, and in my opinion, she's good enough to be the chief chef at any restaurant in New Orleans."

"Where'd you learn to cook like this?" Jack asked.

"I had a partial scholarship at L.S.U., my major hotel and restaurant management," Odette said. "My dad was a roughneck on offshore rigs. During summer breaks, I cooked on the jack-ups feeding hungry crews twenty-four hours a day."

"What's a college graduate doing stripping on Bourbon Street?" Jack asked.

"I haven't graduated yet. A rig explosion killed my daddy. I dropped out of college to help my mom," Odette said.

"Are you going back to college when your mom is on her feet again?" Jack asked.

"She already is. That's why I quit my job. I'll finish my degree someday. Right now, I'm into other things," Odette said.

Their conversation was disturbed when Jimmy's cell phone rang.

"Problems at the plant," he said. "Got to get back. Sorry, Paula. You'll have to do the exorcism later."

"Paula can stay. You can ride back to Chalmette with me, Jimmy," J.P. said. "I have to be at work tomorrow at six. I'm leaving my Airstream here. Paula is welcome to use it."

"Perfect," Paula said. "Odette and I can deal with the ghosts later tonight, and I can return to Chalmette tomorrow. Will you be okay by yourself for one night, Honey Bun?"

Jimmy glanced around to see if anyone was looking. "Baby, I'll be fine. Take care of business. I'll see you tomorrow," he said.

The storm had turned into a thunder boomer, lightning flashing out over the Gulf as rain pelted the roof of Jack's house.

"Lucky and I'll be here next weekend," J.P. said before he, Jimmy, and Lucky left the shelter of the house and hurried to his truck.

Jack, Chief, Paula, and Odette watched through the open door as J.P. and Jimmy disappeared over the bridge to the mainland.

"How are you going to perform the exorcism in this weather?" Chief asked.

"The storm will have passed before dark," Paula said.

"How do you know?" Jack asked.

"I know," she said.

157

"Can you keep Mudbug for me while we're working?" Odette said.

Mudbug was lying in the doggy bed along with Oscar and Coco.

"No problem," Jack said. "I think she likes it here."

"I'm going to my tent on the beach," Odette said.

"I'll join you later," Paula said.

Jack and Chief were playing cards. "Want us to help?" Jack asked.

"Odette and I can handle it, though I need your cooperation."

"Anything you say," Chief said.

"You and Jack must stay here. You may hear strange sounds, maybe even screams. Doesn't matter. Don't try to help, and don't let the dogs out."

"Sure about that?" Chief asked.

"By tomorrow morning, the ghosts will be gone," Paula said. "Of that, I'm very sure."

"You got it, Miss Paula," Chief said. "I'm up fifty cents on Jack. I promise, he's going nowhere until he gets it back, or else I take all his money."

"Be careful," Jack said as Paula disappeared out the door.

Heavy clouds covered much of the waning moon as Paula set across the island to Odette's tent. She didn't need a lot of light to know where she was going. A fire glowed in the darkness, Odette sitting on her blanket in the sand. Paula stripped off her shorts and blouse, Odette watching the transformation.

Paula's everyday persona was that of a prim schoolmarm. That façade quickly disappeared as she untied the ribbon in her hair and let the dark tresses cascade almost to the crack of her ass. Though not very tall, her breasts were large and pendulous, a golden waning moon tattooed on her left breast. Odette's gaze locked on the oddly shaped half-moon aureoles surrounding her erect nipples.

"Take your clothes off," Paula said. "Do you have a witch's tit?"

Odette stripped off her bikini and stood naked in the pulsating glow of the fire as Paula rubbed below her breasts with the palm of her hand.

"What's a witch's tit?" Odette asked.

"An extra nipple. You have one right here."

"I always thought it was a mole," Odette said.

Paula grabbed Odette's hand and guided it to a spot beneath one of her large breasts.

"Can you feel it?" she asked.

Odette nodded. "What does it mean?"

"You don't hear much about witches these days. We avoid persecution because we guard our differences carefully. Even my husband Jimmy doesn't know I'm a real witch."

Paula shook her head when Odette said, "He's surely seen you naked many times."

"In ten years, he's never gotten a good look at my body," Paula said.

"How is that possible?"

Paula smiled. "No one makes love like a witch. When I finish with him, he's good for little else except to close his eyes and pass out. He probably doesn't even realize he's never seen me naked except in the dark."

"Why don't you just let him?" Odette said.

"Can't take the chance, not even with the man I love."

"That's crazy," Odette said.

"Most religions are male-oriented. Pastors, priests, and monks are predominantly males. That's what's crazy."

"Is there not a reason for that?" Odette asked.

"Only one reason," Paula said.

"What is it?" Odette asked.

"Male chauvinism," Paula said.

"We're both going to hell for talking about this," Odette said.

"That's what men want you to believe. It isn't true. Witches are all females. Before there was organized religion, there was paganism. All major Christian holidays are offshoots to pagan celebrations—Easter, Christmas. You get the picture.

"We aren't pagans," Odette said.

"You're wrong about that," Paula said. "Before organized religion, there were no doctors or priests. Sickness, childbirth, and death were all considered the purview of women born with special powers and knowledge. Witches."

"What about men?" Odette asked.

"Men control only the seed; nothing else. Life begins in a woman's womb and is born through the lips of her vagina. Milk dripping from female nipples nourishes life. That particular appendage is worthless on a male."

"I've never heard this," Odette said.

"Because witches still fear persecution," Paula said. "Look at my eyes."

One of Paula's eyes was dark, the other one blue.

"I didn't notice," Odette said.

"No one ever has," Paula said. "I wear a contact to mask my blue eye."

"Why are you so secretive?" Odette asked.

"If people knew what powers I possess, they'd find a way to eliminate me."

"Are there others like you?"

"Many more," Paula said. "You are one of us, though you haven't quite realized it yet."

"You sound as if you hate males," Odette said.

Paula's fury had disappeared, and she smiled. "I love my Jimmy, and it's okay that he thinks he's in control. I want you to know who I am."

"Am I a witch?" Odette said.

"Maybe," Paula said. "Before the night is over, we'll know for sure. At any rate, I'll need your help. Now, let's dance."

Paula began dancing beneath the muted light of a waning crescent moon partially cloaked by damp clouds. Odette joined her. Though having danced on stage, this was different. She could feel the energy emanating from the sky and the tides moving in the Gulf. For the first time in her life, she was one with the earth. The dancing ended when Paula grabbed Odette around the waist and kissed her on the mouth.

"It's time," she said. "Are you ready?"

"My heart is beating so fast it feels as if it's about to burst out of my chest," Odette said.

"The moon is shrinking," Paula said. "It is a time to reflect, purge and declutter. Do you understand?"

"Not really," Odette said.

"There are people you need to let go of and others you need to embrace," Paula said.

"I hope I'm getting the picture," Odette said.

Paula kissed her again. "You are ready. We must dress in black."

Paula had brought a backpack from the house. From it, she handed Odette a swath of black cloth which did little to cloak her nudity.

"Do you have the key for the lighthouse?" Odette asked.

"We won't need it," Paula said. "It'll be open."

A bloodcurdling wail radiated from the stairway when Paula and Odette entered the lighthouse. They needed no light as a blue glow

saturated the inside of the bottom floor. Paula lit
a black candle as they ascended the stairs.

"What's happening?" Odette asked.

"We're about to meet the dead."

"And the candle?" Odette asked.

"A spirit candle. It helps the dead pass to a
different plane of existence."

"I've seen ghosts," Odette said. "What's
making the noise sounds more like demons."

"Take a deep breath, sister, and be brave,"
Paula said.

"Sisters," Odette said, giving Paula a fist
bump.

An unearthly wail echoed off the lighthouse
walls as Paula and Odette ascended the steep
metal stairway. Smoke rising from the candle
affected the two spirits occupying the old
structure as the wail melded into a low moan.
The two women exited the stairway on the second
floor.

The storm had begun again, this time in
earnest. Lightning flashed through the windows,
the metal stairway rattling as thunder rocked the
old structure. When two demons came out of the
walls, Odette stepped behind Paula. Paula held
her ground.

"We are here to help, not harm you. I've
brought a spirit candle to assist in your passing,"
Paula said.

Despite her best efforts, Odette's entire body
was in a tremor. Red and blue smoke rose from
the skull-faced demons. Paula didn't move as the
two creatures towering over her crept ever closer.
An organ began to play, filling the lighthouse with
atonal music. Paula waved the candle.

"This lighthouse isn't where you should
spend eternity," she said. "We are here to help
you cross over."

Instead of engulfing Paula in flames, the two demons began to transform, their images popping and fading. When the smoke and flame disappeared, a man and woman stood before Paula dressed in clothes of a different decade. Tears streamed down the blue-eyed woman's pale face as the man attempted to comfort her.

"They took our Laurel from us," the spirit man said. "We can't leave without her."

"Who took your daughter?" Paula said.

"A gang of evil men," the spirit woman said.

"How old was Laurel when the men took her?" Paula asked.

"Barely fifteen," the spirit woman said.

She nodded when Paula said, "And they killed you and your husband when you tried to protect her?"

"They defiled Sarah before killing her," the spirit man said. "They tied a noose around my neck and tossed me over the banister."

Odette's hand went to her mouth. "Oh my God! Who would do such a horrible thing?"

"A rape gang," the spirit woman said.

"There are graves in Delacroix that bear your names," Paula said. "Your souls are consecrated. You are free to cross over."

"We won't cross without Laurel," the spirit man said.

"You must go now," Paula said. "I will assist in consecrating Laurel's body and make sure her soul crosses over."

"How can we trust you?" the spirit man asked.

"You must because God sent me to help you," Paula said.

The spirit woman was weeping when she looked at her husband.

"I trust her," she said.

"We'll set you free," Paula said. "I'll return Laurel to you. I promise."

Antique glass in a bay window reflected the storm outside the lighthouse. A dust-covered ax lay at Paula's feet. Picking it up, she moved toward the window, leaving Odette alone with the two spirits. They cried as one, Odette hugging the man and woman as Paula sat the candle on the dusty floor, raised the ax, and took a roundhouse swing at the bay window.

When the glass broke, the resultant explosion began forcibly sucking the contents of the lighthouse out the window, dragging Odette and Paula across the floor. Paula let go of the black candle. It flew through the opening, along with the two spirits.

The force of the wind slammed Paula and Odette into the wall, the noise ear-popping. When the suction finally ceased, the couple was gone, Paula and Odette, bloody, sweaty, grimy, and lying naked on the second floor of the lighthouse.

Odette was still crying when she noticed Paula's smile. She gave Odette a fist bump.

"We did it, partner. The spirits have crossed over."

Chapter 20

When Paula tried to stand, her eyes rolled to the back of her head. Odette, holding on long enough to ease her to the floor, grabbed her as she fainted. When she touched the baseball-sized contusion on Paula's forehead, she realized what had happened.

With the spirits gone, there was no light for Odette to see. Knowing she couldn't get Paula down the steep metal stairway alone, she headed for the stairs. After bumping into a wall, Odette waited for lightning to flash. When it did, she crawled toward the stairs.

Afraid of heights, Odette had dreaded climbing the circular staircase behind Paula. Now, unable to see, she clutched the railing as she eased down the stairway, her body shaking as she stepped off the last step. The storm had continued moving up from the Gulf, the door to the lighthouse creaking in the wind, rain pelting Odette's face as she exited the old building.

Paula was lying nearly naked on the second floor of the lighthouse. Even her husband Jimmy had never seen her without clothes on. It didn't matter as Odette knew there was no one to help except Chief and Jack. Her blond hair drenched, she burst through the door.

To say Jack and Chief were surprised seeing Odette naked in the doorway was an understatement. Jack hurried into his bathroom, returned with a robe, and draped it around her shoulders.

"Where's Paula," he asked.

"The second floor of the lighthouse. She's hurt. I couldn't lift her by myself. I need help," Odette said.

Jack tossed his flashlight to Chief as they followed Odette out the door, entered the lighthouse, and started up the circular staircase.

The sound of bats and the din of the storm out the broken window raised their stress levels. Jack and Chief were surprised when they realized Paula was naked. Chief lifted her and started for the stairs.

When they reached the shelter of Jack's house, they were soaking wet. Chief sat Paula in Jack's recliner, covering her with the orange Afghan draping the back of the chair as Jack got ice from his freezer and applied it to her head.

Jack glanced at Odette and said, "You look as if you could use a hot shower. Hand the bathrobe out the door to me. I'll put it in the dryer. It'll be warm and cozy when you finish your shower."

Odette removed the robe and handed it to Jack.

"You've seen me naked."

Jack smiled when Odette shook her ass before closing the bathroom door behind her. Paula was awake and aware when Odette exited the bathroom wearing the dry bathrobe. Jack was still holding ice to Paula's forehead. Her frown indicated she wasn't happy as Chief used a towel to dry her long hair.

"Are you angry about something?" Chief asked.

"You're in on my secret," Paula said.

"Hell, Paula," Chief said. "I always thought you were more than a traiteur. Everyone in Chalmette thinks you're a witch. Now, I'm sure of it."

Paula winced in pain and closed her eyes when she touched the knot on her head.

"Jimmy doesn't," she said.

Paula's reply brought a smile to Chief's usually impassive face.

"You have to be kidding. How could he not know?" Chief asked.

"Because I've kept it from him," Paula said. "He's never even seen me naked."

Jack smirked when Chief said, "Sounds like my ex-wife and me."

"Jimmy and I have a wonderful sexual relationship," Paula said. "Even if it's always dark when we do it."

"Crazy!" Chief said. "Jack and I just had a good look at your body. I think he'd agree you could be the star at any strip club in the country."

"That's a fact," Odette said. "If it were me, I'd never let my husband forget how good my bootie looks."

"People are afraid of witches," Paula said.

"No, they aren't," Chief said. "This isn't the Dark Ages. Most people don't even realize witches exist, or if they do what powers they possess."

Odette said. "I witnessed Paula's powers firsthand. She made a believer of me."

"Powers I'm afraid to let the world know I have," Paula said.

"Hell, Paula, there hasn't been a witch burned at stake in centuries, and Salem's a long way from here," Jack said.

"Maybe," Paula said. "I've never wanted to take the chance."

"There's no maybe about it," Jack said.

Paula's blue eye flashed in the dim light of Jack's living room. The storm had lowered the temperature by more than thirty degrees, and he'd started a fire in the fireplace. Mudbug was in Odette's arms on the couch, Coco, Old Joe, and Oscar lying in front of the fire, the other dogs asleep in the kennel in Jack's backyard. Jack gave Paula two aspirins as thunder shook the house.

"I need arnica," Paula said. "Can you find my handbag?"

Jack knew where it was and handed it to her. Paula put four tablets under her tongue and let them dissolve.

"The spirits are gone," she said. "At least in the lighthouse."

"There are more?" Jack asked.

"The old structure in the bay is full of them," Paula said. "What's the story?"

"The Majestic?"

"Tell me about it?" Paula asked.

"It was a hotel and casino back in the thirties, during Prohibition," Jack said.

"I wouldn't spend the night there if I were you," Paula said. "Some of the spirits haunting the place aren't benevolent, and many of them are ghouls."

"I've never heard rumors about ghosts or ghouls in the Majestic," Jack said,

"You'd never heard rumors about ghosts in the lighthouse until they scared the hell out of you," Paula said.

"You got rid of the ghosts in the lighthouse. Can't you do the same for the ones in the Majestic?" Jack asked.

Paula shook her head. "Not so simple," she said. "The couple in the lighthouse was grieving over their daughter. They'd never harmed a soul. Not so the dead haunting the Majestic. They were bad people and won't respond like normal ghosts. The Majestic is an evil place."

Rain pelted the roof, wind noise intense as Jack glanced at Chief.

"I need a stiff drink," he said. "I only have three bottles of rum left. You have four. Be a good partner and open one of your bottles."

Chief grumbled as he removed the top from a fresh bottle of Dominican rum. Jack poured each of them a mug when Chief handed the bottle to him.

"This rum is so good," Paula said.

"Maybe you'd better go slow," Jack said. "I'm pretty sure you have a concussion."

"I'm a witch," she said. "I have supernatural powers."

"Didn't stop you from getting knocked cold," Jack said.

"I know my body better than you do," Paula said. "Keep the rum flowing and talk to me about the Majestic."

"The U.S. banned the sale and use of alcohol in 1920," Chief said. "The Feds shut down all the bars, breweries, and distilleries across the country. Prohibition lasted thirteen years."

"The Majestic was the largest casino north of Havana, prostitution, drinking, and gambling wide open because of the mob-controlled access to the island," Jack said. "The very rich felt safe here and came from all over the country to enjoy the world-class amenities available."

"How did people reach the island?" Paula asked.

"Yachts and private boats, mostly," Chief said.

"What kept the Feds from raiding the place?"

"There's a secret channel through the barrier islands. When clientele arrived by boat, the casino would send a captain out to pilot it into the bay," Chief said.

"Where did the booze come from?" Odette asked.

Rum runners brought it in from the Bahamas, Cuba, Europe, and the Dominican Republic. The big Coast Guard boats were fast and could catch the rum runners in open waters. If the rum runners made it past the barrier islands, the draft was too shallow for the Coast Guard cutters."

"But some of the rum runners didn't make it," Odette said.

Chief nodded. "If they didn't surrender and agree to let the Coast Guard board them, government cannons blew them out of the water."

"So there are more cases of rum out there in the bay, maybe still in the holds of sunken rum runners?" Odette said.

"Maybe," Jack said.

"Where would you begin to look?" Odette said.

"No idea," Jack said.

"You aren't being truthful," Odette said. "I saw your maps."

"We found them in the lighthouse. Chief and I were thumbing through them when we saw the ghosts," Jack said.

"Were you looking for the maps when you went into the lighthouse?"

Jack glanced at Chief, and neither of them answered her question. Odette decided for the moment to let the matter drop.

Paula knew the rum she was drinking tasted good but had no idea its origin.

"So the old building in the bay was a casino during Prohibition?" she said.

"And a hotel," Jack said.

"I'm not sure I can help you rid the Majestic of its ghosts. As long as it's deserted, you have nothing to worry about," Paula said.

"That's the problem," Jack said. "It won't be deserted for long. One of the new owners is coming to the island. He plans to live in the Majestic while he manages its restoration."

"Then he's in for trouble," Paula said.

"You can help us, can't you?" Jack asked.

Paula winced when she rubbed the bump on her head.

"Do you have keys to the Majestic?" she asked.

"Of course I do," Jack said. "I'm the caretaker."

"Give them to me," Paula said. "I'll take a look."

"Right now?" Jack asked. "It's pouring down outside, and there's no electricity in the building."

"I'm already looped from your rum and half-drowned from the storm," Paula said. "What better time than right now?"

"The Majestic is too far away to walk to in this storm," Chief said.

"If you want to know about the ghosts, there's no better time than now to find out about them," Paula said.

"I'll go with you," Odette said. "I'm not afraid."

"I'm not afraid either," Jack said. "I just don't think it's a good idea."

Paula and Odette started for the door. "Wait," Chief said. "Is the top up on the ATV?"

"You don't know how to drive it," Jack said.

"I'll figure it out," Odette said.

"No one's going anywhere without me," Jack said. "You don't even have clothes to wear."

"My clothes are in Odette's tent," Paula said.

Jack rummaged through his closet, returning with pants and shirts.

"You're about my size, Paula," he said. "Odette, this is the best I can do for you. "Hopefully, it'll fit you like a dress. Put them on, and I'll meet you out front in five minutes."

Jack hurried out the door and fired up the ATV. He waited as rain drummed the vehicle's plastic roof until Paula, Odette, and Chief rushed outside to join him.

"Jimmy's going to kill us," Chief said.

"No, he won't," Paula said. "This is witch business."

After a damp ride through the storm, they reached the Majestic. Jack and Chief, the rain falling in bucket loads, followed the two women down the wooden walkway to the front door of the Majestic. They heard the first wail when Jack unlocked the door and let Paula and Odette into the old building. Jack shined his light in the direction of the howl.

"Turn off the light," Paula said.

The swath of Jack's light disappeared, replaced instantly by colors dancing across the walls, floor, and ceiling. The wails continued though they had no idea from where the sound was coming. A fiery demon popped out of the wall, followed by another.

"Back up," Paula said. "I can't do this without my black candle."

Once they were outside the building, Jack slammed the door and quickly locked it. The rain hadn't abated, heavy winds forming waves that lapped against the stilts the building sat on.

"What'll we do?" Jack asked.

"There's only one option," Paula said.

"Tell me," Jack said.

"Burn this godforsaken building to the ground," she said.

Chapter 21

Paula and Odette spent the rest of the night in J.P.'s Airstream, the sound of rain on the trailer's aluminum exterior lulling them to sleep. Paula was staring out the open door when Odette awoke.

"Thought you were going to snooze all morning," she said.

"This is the first real bed I've slept on in days," Odette said. "Along with the rain on the roof, it made sleeping easy."

"I hear that," Paula said. "It was late when we got here last night, and I was asleep before we had time to look at J.P.'s trailer."

"It's nice," Odette said.

"More than nice," Paula said. "It has gold fixtures in the bathroom. As perfect as the décor and every little detail, I'd almost swear J.P. is gay."

"Maybe he is," Odette said

"I promise you he isn't." Before Odette could comment about J.P.'s sexual proclivities, Paula said, "Jack's up and cooking. Hungry?"

"Starved."

Jack had dropped Chief off the previous night at the foot of his hill, Coco and Old Joe out back with the other dogs. Mudbug came running, leaping into Odette's arms.

"Miss me?" Odette said, kissing the little dog.

Paula laughed when Jack said, "That poor pup has been waiting all morning for you two to get out of bed."

"The kitchen's closed?" Paula asked.

"For everyone except two pretty girls," Jack said. "Need to wash up first?"

"You kidding?" Paula said. "J.P.'s Airstream is like a luxury hotel."

"He even has a built-in hairdryer in the bathroom," Odette said.

Odette and Paula were soon devouring scrambled eggs and grits.

"J.P. has a full head of hair. Some of us should be so lucky," Jack said, stroking his bald spot.

"Your grits are perfect," Paula said.

"Ghost-busting works up an appetite," he said.

"You're the best non-Cajun cook I've ever met," Paula said. "You should open a restaurant."

"Tried it once," Jack said. "Didn't work out."

"Why is that?" Odette asked.

"Let's say there was a woman involved."

Odette and Paula continued eating, though Jack's comment brought knowing smiles to their faces.

"Isn't there always?" Odette said. "Ever been married?"

"Came close a time or two," Jack said. "I never pulled the trigger."

"Then it must have been lust and not love," Odette said.

"When you're in the Merchant Marines, your ship is your wife. You go where she goes, and when she decides to go. Not favorable for a long marriage."

"Some women might like the freedom," Paula said.

Jack snickered. "I've known a few women like that. When I returned to port, I'd usually find them pregnant and married to another man."

"Women get lonely at night," Paula said.

"Tell me about it," Jack said. "That's why I like dogs. Oscar's always happy to see me."

"I don't know what I'd do without my cat, Trixie," Paula said.

"Let me guess," Jack said. "She's solid black."

"Can't be a witch without owning a black cat," Paula said. "They'd kick me out of the union."

"There's a witches union?" Odette said.

"No, baby," Paula said. "I was making a joke."

Jack turned away, hiding his smirk in the palm of his hand.

"You had a few hours to sleep on it," he said. "What do you think now about the ghosts in the Majestic?"

"That building is huge," Paula said.

Jack gave her a nod. "Three stories-worth of hotel and casino."

"Jesus!" Paula said. "No telling how many ghosts there are. When's the new owner getting here?"

Jack shrugged and said, "Can't say for sure."

"Can he sleep on your couch?" Paula asked.

"Mr. Castellano wants to renovate the Majestic and open the island up to tourists. He already has permission to gamble legally."

"How the hell did he manage that?" Odette said.

Frankie Castellano commands lots of power in Louisiana," Jack said.

Jack nodded when Odette said, "The real Frankie Castellano?"

"You must be kidding," Paula said. "The Don of the South?"

"One in the same," Jack said. "He wants to bring tourism and big-time gambling back to the island."

"What does Chief think about it?" Paula asked.

"He's not happy," Jack said. "He says the island was the property of the Atakapa Indians, and since he's the last Atakapa, he's the rightful heir to the entire island."

"Then it should be easy for him to keep Castellano from completing his plans to renovate the Majestic," Paula said.

"Chief's one of the finest persons I've ever met. His problem is he doesn't have a lick of business sense and no idea where the deed is."

"It has to be in the records of the parish courthouse," Odette said.

"It's not," Jack said. "There were mob shenanigans on Oyster Island in the thirties, people bought off, and documents altered or deleted. Going to take someone smarter than Chief and me to straighten things out."

"Does Castellano intend to boot Chief off the island?" Odette asked.

"Mr. Castellano's not a bad person," Jack said. "If he were, I wouldn't work for him. He assigned Chief's land on the hill to him, and he never has to leave."

"Mighty white of him to allow an indigenous person to continue living on his property," Odette said.

"Chief's not happy with the situation. Neither am I," Jack said.

"I know lots of lawyers from my time dancing on Bourbon Street," Odette said. "I'll ask around about a solution."

"You have a higher opinion of lawyers than I do," Jack said. "My experience is most of them would sell you out in a heartbeat."

"You know what they call a lawyer at the bottom of the ocean? Paula asked.

"What?" Odette said.

"A start."

Odette grinned. "At least they tipped big," she said. "Surely, there's an honest lawyer somewhere."

"Maybe so," Jack said. "More eggs?"

"I'm stuffed," Paula said. "I have to get back to Chalmette. No telling what trouble Jimmy is already in."

"Jimmy doesn't seem the type of man who would play around," Jack said.

"All men play around," Odette and Paula said in unison.

"Takes two to tango," Jack said.

"Typical defense," Paula said. "Breakfast was great. I'll wash your shirt and pants and return them to you."

"Then you'll be back?" Jack said.

"You kidding?" Paula said. "I haven't had this much fun in years. Now that Jimmy's a partner in your dog training facility, I'll tag along when he's here on business."

"Then maybe we can figure out what to do with the ghosts in the Majestic," Jack said.

"As I said, don't let anyone stay in the hotel," Paula said. "Their lives, and maybe even their souls, would be in danger."

"Sounds grim," Jack said.

"I'm not exaggerating," Paula said.

"After what I witnessed last night, I believe you. "Our road is getting rougher every day. Be careful going home," Jack said.

Outside, the rain was gone, the sky still cloaked in ominous clouds.

"My clothes are in Odette's tent," Paula said. "Grab Mudbug. I'll get the car and pick you up at the door."

"Aye, aye, captain," Odette said with a salute.

Mudbug and Odette were waiting outside the house when Paula returned with her car. Mudbug wriggled free from Odette's grasp, her tail wagging as she licked Paula's face.

"Cuteness overload," Paula said. "I'll take her if you don't want her."

"Mudbug's my baby. She goes where I go." Paula parked her red vehicle in front of Odette's tent, throwing off Jack's pants and shirt before she reached the front flap. "You have a killer body," Odette said. "Too bad you never tried stripping. You'd have made a fortune in tips."

"I may seem like a prude, but I love being naked as much as you do, baby," Paula said. "It's a witch's thing."

"Except for Jimmy," Odette said.

"Some men require only food and sex from their women, and I make sure Jimmy has plenty of both. I also provide something he can get nowhere else," Paula said.

"Like what?" Odette asked.

Paula winked and said, "Mystery."

"Back in the trailer, you seemed pretty sure J.P.'s not gay. Is that a guess, or do you know for a fact?"

"I wasn't always as straitlaced as I sometimes appear," Paula said. "When I was in high school, I was a real wild child."

"So you and J.P. got it on?"

"Me and practically every other girl at Chalmette High," Paula said.

"But you were different?"

"Hell no. I was as horny for J.P. as he was for me."

"He's so good-looking," Odette said. "How is he in bed?

"The only bed we ever did it in was the back of his old pickup." Paula cracked a smile. "Every time I see J.P., I think about the dirt and hay in my panties when I got home. Good thing I was doing my laundry, or my mother would have skinned me alive."

"I've had a few experiences like that," Odette said. "J.P.'s so handsome he could have been a movie star."

"And don't think he doesn't know it," Paula said. "Not to mention he's hung like a donkey."

"But you left him for Jimmy," Odette said.

"Once love wraps you in its spell, there's no cutting loose," Paula said. "True love lasts forever. Lust ends when you get your rocks off."

"Were you J.P.'s steady girlfriend?"

Odette's question brought a smile to Paula's face. "J.P.s never met a woman he didn't like. Once he'd had you, he was off to his next conquest."

"Sounds like a total asshole," Odette said.

"I'm told he changed after graduating college and joining the Army. He was an infantry officer in Iraq. From what I understand, he doesn't play around anymore," Paula said.

"Except for Bernadine's whorehouse," Odette said.

Paula grinned. "Even Jimmy went there once," she said.

"No way!" Odette said. "And you still love him?"

"Every man's a sinner, baby," Paula said. "He was on a fishing trip with his friends. They were drunk and had to prove to each other which one of them had the biggest dick. It's a man thing."

"That was his excuse?" Odette said.

"At least he confessed," Paula said. "Best sex I ever had the night I forgave him."

Odette was still wearing Jack's shirt, Paula smiling as she unbuttoned it. "I'll wash this for you and return it to Jack."

Paula left the tent, Jack's clothes under her arms and wearing the same demure yellow dress as when she'd arrived on the island.

"I'm worried about you, baby," she said. "You and Mudbug should stay in J.P.'s Airstream. It's too dangerous alone on the beach."

"Mudbug will protect me," Odette said.

"The rougarou will return, and you might not be so lucky this time," Paula said.

"I'm not afraid. You said I'm a traiteur like you."

Paula stared into Odette's eyes. "I was wrong," she said. "You're special, but not a traiteur." Paula kissed her on the mouth. "Take care, baby. I'll be back in a week or so. If you get scared, move to J.P.'s trailer. Promise me?"

Odette and Paula embraced. "We'll be here when you return. Before you go, I have something to ask you."

"Then ask me," Paula said.

"You told the spirits God had sent you to help Laurel cross over."

"A little white lie," Paula said.

Paula grinned when Odette asked, "Aren't you afraid of going to hell for lying?"

"If I can help Laurel cross over, the lie will be absolved," Paula said.

"How do you intend to do that?" Odette asked.

Paula glanced at the dark clouds over the Gulf. "I don't know yet," she said.

After watching Paula's car disappear, Odette grabbed Mudbug, went into the tent, and fell asleep atop her sleeping bag. She'd lost track of time when distant thunder and rain drumming the tent awakened her. A breeze rippled the flap, and Mudbug was barking at something.

"What are you barking at?" Odette asked.

Mudbug glanced at her and then ran outside. Odette followed, cool raindrops dripping down her bare shoulders. Mudbug was near the rolling surf of the beach, pawing at something in the sand. Whatever it was glinted in moonlight peeking through the clouds.

"What is it?"

Mudbug didn't need to answer as Odette picked up a gold doubloon. Forgetting the gentle rain, she began scanning the beach, looking for more gold. As the waves receded from shore, a golden glint caught her eye. She dug another piece of gold out of the sand before the waves rolled back to the beach.

Suddenly caught in the throes of gold fever, Odette ran through the surf, salty water stinging her busted lip from the tumble in the lighthouse. She'd found another piece of gold as dark clouds rolling in from the Gulf made it all but impossible to continue her search.

Mudbug was growling when Odette came dripping out of the breaking waves. When she glanced up and saw the giant rougarou less than ten feet from her, she realized the reason for Mudbug's growls.

Mudbug was between Odette and the ugly creature from hell as it advanced toward them. The beast's red eyes glowed in the muted moonlight. For the first time in her life, Odette regretted being naked. The rougarou was between her and the spear gun propped against the tent. She was reciting the rosary when she touched the dog whistle around her neck. Putting the whistle between her lips, she began to blow.

Chapter 22

Thunder rocked Jack's little house as he and Chief played spades on the plank table. Chief tossed his cards down and pushed three quarters, a nickel, and a dime across the table. Even though it wasn't exactly cold outside, driftwood blazed in the fireplace. The temperature didn't matter because Oscar, Coco and Old Joe were curled up in front of the warm hearth.

"You're a cheater, you know it?" Chief said. "Next time, we're playing gin rummy."

Jack smiled as he added the coins to the pile in front of him.

"Admit it," he said. "When it comes to cards, you ain't shit."

Chief took a drink from his coffee mug. "Shut the hell up," he said. "If we don't stop drinking our profits, we're going to have to go back to the swill you have in your liquor cabinet."

"Don't I know it?" Jack said. "Stop drinking so fast."

"Me? I can barely keep up with you."

"Because you Indians can't hold your liquor."

"Unless you want me to scalp what little hair you have left on your head, then knock it off with the Indian shit," Chief said. "You know I can hold my liquor. You're the only person I ever met I couldn't drink under the table."

"I'm just pulling your chain," Jack said. "When are we returning to New Orleans?"

"We'll have nothing left to sell unless we do it soon," Chief said.

"Then let's run up there this weekend," Jack said. "J.P. will be back, and he can take us to the man in the Garden District with the rougarou medicine."

"I have a feeling we've seen the last of the rougarou," Chief said.

Seeing the card game was over, Jack put the change in his pocket.

"Why do you say that?" he said.

"Indian intuition," Chief said.

Chief smiled when Jack said, "Let's both stop with the Indian bullshit. You're a man, just like me; no more and no less."

"I'm good with that," Chief said.

"If the rougarou never returns, we won't need to visit the scientist with the vaccine," Jack said.

"At least we can hit the strip joint on Bourbon Street," Chief said.

"Don't know if that's a good idea," Jack said. "Ever seen J.P. around a bunch of half-naked women?"

"No, but his reputation precedes him. It's all good. The girls at Rockie's have pretty much seen it all."

"Hope you're right," Jack said. "I don't ever want to spend the night again in the parish hotel."

"Me either," Chief said. "Every drunk in the place tried picking a fight with me."

"If you were small like me," Jack said, "you wouldn't have had that problem."

Old Joe was suddenly awake, emitting a plaintiff howl as he pointed his head toward the ceiling. Within seconds, the outside dogs came running through the doggie door. Chief opened the front door as the howling pack, including Oscar and Coco, raced toward the beach.

"What the hell!" Jack said.

"Guess I was wrong about the rougarou," Chief said.

"Oh, shit!" Jack said.

"Odette's in trouble. I gave her J.P.'s whistle, and she's blowing it. My shotgun's in the teepee. You have a weapon in this place?"

Jack fetched a 1911 Army-issue forty-five from a drawer and followed Chief out the door.

"This baby will stop that bastard in his tracks," Jack said.

"Ever shot that thing?"

"You bet I have," Jack said. "We'll get there faster in the ATV."

Jack and Chief raced across the beach, sliding to a stop in front of Odette's little tent. The lights of the ATV were their only illumination. It was enough.

The beast had backed against the tent, flailing at the pack of dogs nipping at his heels. Odette was outside the circle of chaos, stark naked and circling the dogs in an attempt to reach her spear gun. The rougarou was having none of it.

Jack jumped out of the ATV, dropped to his knees, and pointed the heavy .45 at the beast.

"Odette," Chief called. "Blow the whistle. Get the dogs to back off so Jack can shoot the big fucker."

When the dogs moved away from the rougarou, Jack unloaded seven rounds, none connecting. The dogs momentarily out of the way, the rougarou threw himself on Jack, going for his throat. Chief hit the rougarou with a diving tackle, flailing his fists at the creature's head. Odette blew the whistle again.

Chief and Jack found themselves covered with dogs intent on tearing out the throat of the crazed rougarou. The giant creature was howling, slashing out at his attackers, Jack and Chief alike. Breaking free from the pack, the beast started across the sand. Not before Odette put a spear through his thigh. He didn't bother pulling it out as he raced toward the bridge, the dogs in hot pursuit.

Chief grabbed Odette's arm. "You okay?" he asked.

Jack and Chief had blood all over them from the teeth and claws of the rougarou.

"I'm fine. I can't say as much for you two. Is that your blood or the dogs?"

"Both," Chief said. "Blow the whistle and call the dogs. We don't want to lose any of them."

Rain was falling in heavy drops as the dogs began returning.

"What about the rougarou?" Jack asked.

"He'll be back but likely gone for a while. Odette, you and Mudbug need to spend the night in J.P.'s trailer."

"The rougarou is gone. You said so yourself," Odette said. "Mudbug and I are staying in the tent."

"Then you're going to get wet," Jack said.

"Jack missed the rougarou with his antique pistol though it looks like he blew the hell out of your tent."

Odette's tent was lying halfway on the ground, flapping in the wind and pockmarked with large holes.

"Dammit!" she said. "You destroyed my tent."

"Sorry," Jack said. "Unless you and Mudbug want to sleep in the rain, you better come with us."

Odette rummaged through the ruined tent. A strong wind continued blowing, the rain cold, and Odette noticeably shivering. Chief's shirt was also wet when he pulled it off and draped it over her shoulders.

"Damn, girl, don't you ever wear clothes?" he said.

She grinned as she adjusted the shirt and buttoned it. "It wasn't long ago you and Jack were paying me to dance naked."

"Maybe," he said. "Right now, you feel more like my daughter, and I'm not into incest."

"Well, you're no relation to me, and I lost my innocence long ago. Trust me when I tell you I'd rather have you drooling over my tits than telling me I remind you of your daughter."

Chief came close to cracking a grin. "My daughter is like her mother, who I don't believe has ever had a carnal thought in her head."

Jack was behind the wheel of the ATV. "Stop whining and get in. You can share your heart-warming platitudes when we're dry and sitting in front of the fireplace."

The dogs beat them to the house, shivering in front of the door when they pulled to a stop. J.P.s pickup was also waiting. Everyone, including the dogs, followed Jack into the house when he ran to the front door and opened it.

J.P. wasn't smiling. "What the hell's going on?" he asked.

"The rougarou was back," Jack said.

Jack and Chief were bleeding, as were most of the dogs. Odette found cotton balls and a bottle of rubbing alcohol in the bathroom and began cleaning wounds.

J.P. took some of the cotton balls from Odette. "My Cajun intuition told me something was wrong, not to mention Lucky was acting crazy."

"We're fine," Chief said. "Nothing but superficial wounds."

"No, you're not all right," J.P. said. "You and Jack are infected with the rougarou virus."

"What's that supposed to mean?" Jack asked.

"Not a damn thing," J.P. said, "unless you have a hankering to become a shifter and join the pack."

"You can't be serious," Jack said.

"As a heart attack," J.P. said.

"What'll we do?" Chief asked.

"We have to get some medicine," J.P. said.

"When?" Jack asked.

"Tomorrow isn't soon enough. I just hope and pray Frenette is still alive."

"Who?" Chief said.

"Dr. Kelton Frenette and his wife Latrice. They live in the Garden District. At least they did. I lost touch with them years ago."

Jack brought towels out of the bathroom and began drying and doctoring the dogs. When he handed Odette a plush bathrobe, she dropped Chief's shirt to the floor and put it on. J.P.'s eyes grew large as he watched.

"Damn, girl, you could be a stripper on Bourbon Street with that body of yours," J.P. said.

"You're lucky," Odette said. "Most men pay to see my body."

"I damn sure would," he said.

"The rougarou attack damaged Odette's tent," Jack said. "She's spending the night on the couch."

"I'll take the couch," J.P. said. "You're welcome to sleep in my trailer."

"I'm fine with the couch," Odette said.

"I'll share it with you," J.P. said.

"No, you won't," Odette said. "I'm used to sleeping alone."

187

Oscar, Jack's bulldog, was asleep beside Old Joe in front of the fire. None of the dog's wounds were severe, and those that weren't in front of the fire were sleeping in their warm kennels. Mudbug was still in Odette's arms. When Odette put her on the floor, she joined Coco and Oscar.

"Aren't you going back to Chalmette tonight?" Jack asked.

"The chief relieved me of duty," J.P. said. "Told me to get my head on straight. I'm staying on the island tonight if I'm welcome."

"Of course you're welcome," Jack said. "You're our partner. Chief and I can't do the dog training facility without you."

"Thanks," J.P. said. "I needed to hear that."

"Your boss fired you?" Chief asked.

"He told me to take a week off and decide what I wanted to do with the rest of my life," J.P. said.

"What do you want to do?" Jack asked.

"I wish I knew," J.P. said. "At least I have a week to think about it."

"Odette put a spear through the Rougarou's thigh," Chief said.

"If it's the same Cajun trapper who visited the country doctor, then he'll be back for more care," J.P. said. "I talked to the doctor. This time, he'll get the man's name and find out where he lives."

"And if he does?" Jack asked.

"I'll track down the trapper and see to it he gets the cure."

"Chief and I will go with you to the Garden District tomorrow," Jack said.

"You damn sure are," J.P. said. "How else will you get the rougarou antidote?"

"I'm going, too," Odette said.

"We have other business to conduct," Jack said.

"Like visiting Rockie's on Bourbon Street?" Odette said.

"Maybe," Jack said.

"I'm fine with Rockie's," Odette said. "I told you, I like watching girls dance as much as you do."

"That's not the only business we have to conduct in New Orleans. We need to sell something on Canal Street," Jack said.

"You mean some of your wonderful rum?" Odette asked.

"Maybe," Jack said. "What do you know about our rum?"

"You gave me a taste at Rockie's," she said. "Remember? You'd just sold a bottle. From the money you were flashing around, it wasn't hard for me to deduce it was valuable."

"Damn," Jack said. "It's hell getting so drunk you don't remember what you said or did."

"I don't remember much about our night at Rockie's," Chief said.

"Where do you intend to sell your rum?" Odette asked.

"A place on Canal," Jack said. "It's common knowledge you can sell almost anything there."

"Even this?" Odette said.

"What is it?" Chief asked.

Odette opened her hand and showed them one of her doubloons.

"Where'd you find it?" Jack asked.

"We bargained for a piece of eight when you and Jack visited Rockie's. Remember? I found this one on the beach, near the tent," Odette said. "I'd like to sell it. Take me with you, and I'll buy the first round at Rockie's."

Chapter 23

Everyone had New Orleans on their minds the following morning, and they were on their way to the Big Easy before noon. Jack and Chief sat in the backseat of J.P.'s pickup, J.P. and Odette in the front. Jack's wry comment irritated both of them.

"Those two look like an old married couple, don't they, Chief," he said.

"They do," Chief said. "Now that you mention it."

"Funny," J.P. said. "You might not think it's so funny when I turn this truck around and let you two transform into rougarous."

Chief snickered when Jack said, "Just kidding."

J.P. had slowed the truck almost to a stop. "Sure about that?" he said.

"I'm sure," Jack said.

"Chief?"

Jack hit the gas pedal when Chief said, "Sorry."

"That's better," J.P. said.

J.P. didn't comment when Jack said, "Don't be

190

so touchy. We were only kidding."

Last night's storm had passed, warm sunlight, despite Jack's remark, bolstering everyone's spirits. The stylish dress Odette was wearing helped elevate their moods.

Odette had little more than a pair of cut-off jeans and a yellow halter top to wear and was fretting about their impending trip to New Orleans. Jack saved the day, remembering a closet filled with thirties-era clothes in the Majestic's storage building.

Odette was like a child in a candy shop as she sorted through the beautiful dresses, finally deciding on a figure-hugging cocktail dress adorned with sparkling gold sequins, adjustable spaghetti straps, and a scoop neckline. Odette looked exotic and sleek and knew it when she emerged from the bathroom.

Dressed in starched jeans, a black Western shirt, and snakeskin boots, J.P. was Mark Anthony to Odette's Cleopatra. They both seemed to know they were going to catch everyone's eye in the French Quarter.

"When they reached the outskirts of town, Jack said, "We need to conduct a little business on Canal. You know where the shop is?"

"Me and everyone else in New Orleans," J.P. said. "Want me to come in with you to make sure he doesn't rip you off?"

"I only need to hand him the bottle and then take the money," Jack said. "The price is already set. Odette might need some help."

"I'll do my own negotiating, thank you," she said.

"Let me do it for you," Jack said. "I'll get you top dollar."

Odette laughed. "You left money on the table. If I were you, I'd be embarrassed."

"You don't know how much I got," Jack said.

"You told everyone at Rockie's who would listen," she said. "You got two thousand for the doubloon and four thousand for the bottle of rum."

"So?" Jack said. "The man I sold it to would have to make money, or he wouldn't have bought the rum and gold."

"What condition was the doubloon in?" Odette asked.

"It didn't have a mark on it," Chief said.

"Was there a date on the coin?"

Chief nodded. "I think it was 1588."

"Though I didn't see the coin, I'm guessing it was probably worth twelve grand," Odette said.

"Get out of here!" Jack said.

"A similar bottle of rum as yours recently sold at a Sotheby's auction for more than sixty-thousand dollars."

Chief gave Jack a dirty look. "You gave Bernadine sixty grand to have sex with you?"

J.P. slowed the truck again, turned, and glanced at Jack. Odette was also staring, her eyes boring directly into Jack's innermost thoughts.

"You paid Bernadine sixty grand for a roll in the hay?" J.P. said.

"They had no roll in the hay," Chief said. "All they did was hold hands. Bernadine didn't know how much the bottle of rum was worth."

"Bernadine didn't drink the rum," Jack said. "It was you and the bartender. Bernadine barely got a sip."

"Does it matter who drank the rum?" Odette asked. "None of us knew how much a bottle is worth. It's water under the bridge."

"Odette's right. We've drunk more than one bottle," Chief said. "Both of you and Odette helped us do it. Let's forget about it and move on."

"Whatever," J.P. said. "I'm not letting you sell another for four thousand dollars."

"We were going to use the money to celebrate at Rockie's," Chief said.

"Tell you what," Odette said. "There's more rum on Oyster Island or in the nearby hull of a sunken ship. Cut me in on the deal, and let me help you find it. I'll sell my doubloon and pay for everything at Rockie's tonight."

"Hell, Odette, I was planning on spending at least a grand myself," Jack said.

"Trust me when I tell you I'm going to get considerably more."

"And how do you plan to do that?" Jack asked.

"It's worth twelve-five," Odette said. "I'll get ten for it."

"How do you know what it's worth?" Chief asked.

"I researched it on the Internet," she said.

"You have a computer?" he said.

"I have access to the Internet on my cell phone," Odette said.

J.P. turned on Canal Street, slowing in front of the camera shop to let Odette out of the truck.

"We'll drive around the block," he said.

"I won't be long," Odette said before shutting the door.

J.P. circled the block for the second time, Odette still in the camera shop.

"The owner of the shop knows how to horse trade. Odette's pants will be gone when she comes out," Jack said.

"She's wearing a dress," Chief said. "Not pants."

"You know what I mean," Jack said.

Odette was exiting the door of the camera shop when J.P. slowed after his third rotation of the block. The grin on her face spoke volumes when she climbed into the front seat.

"Did you get ten grand?" Jack asked as she buckled her seatbelt.

"Yes," she said. "He lost his concentration when I showed him a little leg."

"You had an unfair advantage," Jack said.

"Your body doesn't last forever," Odette said. "You have to use it while you can."

"Want me to hold the money for you?" J.P. asked.

He laughed when she said, "Your ass!"

"Then let's head over to the Garden District," J.P. said. "It's been a while since I saw Dr. Frenette. He may not even be alive."

"Don't even think it," Jack said. "Growing fur and fangs doesn't appeal to me."

When Americans began moving to New Orleans after the Louisiana Purchase, they didn't want to live with the Creoles in the French Quarter. They bought plantations west of the city and subdivided them to avoid it. After turning off Canal and heading down St. Charles Avenue, J.P. passed a slow-moving streetcar.

Stately mansions with extensive gardens soon dominated this area, eventually annexed by New Orleans. As the large tracts became even more subdivided, the gardens disappeared, replaced by more houses. It didn't matter because the name Garden District stuck.

Odette had driven through the neighborhood many times and was still in awe of the old neighborhood's beauty, architecture, and history. The lack of Garden District construction rules had resulted in a conglomeration of eclectic architecture.

On the way to the Frenette's, they passed Greek Revival, Victorian, and even plantation-style houses. J.P. parked in front of a home needing a fresh coat of paint. The group avoided the broken boards on the porch, and Chief pointed out the cracked panes of glass in the windows. The massive trees in the yard could have used a good pruning.

"Are you sure someone lives here?" he asked.

"It hasn't changed much since the last time I was here," J.P. said. "Frenette's in a wheelchair. At least he was last time I saw him."

They found the beautiful old cut-glass door ajar. No one came when J.P. pounded on it.

"What now?" Chief asked.

J.P. pushed open the door and entered the house. "I'm a cop," he said. "Looks suspicious, and I'm duty-bound to investigate."

They followed him into an alcove, large potted plants growing profusely in the light filtering through the antique glass of the front door. J.P. stopped to look.

"What?" Jack said.

"There were no plants in the pots last time I visited. It's a good sign someone is taking special care of these big babies," J.P. said.

"I don't know about that," Odette said. "Except for watering, no one seems to have cared for them. It's like a jungle in here."

"At least someone's watering them," Chief said.

Leaving the alcove, they entered a cavernous room with off-pink walls. The couch, settee, and chairs were all antiques, Chief feeling as if he'd time-traveled to a different era. Odette voiced his thoughts.

"This room probably hasn't changed much since before the Civil War," she said.

"No dust," J.P. said. "Someone is living here and taking care of the place."

Down to the polished brass doorknobs, everything was spotless, only the patina of age and decades of use tarnishing the furniture.

195

Odette heard something down the hall.

"Hello," she called.

"Hear something?" Jack asked.

"Sounded like the barking of a dog and someone crying," Odette said.

J.P. was already heading down the hall, Odette and the others following. J.P. traced the sound of a crying woman and barking dog to the kitchen.

Unlike the rest of the house, the kitchen spoke of a remodel. Judging from the honeycomb tile floors and green Formica cabinet tops, probably done in the fifties or sixties. A rotund black woman was sitting on the floor, her face in her hands, a black pug with a white chest guard-dogging her. J.P. knelt beside her and put his hand on her shoulder. The small dog jumped into J.P.'s arms and licked him on the mouth.

"Latrice, are you okay," he asked.

The woman opened her eyes and looked at J.P. "Who are you?" she said.

"Jean Pierre Saucier. A lieutenant with the Chalmette Police Department. I met you and your husband several years ago when we had a rougarou problem on Goose Island."

A flicker of recognition registered in the woman's eyes. "Now I remember you," she said.

"Latrice Frenette, this is Odette, Jack and Chief."

"What are you doing here?" Latrice asked.

Before answering, J.P. and Chief helped the woman to her feet and into a chair at the kitchen table. Latrice reached down and picked up the pug. The little dog's face was white with age though she still had a throaty bark. When she realized Latrice was okay, her little tail began to wag.

"This is Princess. She's old as the hills, deaf and blind as a bat, but still the best little watchdog you could ever want."

J.P. was smiling as he petted Princess and said, "We have another rougarou problem on an island near the Gulf. We need your husband's help," J.P. said. "Is he . . . ?"

Latrice continued to cry. Odette found a bottle of water in the refrigerator, holding it to the big woman's lips until she took a drink.

"Tell us why you're crying," she said.

"Kelton's alive but non-responsive," Latrice said. "He hasn't spoken in two days."

"Maybe we better call 9-1-1," J.P. said.

Latrice took another drink from the bottle of cold water. "Kelton made me swear not to take him to the hospital," she said. "He wants to die in his bed."

"I'm so sorry," J.P. said, patting her hand.

Odette put her arms around the woman's large neck, and hugged her. "Is there anything we can do?" she asked.

"Are any of you doctors?" she asked.

"We aren't," Odette said, "but we can pray with you."

Odette's offer seemed to lighten Latrice's burden. "Then come with me," she said.

They followed Latrice down a darkened hallway to the master bedroom, its curtains drawn, the lighting dim. Latrice lit a candle on the nightstand by the four-poster bed. Princess was slightly overweight, unsteady on her feet as she followed them into the bedroom.

The eyes of the man lying in bed beneath a white crocheted spread were closed, his gray hair mussed, beard untrimmed. Unlike Latrice, his skin was white, though showing signs of jaundice. J.P. was staring at him.

"Last time I saw Dr. Frenette, he looked as though he weighed over three-hundred pounds," he said.

"Cancer has withered him," Latrice said.

"He's had no chemotherapy or radiation treatments?" J.P. asked.

Latrice lifted Princess off the floor and put her on the bed. She lay beside the stricken man, her head nestled against his neck. Dr. Frenette didn't respond when the little dog licked his face.

"Kelton said he'd rather die of cancer than have his body and immune system destroyed with injected poisons."

"But he's a doctor," J.P. said.

"A biologist with a Ph.D. Not a medical doctor," Latrice said.

Odette put her arm on Latrice's shoulder, took her hand, and squeezed it. "I'm so sorry," she said. "We'll pray with you."

Latrice knelt beside the bed and bowed her head. "Please take my hands," she said.

Jack, Chief, J.P., and Odette joined hands. Their heads bowed as Latrice began to pray. When she'd finished the prayer, Odette handed her a glass of water from the stainless steel pitcher on the stand beside the bed.

"Are you sure you won't allow me to call an ambulance?" J.P. asked.

"I can't," Latrice said. "You said you have a problem. Perhaps I can help."

"Chief and Jack suffered wounds in a rougarou attack," J.P. said. "Unless we get the cure, they're both going to become rougarous. Dr. Frenette had medicine that would cure the disease. We were hoping you might have some."

Latrice glanced at the floor and shook her head. "Kelton only made a single batch of the medicine. The cure is in his head; he never wrote it down."

"You're a nurse," J.P. said. "Did you help him prepare it?"

"I am a registered nurse and Kelton's

assistant," Latrice said. "Kelton mixed the batch of medicine while I was fixing dinner. I never recorded the ingredients or procedure."

"Damn!" J.P. said. "We're screwed!"

"Maybe not," Chief said. "I have an idea that might work."

Chapter 24

The group waited for Chief's explanation. "I
was a kid when I first heard about
rougarous. My grandmother told me they
were immortal."

"Nothing's immortal," Odette said.

"Not true, baby," Latrice said. "Cancer cells
are immortal. That's why the disease is all but
impossible to cure."

"So, Chief," Jack said. "What's your point."

"The rougarou disease is coursing through
our bodies," Chief said. "If what J.P. says is true,
we'll soon begin transforming."

"That's a horrible thought," Jack said.

"Unless we take the medicine that cures the
disease," Chief said.

"Only Dr. Frenette knows the formula,"
Odette said.

"Then we revive him," Chief said.

"I won't allow you to take Kelton from this
house," Latrice said.

"That's not what I'm suggesting," Chief said.

"What are you suggesting?" Jack asked.

"My blood type is O-negative. I'm a universal
donor and can give blood to any blood type. Inject
some of my blood into Dr. Frenette. Hopefully, it

will render him immortal and revive him to recreate the rougarou cure. Who knows, it might even cure his cancer."

"Sounds sort of loopy to me," J.P. said.

"It's worth a try," Jack said. "I don't want to terrorize people beneath a full moon."

"I think it's a wonderful idea," Latrice said. "Kelton's medical lab is in the basement. No one has been down there since we inoculated the rougarou frozen in our basement freezer."

"You had a rougarou in your basement?" Odette said.

"Long story," Latrice said. "Kelton cured him, and he's no longer there. I'll get a gurney."

They waited until Latrice returned with a medical gurney. After Latrice had pulled down the bedspread, J.P. and Chief lifted the withered body of Kelton Frenette out of bed and onto the gurney.

"This way," Latrice said as she pushed the gurney into the hallway.

Latrice stopped in front of a door, beside it an oversized dumbwaiter. After wheeling Frenette into the dumbwaiter, she pushed a button. An electric motor grated as the cab of the dumbwaiter began descending into the basement.

When she heard the apparatus thud to a halt, she lifted the metal bar across the door leading into the basement. The ring of keys hanging on the wall rattled as she unlocked three padlocks and switched on an overhead bulb that dimly illuminated the musty stairs.

"The steps are steep and slick, the overhead light barely bright enough to illuminate the descent. Be careful. Though I'm a nurse, it has been a while since I set a broken bone."

Chief led Latrice, Odette, J.P., with Jack following. Latrice hadn't lied about how slick the bare concrete steps were, his mocassins barely allowing him to make it to the bottom of the stairs without busting his ass. If he had been claustrophobic, he would have turned and hurried up the stairs. He let Latrice walk past him and flip on the overhead fluorescent lighting when he reached the basement floor.

"Oh my God!" Odette said. "It's like something out of an old Frankenstein movie."

Dust-coated beakers, test tubes, and medical paraphernalia littered the dark medical lab. A dissection table still reeked of formaldehyde.

Latrice smiled. "When we were spending lots of time down here, Kelton would jokingly call me Igor."

Latrice wheeled the gurney to the center of the dank basement, Chief jumping when a rat scurried across his foot.

"You'll need to lie on your back while I draw the blood," Latrice said.

"You need that much blood?" Chief asked.

"Don't want to take any chances," she said. "Sorry, there are no chairs. We'll all have to stand while we're down here."

Latrice smiled when Chief said, "You aren't going to make me lie on that thing, are you?"

"The dissection table is only for cadavers. There's a portable gurney in the corner."

"Good," Chief said. "I was about to change my mind about giving the blood."

Latrice wheeled the extra gurney to the one bearing Kelton Frenette.

"Lie down and roll up your sleeve," she said. "It'll take me a moment to gather the needed apparatus."

Latrice pulled an armload of medical equipment out of a cabinet. Jack helped her carry it to the two gurneys.

"Are you a nurse?" Latrice asked.

"No, but when I was in the Merchant Marines, we were always shorthanded at everything. I assisted on several medical procedures," Jack said.

"Then you must be knowledgeable," Latrice said.

"I take good directions," Jack said with a smile.

"We're going to draw blood from Chief and then drip it into Kelton's vein. Hope you're not the impatient type because it's going to take a while."

She smiled when Jack said, "Time is cheap and something of which we have plenty."

"Then hook up the intravenous apparatus while I fetch the blood pressure meter."

"Who's the meter for?" Jack asked.

"Chief," Latrice said. "Don't want him to have a heart attack. You're okay with the sight of blood, aren't you?"

Jack nodded. "As long as it's not my own."

"There's a coffee pot under the sink," Latrice said. "Someone will have to return to the kitchen to get the coffee."

"Not me," Odette said.

"I'll get it, though I'd rather have something stronger," J.P. said.

"Amen to that," Jack said.

"Kelton loves his brandy though there's none here in the basement," Latrice said.

J.P. glanced at Jack. "You still have rum in your flask, don't you?"

"It'll just make us want more," Jack said.

"If we need more, you can run out to the truck and get the bottle," Chief said.

"You kidding?" Jack said.

"It's going to do neither of us any good if we both turn into rougarous," Chief said. "We may as well go down happy."

"Can't you wait until we get to Rockie's?" Odette said.

"I'm beginning to feel a little queasy," Chief

said. "I don't think I can do this without a shot of rum."

Jack pulled the flask from his back pocket, opened it, and took a swig."

"Kelton always drank when he was experimenting," Latrice said. "I have glasses in the cabinet for the rum."

"No use dirtying your glasses," Jack said, handing the flask to Latrice. "If you don't mind drinking after a future rougarou, that is."

Latrice smiled as she took the flask. "Hopefully, none of us will become a rougarou."

Jack finished assembling the U.V. drip as Latrice sipped the rum and then handed the flask to Chief.

"Wonderful," she said. "Where did you buy it?"

"We didn't buy it," Chief said.

He shook his head when she said, "You stole it?"

"We found it on Oyster Island," Chief said. "It's Prohibition-aged rum distilled in the Dominican Republic and then bootlegged by rum runners to the island."

"Illegal rum?" Latrice said.

"Fruit of the forbidden vine," Chief said. "Nothing sweeter."

Latrice had shut out the rum talk and was trying to insert the needle into Chief's vein.

"What's the problem?" J.P. asked.

The look of exasperation on Latrice's face said it all. "He's starting to transform."

"Impossible," J.P. said. "He was infected last night, not a week ago."

"Are you a virologist?" Latrice asked.

"No," J.P. said.

"Then see if you can insert the needle," she said.

Odette drew closer, watching as J.P. forced the

needle into Chief's vein.

"Sorry if I hurt you," J.P. said.

"I didn't feel a thing," Chief said.

J.P.'s smile was gone. "That's what I was afraid of," he said.

Odette grabbed Jack's arm and said, "How do you feel?"

"Like I could rip the door off the hinges with my bare hands," he said.

Jack glanced at the back of his hands as patches of heavy fur began to appear.

"What the hell are we going to do now?" Jack asked.

A white porcelain freezer occupied a corner of the basement.

"Get in the freezer," Latrice said.

"You kidding?" he said. "I'm not getting in there."

"You'll be fine," Latrice said. "The freezing temperature will halt your transformation until we get the cure."

Latrice smiled when Jack said, "And what if you don't?"

"Trust me," she said. "You won't know the difference."

"Do it now," J.P. said to the hesitant Jack.

Jack's eyes were large as he crawled into the freezer using the stepstool Latrice provided.

"Oh, shit!" he said when Latrice shut the top of the freezer with a decisive slam. "Let me out of here," he called as she turned the lock.

"We can't lock him in there," Odette said. "He'll go crazy."

"Chief's going to join him soon as we get enough of his blood," Latrice said.

"If he doesn't kill us all first," J.P. said.

Dark hair was already growing on Chief's face, his dark eyes turning red.

"What the hell do we do now?" J.P. asked.

205

Odette pulled the needle from Chief's vein. "This will have to be enough blood," she said.

J.P. helped her lead Chief to the freezer. "Latrice, throw me the key."

"I don't think I can do this," Chief said.

"Get in there," Odette said. "When you awake, I'll give you a special table dance at Rockie's as a reward."

J.P. pushed Chief into the big freezer, slammed the top, and locked it.

Growls, moans, and pleas for help emanated from the freezer as J.P. said, "Turn that puppy up to high."

Latrice had already taken the bag of blood she'd drawn from Chief's arm and situated it above her husband's gurney. She inserted the needle into a vein in his arm and started the drip as J.P. and Odette watched.

"Now what?" Odette said.

"Might not hurt to do more praying," Latrice said. When she finished a short prayer, she grabbed Jack's flask from the side of the gurney. "There's not much left," she said.

"Drink it," Odette said.

Latrice handed J.P. the flask after drinking the last of the rum. "I'll be back," she said, starting up the dark stairway. She returned with a bottle in her hand. "You like brandy?"

"I'd drink a glass of rubbing alcohol right now if I had it," J.P. said.

Latrice smiled as she opened the bottle and then poured them a snifter.

"Pierre Ferrand, vintage 1972," Latrice said. "Kelton made me promise to save him a bottle until we could drink it together."

"You think Chief's blood will revive him?" Odette asked.

"Don't know. It's now or never," Latrice said. "Either way, we can't go wrong."

As the temperature in the freezer grew frigid, Jack and Chief stopped banging on the walls. Latrice sat on Chief's vacated gurney, her head tilted forward and her eyes closed. Odette was also asleep, her head on J.P.'s shoulder. Half asleep himself, J.P.'s eyes popped open when the sheet covering Dr. Frenette began to move. He nudged Latrice until she opened her eyes.

Latrice was instantly awake when J.P. said, "He's moving."

When Dr. Frenette sat up in bed, Latrice hugged him and then handed him a snifter of brandy.

"Oh, Kelton, I can't believe it," she said.

Frenette kissed Latrice and sipped the brandy with a smile on his face.

"Have I died and gone to heaven?" he asked.

"You're very much alive," she said. "And you have problems to solve."

Frenette glanced across the dimly-lit room and saw J.P. and Odette for the first time.

"Wonderful to see you again, Lieutenant Saucier. Who is the lovely young woman with you?"

Odette was just waking up, giving J.P. a dirty look when she realized she had her head on his shoulder. Her frown turned to a smile when she realized Dr. Frenette was conscious.

"This is Odette," J.P. said. "Trust me when I tell you I'm happier to see you again than you are to see me."

"I'm alive and feeling better than I ever have in my life. I'm assuming you and the young lady have something to do with my recovery."

"We got a big problem, Doc, and you're right in the middle of it," J.P. said.

Frenette pulled the sheet off his legs and slid off the gurney to the floor. His polka dot pajamas engulfed him.

"If I have a problem, I love it. I haven't been this slender since I was in my thirties, and I can't remember the last time I stood on my own two feet."

Latrice backed up a few steps and beckoned Frenette with open arms to walk to her. He did, barely stumbling before reaching her.

"Now," he said. "Please tell me why I feel so good."

Latrice looked at J.P. to answer the question for her.

"You feel immortal because you are," he said. "Latrice infused you with rougarou blood. The two good men responsible for bringing the infection into your home are little more than blocks of ice in your freezer."

Chapter 25

D r. Frenette kissed Latrice and returned to the nightstand to retrieve his brandy, which he finished in a single drink.

"I understand the gravity of the moment, Lieutenant Saucier. Latrice, we're going to need more Pierre Ferrand."

Latrice shook her head. "Baby," she said. "You drank the last of it."

Dr. Frenette set the empty snifter back on the nightstand as the smile disappeared from his face.

"What good is immortality if I have no Pierre Ferrand?" he said.

"Your brandy was wonderful," J.P. said. "We have a sixty-thousand dollar bottle of Dominican rum in the truck that will make your brandy taste like swill."

"You must be kidding," Dr. Frenette said.

"I'm not," J.P. said.

"Then I accept the challenge," Frenette said, his smile returning.

"I'll run out to the truck and get the bottle," J.P. said.

Odette grabbed his elbow. "I'll go with you," she said.

They were barely up the stairs when Odette released J.P.'s arm and moved away from him.

"I was beginning to think you like me," he said.

"Don't get your hopes up," Odette said. "I wanted to hear your take on our situation."

"Not good," J.P. said.

"Jack and Chief didn't deserve this."

"Frenette will save them," J.P. said.

"How can you be so sure?" Odette said.

"Though Frenette seems like a mad scientist, he's a genius. He'll figure something out. We have to stay positive," J.P. said.

"If he doesn't, that freezer will be Jack and Chief's tomb. I can only imagine what they thought as their body parts began to freeze."

"You've witnessed a rougarou more than once. That beast you put a spear through has a normal life when he's not terrorizing the countryside. If we hadn't put Jack and Chief in the freezer, they would have tried to kill us. That's a fact," Jack said.

"I don't know. . ." Odette said.

"Yes, you do," J.P. said. "In this life, you play the cards you're dealt. No matter how weird and eccentric Latrice and Dr. Frenette seem, they are the hand we're holding."

"Great speech, coach. It doesn't make our situation any less serious," Odette said.

J.P. unlocked the door to his truck and handed the bottle of rum to Odette. Popping it open, she took a drink.

"Feel better?" J.P. asked.

"You're a cop and used to situations like this. I'm not." Odette said.

"I've seen my share of murder scenes," he said. "You never get used to it."

"Is that why you want to train dogs?"

"One of the reasons," he said.

210

"What other reasons?" she asked.

J.P. turned his head away from Odette. "I'd rather not say."

Odette stood on her tiptoes and gave him a peck on the lips.

"I've never in my life been nervous around a man," she said.

"Does this mean I have a chance?" J.P. asked.

Odette took another swig from the bottle of Dominican rum. "Not a snowball's chance in hell," she said.

J.P. was grinning as he followed Odette back down the slick stairs to the basement lab where she handed the bottle to Frenette.

"You don't need a snifter for this," she said. "It's wonderful straight from the bottle."

Dr. Frenette took Odette's advice. "I truly have died and gone to heaven," he said. "Latrice, we need music."

"Yes, my dear," she said.

"Beethoven's Bagatelle No. 25 in A minor," he said. Dank basement walls began to resonate with a haunting melody. "The two men weren't fully transformed, or you'd never have managed to get them into the freezer."

"They were only beginning to transform," J.P. said.

"I'll have to mix a batch of the cure," Frenette said. "Once I finish, we'll lay them out on the gurneys and wait for them to thaw. Latrice, will you please bring me the formula?"

He frowned when she said, "You never wrote it down."

"Are you sure?" he said.

When Latrice nodded, Frenette closed his eyes and began massaging his temples. When he opened them, he grabbed the bottle of rum and took another drink.

"Baby," Latrice said. "Are you okay?"

211

"Physically, I feel wonderful. My thinking is beginning to blur."

Odette cast Latrice and J.P. worried glances. Latrice was also worried.

"Baby," she said, "I think you're beginning to transform."

Dr. Frenette winced and grabbed his head. "I'm not thinking straight, and we need the formula to proceed."

"Mama Malaika, a voodoo woman on Goose Island, soaked the buckshot in the shells of her son's shotgun in a concoction made from wolf's bane," J.P. said. "The buckshot wouldn't kill a rougarou but would stop it in its tracks long enough so you could at least have time to run away."

"Aconite," Frenette said.

"Pardon me?" J.P. said.

"Wolf's bane belongs to the genus Aconitum. Aconite is the active ingredient in wolf's bane," Frenette said. "Latrice, bring me the Martinsdale."

"You left it in the corner last time you were down here."

Odette saw the book in a dark corner of the basement, retrieving it for Dr. Frenette.

"This book weighs a ton," she said.

"Eleven pounds of knowledge," Dr. Frenette said.

"What is it?" she asked.

"Martindale: The Complete Drug Reference," he said. "Worth its weight in gold."

Dr. Frenette thumbed through the thick book. Finding a sheet of paper, he began to read it.

"What is it?" Latrice asked.

"The formula for the rougarou vaccine," he said.

"Wonderful," Latrice said.

"I knew I had written it down somewhere,"

Frenette said.

Laying the book on one of the gurneys, he began shuffling through bottles of chemicals in the cabinets.

"Can I help?" Odette said.

"Are you a chemist?" Frenette said.

"I'm a cook and can follow a recipe," she said.

Frenette handed her a scrap of paper. "In the cabinets, there's every receptacle you need to mix the ingredients. I'll get the chemicals. You mix them."

J.P. sidled up beside Odette. "Don't you think you should let Dr. Frenette prepare the medicine? It's kind of important."

"Dr. Frenette trusts me. Maybe you should, too," she said.

"Uncle!" he said. "Can I help?"

Odette pushed a mortar toward him and filled it with a white chemical. When she handed him a pestle, she said, "Grind this to a consistency of fine powder. When you finish, I'll give you something else to do."

Everything halted when Dr. Frenette fumbled a jar of chemicals, shattering when it hit the concrete floor. Latrice hurried to help. Grabbing Frenette's shaking arm, she stared into his eyes.

"We must hurry," he said. "How are you coming on the concoction?" he asked Odette.

"Waiting for it to dissolve in the distilled water," she said.

Taking the flask from her, he said, "My centrifuge will speed things up. Lieutenant Saucier, Latrice will help you get the men out of the freezer."

The music from Beethoven was looped and continued to play while J.P. waited for Latrice to open the freezer. They both were shocked when she opened the lid.

Ice, reflecting in the overhead lights, covered

both men. The grimaces on their faces told the story of how they must have felt as their flesh and blood became frozen chunks of ice.

"They're going to be dead weight and all but impossible to lift out of there," Latrice said.

Latrice was correct, and it took all of their strength to wrestle Chief's frozen body out of the freezer and onto the gurney. Getting Jack out of the freezer was more manageable, though not much. Dr. Frenette stopped what he was doing to glance at the bodies.

"I should have helped," he said. "I keep forgetting I'm no longer in the wheelchair."

"It's all right," Latrice said. "We managed."

"Will they be alive when they thaw?" J.P. asked.

"Oh, yes," Dr. Frenette said. "They are immortal until I vaccinate them."

Odette stopped what she was doing and joined them.

"How long will it take Jack and Chief to thaw?" she asked.

"Hours," Dr. Frenette said.

"What'll we do till then?" J.P. asked.

"Go upstairs, freshen up, and get something to eat. In a couple of hours, we'll need to start taking shifts watching them until they begin to thaw."

"There's another problem," J.P. said. "The creature that infected Jack and Chief is still loose. I need some of the pneumatic shells like I used when we had the rougarou problem on Goose Island."

Dr. Frenette searched through a cabinet. "I only have one casing left," he said. "Can you stop the creature with one shot?"

"Sounds as if I don't have a choice," J.P. said.

"I had the injection cartridge made especially for the pneumatic pistol you used. It'll take a week or ten days to have more made," Dr. Frenette said. "Can you wait that long?"

"We need to stop the rougarou before it infects someone else. That's a problem because we still don't know who it is or where to find him."

Dr. Frenette loaded the injection cartridge into a pneumatic pistol and handed it to J.P.

"This is guaranteed to stop a rougarou in its tracks. Just don't miss. I trust you remember how to use it?" Dr. Frenette said.

"It's something you never forget," J.P. said.

The sky outside had begun to darken as they ate pork and beans out of a large can.

"Sorry," Latrice said. "My mind has been elsewhere, and it has been a while since I visited the market."

"Best can of pork and beans I ever ate," J.P. said with a wink. "Guess we're going to miss out on Rockie's."

"I'm more worried about missing dinner. A can of pork and beans split four ways doesn't go very far," Odette said.

"It can't be too much longer," J.P. said. "Jack and Chief were dripping water on the floor."

"I feel so guilty," Odette said.

"About what?"

"They were protecting me from the rougarou and got infected. I didn't."

"I've known Chief all my life," J.P. said. "He's the salt of the earth. I just met Jack, but he and Chief are two of a kind. When those two have your back, you don't have much to worry about."

"I'm not worried about me. I'm worried about them," Odette said.

"Is there any rum left?" J.P. asked.

"Frenette was hogging it," Odette said. "It's almost gone."

"Too bad," He said. "I'm as hungry as you are

and craving a drink."

"Are you an alcoholic?"

"Hell, I guess I must be," he said.

"When did you start drinking?" Odette asked.

"Two or three," he said.

"You're full of shit," Odette said.

"Mama told me Grandma used to put it in my bottle to stop me from crying."

Odette shook her head. "You've been drunk since you were three?" she asked.

"Pretty damn much," he said.

"Ever been married?"

Odette's question brought a big grin to J.P.'s face. "I never found the woman I want to have kids with," he said.

"I've always thought men's dicks controlled everything about them," Odette said.

J.P. snickered. "Then you know less about men than I know about women," he said.

"I know about men," she said. "They're all the same."

Odette's smile disappeared when J.P. asked, "Did your daddy abuse you?"

"Hell no!" she said. "Did your mother abuse you?"

J.P. grinned. "She paddled my ass a time or two. I probably deserved it."

"And your dad?" Odette asked.

"I related to my mother more than my dad," he said. "I imagine that's pretty common."

"My dad defined my mom," Odette said. "She fell to pieces when he died."

J.P. clutched her hand. "I'm so sorry you lost him, and please forgive me for my rude suggestion."

"My dad never molested me," Odette said. "Why did you even suggest such a thing?"

"I'm a law officer and trained to recognize certain traits in people."

"Dad was no abuser."

"But someone else was?" he asked.

"You're an asshole!" she said.

"Well?"

"My grandfather. He lived in the house across the street from us. Grandma died when I was young. My parents used to leave me with grandpa."

"What did he do to you?" J.P. asked.

"What difference does it make?"

"Maybe you want to get it off your chest," he said.

Odette took a moment to answer. "He'd have me sit in his lap. Though I was only five or six, I remember him putting his hand where it shouldn't be."

"Odette, I'm so sorry," J.P. said.

"I know now grandpa was in the early stages of dementia. What makes me angry is dad knew and never did anything to protect me."

"Your mom didn't know?" J.P. asked.

"If she knew, she never let on," Odette said.

"You never confronted her with it?"

"I couldn't," Odette said.

"Not all men are bad, and not all women are good," J.P. said.

"I'm not an idiot," Odette said.

Dr. Frenette disturbed their conversation. "We need to get to work. Odette takes the first watch, relieved by Latrice. J.P. takes over from Latrice. I'll spell J.P. and watch the two men through the night. Call me on the intercom if they begin to move. I'll come down and administer the vaccine."

"No use risking everyone," J.P. said. "Show me how to do it. I'll stay with Jack and Chief until they begin to revive."

"No way!" Odette said. "I'm not afraid."

"I know you're not afraid," J.P. said. "It's just

that. . ."

"That I'm a woman?" Odette said, finishing his sentence.

"Not what I meant," he said.

"I'm having none of it," Odette said.

"Then head to the basement," Frenette said. "I have no idea how long it takes a human body to thaw."

Odette gave J.P. a dirty look as she walked out the door.

"Wait," J.P. said. When Odette turned around, he showed her the bottle of rum. "Have a swig before you go. There's still plenty in the bottle."

Odette took a drink, though she never stopped frowning at J.P. Latrice and J.P. rested their heads on the couch and closed their eyes. After two hours had passed, Frenette woke Latrice and she went to the basement to relieve Odette. J.P. and Odette were asleep on the couch when Dr. Frenette awakened J.P. with a shake of the shoulder.

"Your turn in the barrel, Lieutenant," Frenette said.

Chapter 26

J.P. returned alone to the dank basement where Latrice had placed sunlamps above Jack and Chief to facilitate their thawing. J.P. sat on the floor, his back propped against the concrete wall. Frost covered their hair and eyelids, their lips blue and faces frozen in tortured masks.

Beethoven's bagatelle had ended, the only sound a tiny mouse scurrying across the floor. Total darkness followed a loud pop echoing off the concrete walls. A fuse had blown, leaving J.P. in complete darkness. He grabbed his cell phone before remembering he didn't have Odette's number or anyone else's who could provide immediate help.

J.P.'s phone had a flashlight app. Something kept him from using it. Instead, he followed the wall until he found the door leading upstairs. When he reached the top of the slick concrete stairway, he found the basement door locked.

J.P.'s years of detective work told him something was afoul. Stepping back against the wall, he listened as someone outside the door rattled a set of heavy keys. He remained silent, his police-issue .45 revolver in his hand when the heavy metal door creaked open.

"J.P.," a voice said.

It was Latrice, the candle she carried casting dancing shadows on the concrete walls.

"Latrice, what the hell's going on?"

Latrice clutched his hand. "Kelton has transformed. He's going to kill us."

J.P. squeezed Latrice's hand. "Get a grip and tell me what happened."

"Kelton told me he took the cure. He lied. He apologized before he fully transformed. He said after experiencing immortality, he couldn't return to cancer and a wheelchair."

"How did you get away from him?"

"Odette interrupted us. Kelton had all but transformed and looked terrifying. When she ran upstairs, he forgot about me and followed after her."

"What happened to the lights?" J.P. asked.

"The breaker box is in a kitchen closet. Not knowing what else to do, I tripped the main breaker thinking it would be harder for Kelton to find us in the dark."

"You did good," J.P. said.

"I don't know," Latrice said. "Kelton's a wolf now and can probably see in the dark."

"Is the pneumatic pistol still on the coffee table?" J.P. asked.

Latrice pulled the weapon out of her apron. "I grabbed it when Kelton ran upstairs.

J.P. put away his .45 and took the pneumatic pistol from Latrice.

"Hope it works," he said.

"I know," Latrice said. "Sounds as if he was planning to transform all along, the pistol probably inoperative."

"I'm going to find out," J.P. said.

"Assuming the pistol does work, you can't take a chance hitting Kelton in the dark," Latrice said.

"What else can I do?" J.P. asked.

"I have a plan," she said.

"Then tell me, and make it fast. The beast could be ripping Odette apart as we speak."

"I'll see if Jack and Chief have thawed enough for me to vaccinate them."

"Then what?" J.P. asked.

"You hide in the kitchen with the pistol. I'll wheel Jack and Chief into the dumbwaiter, take them upstairs to the kitchen and then restore the electricity," she said. "When Kelton appears, shoot him with a dart."

"Your plan has a flaw," J.P. said. "The transformation will give him superhuman powers and the speed of a scalded cat. We'll be sitting ducks."

"What else can we do?" Latrice asked.

"You stay in the dumbwaiter with Jack and Chief," J.P. said, returning the pneumatic pistol to her. "I'll get Dr. Frenette to follow me into the basement. My cell phone has a flashlight app that's as powerful as a floodlamp. I'll lead him to the dumbwaiter. When I yell now, turn on the light and pop a dart in your husband's chest."

J.P. showed Latrice how to activate the flashlight. "What about you?" she asked.

"Don't worry about me. After you put the dart in the beast's chest, shut the dumbwaiter door and take it upstairs. Lock the basement, go to the breaker box and turn on the lights."

"What if I miss?" Latrice asked.

"Don't miss," J.P. said.

When Odette returned from the bathroom, she walked in on Latrice and Dr. Frenette as Frenette was transforming into a rougarou. She screamed when she realized he was about to maul Latrice. When the transformed beast wheeled around and saw Odette, he started across the room after her. Having no weapon, she ran upstairs.

The old Garden District house was a maze of hallways and corridors. Finding a door in the hallway opened a crack, she hurried inside, shutting the door behind her.

Though dark outside, the light from a streetlamp shining through an open curtain provided scant illumination. It was enough for Odette to tell it was the Frenette's bedroom where she'd first seen him. She slid under the four-poster bed and found she wasn't alone. Princess, Latrice's little pug, licked her face.

"Hey, baby," Odette said. "Don't be scared."

Princess barked as the door to the bedroom opened, and the rougarou entered. It became quickly apparent the angry creature retained no memory of the room as it tripped over a nightstand, its growls rumbling against the walls.

The angry creature tossed a chair through the window. Before the crash of breaking glass ended, the beast grabbed the edge of the bed, turning it upside down. Suddenly exposed, Odette grabbed Princess and scooted against the wall. The changeling raised his muzzle to the ceiling and howled.

J.P. was opening a curtain in the living room when the roar of the rougarou punctuated the silence. Grabbing his service revolver, he headed up the stairway. Barely able to see in the muted light of a streetlamp outside the house, he ascended the stairs one step at a time. When he reached the second floor, two distinct sounds penetrated his psyche: the howl of the wolflike-creature and a small dog whose bark was bigger than her body.

Glass crunched beneath his boots when he kicked open the door to Frenette's bedroom. A chill breeze blew through the window broken by the rougarou. The beast wheeled around, red eyes glaring when J.P. unloaded his pistol into his back. The bullets didn't kill him but knocked him to the floor, murder in his glowing eyes as he sprang to his feet.

As the beast lunged for him, J.P. could do little more than throw his pistol at him. The heavy revolver bounced harmlessly to the floor as Princess wrestled loose from Odette's arms and began biting the rougarou's ankles.

Princess wasn't big enough to do any damage to the creature. She didn't seem to know it, and neither did the rougarou. Shunting past J.P., the creature ran out of the bedroom and down the stairs, Princess close behind. J.P. grabbed Odette when she tried to follow them.

"Where do you think you're going?" he asked.

"We have to save Princess," Odette said.

"Princess doesn't need saving. She's a dog. That monster, just like the one on the island, is afraid of dogs. She'll be fine."

"He'll kill her," Odette said.

"No, he won't," J.P. said.

"Then what are we going to do?" she asked.

"Latrice and I have a plan. I'll get the creature to chase me into the basement. Latrice has inoculated Chief and Jack and wheeled them into the dumbwaiter. When he follows me to the door of the dumbwaiter, Latrice is going to blind him with the flashlight app on my cell phone and then blast him with the pneumatic gun."

"I'm going to help you," Odette said.

"Fine," J.P. said. "You can be a big help if you follow orders."

"Then stop with your insinuations and tell me

223

what you want me to do," she said.

"There's a breaker box in the kitchen closet. Latrice threw the breaker so we'd have the cover of darkness from the rougarou. Go to the kitchen. Flip the breaker when you hear me call."

"What about Princess?" Odette asked.

"Her barking won't keep the creature at bay forever. When it realizes as much, it will kill her," J.P. said.

"What, then?"

"Princess is in the doorway, right around the corner. You grab her when we go up behind her and run like hell for the kitchen."

"What's going to stop the creature from chasing after Princess and me?" Odette asked.

"At least for the moment, Princess has her bluff in on the rougarou. He won't follow you because he's scared of Princess. He'll follow me instead," J.P. said.

"He's unearthly fast," Odette said. "He'll catch you before you get out the door."

"Then you and Princess will have to hold him at bay for a bit. I'll have enough time to get into the basement before he does."

Odette slapped his hand. Though it was too dark to tell, he took it as a high-five.

"Then let's do it," she said.

Odette grabbed J.P.'s hand and pulled him toward the sound of rougarou's growls and the little dog's barks. Princess didn't stop barking when Odette lifted her into her arms. J.P. hoped for the best as he slipped out the door and began shouting as he headed down the dark hall to the entrance to the basement.

"Come get me, you sorry sack of shit!"

Slipping past Odette and the barking pug, the rougarou bounded for the door. The beast was as fast as Odette had said and could see in the dark. He caught J.P. at the top step of the slick stairway.

Razor-like claws tore off J.P.'s fancy shirt as it raked down his back. Trying to get away from the rougarou's grasp, J.P. slipped on the narrow concrete stairs and tumbled headfirst into the darkness. If the rush of adrenaline hadn't begun surging through his system, he would indeed have broken his neck. Instead, he flipped over on his back and awaited the next attack. He didn't have long to wait.

The beast charged down the stairs, lifted J.P. off the floor, and shot-putted him into a cabinet laden with bottles and beakers. J.P. grimaced when broken glass bit into his arms and chest, though he was grateful it wasn't the fangs or claws of the rougarou.

Suddenly aware of J.P.'s life-threatening peril, Latrice came out of the dumbwaiter and activated his cell phone flashlight. By now broken glass and toxic chemicals had covered the basement floor, and J.P. was bleeding.

Latrice tried to draw a bead on the fast-moving creature, her efforts meeting with no success. In frustration, she began screaming, trying to get its attention and draw it away from J.P.

"Stop it, Kelton!"

Her cry had no impact on the rougarou, though it revived Jack and Chief. At first, they were dazed and confused. Their conditions changed when they saw the rougarou in the strobe-like light issuing from J.P.'s cell phone. Chief was the first to react.

Diving on top of the creature, he began pummeling him with his fists. Jack joined the fray, breaking a large bottle of chemicals over the rougarou's head. They were soon as bruised and bloody as J.P.

Standing in a shooter's stance, Latrice held

225

the pneumatic pistol in both hands, trying to get a clear shot at the beast. It didn't come.

The rougarou was more potent than all three men combined. It didn't matter because the floor was so slick that every time it managed to get to its feet, it would slip and fall again. When Latrice got too close to the action, she had the pneumatic pistol knocked across the floor. Jumping into the fray, she began flailing and clawing with her nails.

J.P. was in pain as the fight continued in almost total darkness. He somehow managed to pull free of the melee and sprint up the slick stairs. When he reached the top, he began to yell.

"Odette. the lights!"

When fluorescent lighting illuminated the basement, J.P. hurried down the slick stairway. Slipping hard on the last step, he crashed into the wall. The tumble knocked him out. It was the last thing he remembered for a while.

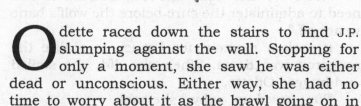

Odette raced down the stairs to find J.P. slumping against the wall. Stopping for only a moment, she saw he was either dead or unconscious. Either way, she had no time to worry about it as the brawl going on in the center of the basement seemed more important to her.

Latrice, Jack, and Chief were on the concrete in a life or death battle with the rougarou. The floor was sticky with blood, toxic chemicals and strewn with broken glass. Odette's first impulse was to dive into the fray. She quickly decided it wasn't a good idea.

Though immensely powerful and physically dominant, the rougarou couldn't get up off the floor. Every time it tried, Jack, Chief, or Latrice would wrap their arms around its legs and drag him back to the concrete. Despite managing to keep the creature on the floor, it was only a matter of time before the rougarou's strength would prevail.

When Odette spotted the pneumatic pistol, she scooped it up. Jamming the gun to the creature's neck, she pulled the trigger. The result of the dart wasn't instantaneous.

The creature clutched the projectile and emitted a primal wail. Yanking the dart out of its neck, it glared at Odette with angry red eyes. For a moment, Odette thought he was going to bound up off the floor and attack her. Instead, the creature's head nodded as his glaring eyes shut, and he slumped to the floor.

Latrice, Jack, and Chief were still punching the creature even though it was out like a light. Odette grabbed Latrice's arm, pulled her to her feet, and shook her back to reality.

"It's over," she said. "The rougarou is out. You need to administer the cure before the wolf's bane wears off."

It took a moment for Latrice to realize the rougarou was down. When she did, she smiled and hugged Odette.

"You saved us, baby," she said.

"No, the four of you saved us. I only put the dart in the creature's neck. If I could, I'd have shoved it up its ass."

Jack and Chief pulled themselves off the floor and joined the group hug, the remains of their shredded clothes stained with blood and toxic chemicals.

"Holy hell!" Odette said. "You guys look like you were on the losing end of a knife fight."

"You aren't far wrong," Jack said, pulling a sliver of glass from a cut on his arm.

Latrice broke away from the group and began looking for a cure bottle, finding all she needed in the corner refrigerator. Kelton Frenette was slowly transforming into human form and was the first to receive a dose.

"I vaccinated Jack and Chief," Latrice said. "That leaves you, me, and J.P. Stick your arm out."

"Where is J.P.?" Jack asked.

After receiving her shot, Odette hurried to

J.P.'s crumpled body in the corner.

"He took a nasty stumble down the stairs," she said.

Latrice felt a vein in his wrist. "He's alive," she said. "His pulse is strong."

"Thank God!" Odette said.

Pulling up J.P.'s sleeve, Latrice administered a dose of the vaccine. Odette swabbed J.P.'s face with a wet cloth until he opened his eyes. When he did, he came up swinging. Chief pinned his arms.

"Whoa, buddy. The fight's over. You okay?"

J.P. rubbed his swollen forehead. "Just got the sense knocked out of me."

"That happened years ago," Odette said with a smirk.

"No comments from the peanut section," J.P. said.

"What the hell does that even mean?" Odette asked.

"Hell if I know," J.P. said. "Something, my mama always used to say."

J.P. nodded when Latrice asked, "Can you stand? Then let's go upstairs. I'll get us all cleaned up. Kelton has a closetful of clothes to wear until you get home. Everyone except Chief. He's so big; he'll have to make do with a bathrobe."

Chief almost cracked a smile. "Won't be the first time," he said.

Though Dr. Frenette had begun to transform, he was still unconscious as they loaded him on a gurney and wheeled him into the dumbwaiter.

"I'll take him," Odette said. "Meet you at the top of the stairs."

When the door closed, the inside of the dumbwaiter went dark, only the whine of the electric motor punctuating the silence. Latrice met her at the upstairs door.

"You okay, baby?"

"That was about the creepiest two minutes I've ever spent," Odette said.

Latrice grinned. "Let's get everyone cleaned up, doctored, and new clothes to wear. First, I need to find Princess."

Latrice turned with a smile when Odette said, "She's behind you."

The pug's curly tail was wagging when Latrice lifted her off the floor and hugged her in her big arms.

"I was so worried," Latrice said as the little dog squirmed and licked her face.

"I'm not exaggerating when I tell you she saved my life and J.P.'s," Odette said. "None of us would be alive now if it wasn't for her."

They were relaxing in the living room when Dr. Frenette began to revive. When he became fully conscious and saw everyone's condition, he said, "I'm so sorry."

"What the hell were you thinking?" J.P. said. "Why didn't you inject yourself?"

Frenette looked small and weak, nothing like the vibrant creature he'd been.

His voice was measured when he said, "I didn't want to die of cancer or go back to the wheelchair. I chose to live, even if it meant becoming a rougarou."

"That wasn't fair to Latrice," J.P. said. "It damn sure wasn't fair to the rest of us."

"I meant to infect Latrice. We'd have been together forever."

Frenette sank back into the gurney, pulling the rubberized sheet around his neck.

"Everything worked out," J.P. said. "We survived, and now we're all inoculated. Latrice refilled the dart. We're going to leave and let you get some rest."

Chief caught J.P.'s eye and shook his head.

"Not that easy," he said.

"What?" J.P. said.

Chief motioned J.P. to join him in the corner of the living room. Odette, Jack, and Latrice also wanted to hear.

"What the hell, big boy?" Jack said.

"Frenette's a smart man. He tasted immortality, and it doesn't take a genius to realize he's never going to be happy returning to his death bed."

"Your point?" J.P. asked.

Chief tried unsuccessfully to close the red velvet bathrobe. "It won't be tonight, or maybe even next week, but you can rest assured he'll figure out how to regain his lost immortality. We can't take a chance on him becoming a rougarou again."

"Are you suggesting we kill him?" Odette asked.

"Return him to his former health and vitality as a human," Chief said.

"How do we do that?" J.P. asked.

"I'm betting the virus won the immortality battle, his cancer cured," Chief said.

"What if it isn't?" Jack said. "He refuses to go to a doctor to find out."

"Then it's up to us to convince him," Chief said.

"How in the hell are we going to do that?" Jack asked.

"By performing the Atakapan cleansing ceremony," Chief said.

"We're dealing with reality here," J.P. said. "Not gobbledygook."

"My beliefs aren't gobbledygook," Chief said.

"Beliefs are important," J.P. said. "We all have them. None of ours are ever the same, so don't get your breechcloth in a wad."

"You know I'm not a religious person, Chief,"

231

Jack said. "Do you believe a cleansing ceremony is going to make an iota of a difference in Frenette's health?"

"I've seen it work," Chief said. "Even if you don't believe it, the Great Spirit exists. The earth and universe are too complex for mere mortals to comprehend. Magic is real. I believe it, and so should you."

"Chief is a spiritual person," Odette said. "If he believes the Atakapan cleansing ceremony will keep Dr. Frenette from becoming a monster again, I'm all for giving it a try."

"Latrice, what do you think?" J.P. asked.

"I'm like Jack," Latrice said. "I haven't been to church in twenty years."

"Then are you saying no?" J.P. asked.

Latrice glanced at her husband on the gurney. "As a hospital nurse, I saw my share of unexplained miracles. If Chief has faith, then so do I."

"You look skeptical, J.P.," Jack said. "Tell us what you think."

"Dr. Frenette is vaccinated. He can't become a rougarou again until the vaccine wears off. That may be years away. Even then, he'll have to come in contact with the virus, and that presumes he survives his cancer."

"Yeah," Jack said. "Let's get out of here."

Chief looked dejected as Jack and J.P. started for the door. Still in her retro dress, Odette was the only person wearing the same thing she'd had on when she left the island.

Jack and J.P. stopped when she said, "Wait a minute. What's it going to hurt to perform the cleansing ceremony? It's three in the morning. Looking the way you do, you're going nowhere except back to the island."

"Latrice?" J.P. said.

"I have no clue if Chief's cleansing ceremony

232

will change anything. All I know is Kelton needs all the help we can give him."

"You two get out of here," Odette said. "I'm staying with Chief to help him with the ceremony. We'll hitchhike back to the island tomorrow."

Jack looked first at J.P. and then back at Odette.

"Dammit!" he said. "I need rum."

"Kelton's out like a light," Latrice said. "I'm all for Chief performing the ceremony. Just not tonight. Will you do me a favor, though?" Latrice asked.

Latrice smiled when Jack said, "Hell, I'd fight the rougarou again for a sip of Dominican rum."

"They won't have your rum, but there's an all-night liquor store on St. Charles, about a mile from here," Latrice said. She handed Jack a wad of cash. "Get Kelton several bottles of 1972, Pierre Ferrand."

"I'll drive us to the liquor store, but I'll be damned if I'm going in wearing clothes five times too big for me," J.P. said.

"What makes you think they have Pierre Ferrand, 1972?" Jack asked.

"The owner of the liquor store stocks it for us," Latrice said.

"You two don't work," Jack said. "Mind if I ask how you can afford such expensive brandy?"

"Kelton is an inventor. He owns dozens of patents. We never come close to spending the mailbox money we get every month."

"Must be nice," Jack said.

"All the money in the world won't cure Kelton's terminal cancer. Perhaps Chief's ceremony can," she said.

"I'll go into the liquor store," Odette said. "At least I'm wearing the same clothes I had on when I left the island."

"We'll drop off your Pierre Ferrand. Will you

233

be awake?" J.P. asked.

"I'm tired as hell," Latrice said. "Makes no difference. I won't crash until after you bring the brandy."

Rain drizzled on the windshield of J.P.'s truck as they headed out of the Garden District to St. Charles Avenue and the liquor store. There was a chill in the air as he turned on the heater.

"There's something I need to tell you," J.P. said. "I was going to wait until tomorrow. Seems about right, I tell you now."

"What?" Chief asked.

"Bad news," J.P. said.

"What could be worse than fighting a rougarou, getting burned by toxic chemicals and shredded with broken glass?" Jack asked.

"The State rejected our dog training grant application," J.P. said. "We're not going to have enough money to make the project work."

"Damn!" Jack said. "I wasn't expecting that."

"We'll come up with the money some other way," Chief said. "We've already made a start. How much do we need?"

"More than a hundred grand," J.P. said.

"That's crazy," Jack said. "Why do we need that much money?"

"Trust me," J.P. said. "That may not even be half enough."

"Where are we going to raise that kind of money?" Jack said. "I can't even get a higher limit on my credit card."

"The rum," Chief said. "If we sell the rest of the bottles, we'll have more than enough money to fund the training center."

"If we don't drink it all first," Jack said.

Odette reached in her purse and pulled out a wad of bills.

"Here's the ten grand I got for the doubloon. I have three more doubloons in my tent I'll sell and contribute to the cause. Though it isn't enough, it will help. Take it," she said.

"You don't have to do that," J.P. said.

"I don't have to do anything," she said. "I had no money when I came to the island. I didn't need it then. I don't need it now. Take it."

"What about Rockie's?" Jack said.

"No one's going to Rockie's tonight," J.P. said. "Have you looked at yourself in a mirror lately?"

Jack glanced at Chief in the red velvet bathrobe, and then at the oversized pants and shirt, he was wearing.

"Dammit!" he said.

"You can't take Odette's money," Chief said. "It's not right."

"It's okay, Chief. I want to do this," Odette said.

J.P. took the money and stuffed it in his shirt pocket.

"Don't give up your dream," she said. "Things will work out."

"Odette's right. We'll figure something out," J.P. said.

"Thanks, Odette," Jack and Chief both said.

They found the liquor store at an intersection with St. Charles Avenue. The parking lot was dark, not a car there. Shells covering the lot crunched beneath the wheels of J.P.'s truck as he parked in front of the door.

"Now," he said. Who's going into the liquor store?"

Chapter 28

The wood-framed liquor store bore the name Junior's International House of Liquor, the iron bars on the picture window and door suggesting Junior's clientele were anything other than jet setters. J.P. handed the wad of cash Latrice had given him to Odette.

"If any of us other than you walk in there this time of night, the cops will be swarming the place in ten minutes," he said.

"I can handle it," Odette said.

When a chopped Ford with twelve-inch wheels and loud exhausts slowed as it passed the liquor store on St. Charles, Chief opened the door and stepped out.

"It's not safe for Miss Odette to go in alone," he said. "I'm going with her."

Jack glared at J.P. and opened his door. "Me too," he said.

"Suit yourself," J.P. said.

"You're the cop," Jack said. "Don't you feel even a little bit guilty?"

J.P. frowned and followed them out of the truck. "Cops are human, too," he said.

A tall man behind the counter was reading a racing form when the crew entered the liquor store.

His frown never disappeared when he said, "Help you?"

"Your best bottle of rum," Jack said.

"Second aisle to your right," the man said.

His expression changed when Odette said, "We also need several bottles of Pierre Ferrand, vintage 1972."

Before they could say scat, they were staring into the barrel of a sawed-off, twelve-gauge double-barrel shotgun.

"Up against the wall," the man said.

"Now wait just a minute," J.P. said. "I'm a police officer. My badge is in my pocket."

"Hands behind your heads. You come close to that pocket, and I'll blow you away. I'm calling the police."

"You crazy?" Jack said. "We didn't do anything."

"The only people I know who drink Pierre Ferrand are Dr. Frenette and his wife Latrice," the man said. "From the looks of the four of you, I'm guessing you just came from there."

J.P. recognized something about the tall, slender man with the Chalmette accent.

"You're Junior Portie," he said. "I'd recognize your voice anywhere."

"Who the hell are you?" the man asked.

"Jean Pierre Saucier. Your last day as a cop in St. Bernard Parish was my first. I was at your going away party."

"I'm not buying it," the man said. "Everyone in the neighborhood knows I'm Junior Portie and that I was a cop. You could have heard it anywhere."

"You know the Frenette's," Odette said. "Latrice is awake. Call her. She'll vouch for us."

"You're the only decent-looking person in the bunch," Junior said. "Did these felons kidnap

237

you?"

"No, sir," Odette said.

"Then why do those three look as if they just came from a double homicide?"

"You wouldn't believe it if I told you," J.P. said.

"Try me," Junior said.

"We were wrestling a rougarou in the Frenette's basement," J.P. said.

J.P.'s words resulted in something unexpected. Junior grabbed his cell phone from the counter and speed-dialed Latrice.

"Latrice," he said when she answered. "It's Junior Portie. I got three vagrants and a pretty little girl here in the liquor store. Are you and the doc okay?"

Junior finished the conversation and set the shotgun on the counter.

"Latrice sounded okay," he said. "I'm shutting down the place, taking my shotgun, and going with you. You need to prove to me there's no one there with a knife to Latrice's throat."

J.P.'s hands were still on his head. "Reach in my pocket. You'll find my badge."

Junior removed J.P.'s badge with the deft hands of a police professional. After staring at it for a moment, he returned it to J.P.'s pocket.

"Makes me even leerier of you," Junior said. "You could be a cop killer for all I know."

Junior managed a smile when J.P. said, "I've never killed anyone except bad guys. You know my boss Captain Comier. Call him. He'll vouch for me."

"It's almost four in the morning," Junior said.

"Hell, Junior, you've been retired too long. Captain Comier has been up for thirty minutes and has probably already fielded a dozen calls."

Junior redialed his phone, his face soon awash in a broad grin. The ensuing conversation lasted ten minutes, Junior still grinning when he returned the phone to the counter.

"Put your hands down, Jean Pierre. Champ said you were a little strange but told me you are the best man on his force. Now, tell me, why the hell are you, except for the pretty young lady, scratched to hell and dressed like circus clowns?"

"You know Dr. Frenette is a rougarou researcher?" Odette said.

"I've heard, though Kelton and Latrice have never talked about it," Junior said.

"Dr. Frenette's work was discredited, partly because of their mixed marriage."

"They are two of my favorite people," Junior said. "Mixed marriages are common these days. Not so common when I was a kid."

"Latrice and Dr. Frenette love each other," Odette said. "That's all that counts."

"What's your name, pretty girl?" Junior asked.

"Odette," she said. "This is Jack, and you can call the big Indian Chief."

"My wife and I have been married almost forty years, and we're both tolerant of everyone's sexual preferences. It's pretty damn obvious he's big enough to kick my ass. I'll call the big one anything he likes," Junior said, shaking their hands.

Junior smiled when Jack said, "I need a drink. Got anything alcoholic in this place?"

"You said you wanted rum," Junior said. "I have some of the best."

"Expensive?" Jack asked.

"Liquor doesn't always work that way," Junior said. "This rum isn't also the best. It's the cheapest."

"Suits me," Jack said with a smile.

"I guess you know Dr. Frenette has cancer," J.P. said.

"I heard," Junior said. "I'm shutting down for

239

the night. I'd be happy to drop off the Ferrand to Latrice and the doc."

"Thanks, Junior," J.P. said.

"Don't forget the rum," Jack said

"You like Dominican Rum?" Junior asked.

"You kidding? It's our favorite," Jack said.

"Then you'll like this," Junior said, showing them a bottle. "This is the same recipe as the defunct Whistling Winds distillery used. Heard of it?"

"You bet we have," Jack said. "How did they get the recipe?"

"Don't know. It's the best rum I ever tasted," Junior said. "Like to try it?"

"Thought you'd never ask," Jack said.

Junior opened the bottle. Finding tumblers under the cabinet, he poured two fingers for each of them.

"Enjoy," he said.

After taking a sip, Jack said, "I think I've died and gone to heaven. What's the name of the brand?"

"Island Rum. It's kind of pricey," Junior said with a snicker.

"How much?" Chief asked.

"Fifteen bucks for a half," Junior said.

"You're kidding," Chief said. "Sounds like the owners of the distillery have no idea what they have."

"So stop complaining," Jack said. "All the better for us."

"Most people never try this brand because it's so cheap. I have ten bottles in back I'll never sell."

"Double the price, and it will sell twice as fast," Odette said.

Odette's suggestion brought a broad grin to Junior's big face. "If I do that, it'll soon be a hundred bucks a bottle."

"Give us all ten," Jack said.

Junior brought the two boxes of rum from the back and set them on the counter.

"Anything else?" he asked.

"We're worried about Kelton and Latrice," J.P. said. "Can you keep an eye on them for a week or so?"

"What's your cell phone number?" After exchanging numbers, Junior asked. "Why do I need to keep an eye on them?"

"Long story and we need to get on the road," J.P. said. "I'll call and tell you all about it tomorrow."

"You got it," Junior said.

Chief carried the boxes of rum to the truck, stowing them in the backseat between him and Jack. They had barely buckled up when Jack opened one of the bottles.

"Save some for us," Chief said.

"You'll get your share. This rum is as good as ours is," Jack said.

"You're right," Chief said. "I can't believe we've been swilling sixty-thousand dollar booze when we could have drunk the same thing for the price of rotgut."

Chief handed the bottle to Odette. "Wonderful," she said.

"This is tasty," J.P. said. "How many bottles of the real stuff do we still have?"

"Jack and I each have three bottles left," Chief said.

"That'll give us more than enough money to fund the dog training facility," J.P. said.

"And we won't have to drink up any more of the good stuff," Jack said.

"The rum is good," Odette said. "What I need is something to eat."

"Me too," Chief said.

"We're halfway to Chalmette," Jack said. "Wait till we get back to the island, and I'll cook

241

us a breakfast to die for."

"I'll help," Odette said.

"Step on it," Chief said. "I'm not sure I can wait that long."

"Don't eat the seat covers," Jack said. "Another slug of rum will tide you over until we get back to the island."

Odette and Jack were asleep when J.P. crossed the bridge to Oyster Island. The sun had popped up from the depths of the Gulf of Mexico, setting ablaze the morning sky. A truck with a camper in the back was waiting at Jack's house. J.P. eased his vehicle beside it, knowing something was wrong before it came to a stop. When he caught a glimpse of his Airstream trailer, he realized it was something terrible.

"What the hell?" he said as he jumped out of the truck to examine his trailer's dented metal door.

Paula and Jimmy joined him from the other truck. "We brought our camper so we can stay awhile," Paula said.

"You had a visitor last night," Jimmy said.

J.P.'s hands were on his hips as he studied the damage. "Damn it! That's going to cost a month's salary to fix."

"At least the beast didn't manage to get inside. More than I can say for Jack's house," Jimmy said.

Jack and Odette were rubbing the sleep from their eyes as they climbed out of J.P.'s truck.

"What in holy hell?" Jack said.

He didn't wait for an answer as he burst through the door, flapping in the morning breeze. Stunned by the damage, he halted in his tracks.

"The dogs," J.P. said. "Where the hell are they?"

Still outside, Chief pointed at the jumble of tracks in the sand.

"The dogs chased the rougarou to the bridge," he said. "We need to hurry before he kills some of them."

J.P. grabbed the pneumatic pistol from the front seat of his truck.

"I'm on it," he said.

"Once you get off the dirt road, it's more swamp than dry land. You'll need a tracker," Chief said.

"I'm coming with you," Jimmy said.

"Then let's go," J.P. said.

"Me too," Jack said.

"The beast might double back," J.P. said. "You need to stay behind in case he does."

Jack, Odette, and Paula watched as the three men disappeared over the bridge."

Paula and Jimmy's camper occupied the bed of his pickup. Paula climbed inside, returning with a box.

"Brought you a new tent from the Army-Navy store," she said.

Odette smiled and hugged her. "You are so thoughtful," she said.

"Put it in the ATV," Jack said. "You can set it up later. Right now, we need to check the house for damage."

J.P.'s damaged Airstream didn't prepare them for the mess they found inside Jack's house. Furniture and trash lay strewn across the floor.

"Good Lord," Paula said. "The creature did a number in here."

"Wonder how he managed to do so much damage before the dogs chased him away?" Odette asked.

"He pushed my recliner against the doggie door," Jack said. "The dogs were probably going crazy trying to get in. The creature did lots of damage, though probably not as much as he would have if the dogs hadn't managed to get through the doggie door."

"It means the rougarou is capable of thinking like a human and not simply a wild beast. "Odette said.

"That's scary," Paula said. "Is it possible he planned these attacks?"

"If he did," Jack said. "They aren't going to end until we kill it, or he kills us."

"Or J.P. inoculates it," Odette said.

"He pissed on the front door, and it stinks to high heavens," Paula said.

"Marking his territory," Jack said. "I'll get a mop."

An hour had passed before they had the broken glass swept up, the floor mopped, and the trashed furniture hauled outside.

"We're lucky," Paula said. "He could have destroyed your house if the dogs hadn't chased him away."

"I'm worried about Mudbug," Odette said. "She's not big enough to keep up with the full-grown dogs. I'm going to look for her."

"They'll find her," Paula said. "She'll be fine."

"You sure?" Odette said.

"Positive. Let's help Jack cook breakfast. Everyone will have an appetite when they return with the dogs."

Chapter 29

O nce J.P., Chief, and Jimmy crossed the bridge, the terrain changed. The beach was gone, the sand gone. What was left were vines, ferns, and stagnant water.

"This is the first time I've been afoot on this side of the bridge," J.P. said.

Stunted trees and marshy vegetation bordered both sides of the road. A sunning snake slithered off into the shallow water and swam away.

"Cottonmouth," J.P. said.

"Hope you're not afraid of snakes. There are more of them than there are of us," Chief said.

"How do you know?" J.P. asked. "You can't see much more than ten feet from the road."

"Things get marshy and then swampy pretty quick," Chief said. "The sand on the road came from the island. The Parish added the shells. The rains hardened the road making it the only way into the island without a boat or chopper."

"Have you been in the swamps?" J.P. asked.

"Got lost in there more times than I can count. The last time I did, Grandpa banned me from doing any more exploring."

245

"You think the rougarou is somewhere in the swamp?" J.P. asked.

Chief nodded. "I'd bet money on it."

"How do you know the dogs haven't left the road already?" J.P. asked.

"Grandpa could track a butterfly through a field of clover. He taught me everything he knew," Chief said. "I'll tell you when we reach the spot where they leave the road."

"I hear a dog," Jimmy said.

When they rounded a bend in the road, they saw the dog making the noise. It was Mudbug, her whines turning into a wagging tail and barks of joy when she saw Chief, J.P., and Jimmy. Jimmy picked up the little dog and began comforting her.

"We can't take her with us," Chief said. "You'll have to take her back to the island."

"To hell with that," Jimmy said. "You need me."

"Chief's right," J.P. said. "We can't leave Mudbug here, and you won't be much help with her in your arms. Chief and I'll find the rougarou."

"Then wait on me until I get back," Jimmy said. "I'll bring my 30-30."

"We don't have time to wait on you," J.P. said. "Every minute we waste means more danger for the other dogs."

Though anything but happy, Jimmy headed back to the island with Mudbug. Chief and J.P. continued ahead for another mile when they began hearing the barks and howls of dogs. Around the next turn, they found the pack barking at something off the road. Coco stopped barking when he saw the two men, ran, and jumped into Chief's arms.

"You little warrior," Chief said. "Were you leading the pack?"

J.P. made a quick count. "They're all here," he said. "None of them are bleeding."

"Good," Chief said. "Give me the pistol, and then take them back to the island with you."

"Your ass!" J.P. said. "You take the dogs."

"You'll never find your way into or out of the swamp alone," Chief said. "Give me the pistol. I can handle things from here by myself."

"Not going to happen," J.P. said.

"The dogs won't stay on the road and wait for us. With the possible exception of Old Joe, they wouldn't survive the swamp," Chief said. "Someone needs to return them to the island."

"Then you take them," J.P. said.

"I know the swamp. You don't," Chief said.

"I'm Cajun," J.P. said. "Swamp water's coursing through my veins."

Chief almost smiled. "We need a boat. I have a pirogue. Let's both go back with the dogs. We can return with the pirogue in the back of your truck. We're going to need a spotlight."

"The rougarou will be gone by then," J.P. said.

"No, he won't," Chief said. "He's not far away. I wouldn't doubt if he's watching us right now. He'll be here when we return."

"Hope you're right," J.P. said.

"What I hope is Jack has grub ready," Chief said. "I'm starving."

The dogs were happy heading back to the island. They ran ahead of Jack and Chief, occasionally slowing to bark at squirrels, snakes, or waterfowl. They crossed the bridge to the house before Chief and J.P. reached it. Because of their barking, everyone was waiting outside for J.P. and Chief when they arrived.

"Well?" Jack said.

"We found the dogs but not the rougarou," Chief said. "We're going back with my pirogue after we get something to eat."

"Then you came to the right place. We've all eaten. We left plenty for you and J.P.," Jack said.

"Thanks for finding Mudbug," Odette said as they entered the front door.

"We weren't coming back without her," J.P. said.

Everyone was standing around watching as Chief and J.P. ate bacon and eggs and homemade biscuits and gravy.

"What?" J.P. asked. "Don't you all have something else to do besides watching Chief and me eat?"

"We have bad news," Jack said.

"More bad news?" Chief asked.

"The rougarou broke every bottle of our Dominican rum. We didn't realize it until we checked the pantry."

Chief stopped eating, closed his eyes, and rubbed his forehead.

"Are you kidding?" J.P. asked.

"Would I kid about something that important?" Jack said.

"Guess not," J.P. said. "Did you tell Paula and Jimmy we didn't get the grant from the State?"

"We heard," Paula said. "Jimmy and I have some extra money we can contribute. Not nearly as much as we need, though."

"Odette sold her gold doubloon for ten grand and contributed the money to the cause," J.P. said. I vote we make her a full partner. Anyone opposed?"

When everyone agreed, Odette kissed J.P. on the cheek.

"Thank you all," she said.

"Does it mean you like me now?" J.P. asked.

"Yes, but I never fraternize with business associates."

"Damn it!" J.P. said as he returned his attention to the scrambled eggs.

"That's not your only problem," Odette said. "If we can't figure a way to raise an extra hundred grand or so, there won't be a canine training center."

"Let's not get down in the dumps," Chief said. "Something will work out."

"Indian intuition or just a wild-ass guess?" Paula asked.

Everyone grinned when he said, "Just trying to make you feel a little better."

"At least we still have rum," Jack said. "Even if it isn't worth much."

"That's a plus," Chief said. "Why haven't you broken out a bottle?"

"It's still in J.P.'s truck," Jack said.

Chief sat his utensils beside the plate, returning from the truck with a box of rum under each arm.

After placing the boxes on the counter, he said, "Got any more bacon and eggs?" When he finished eating, he started for the door. "I have to feed my chickens and take care of a few things. I'll be back with the pirogue."

"I'll drive you in the ATV if Jack lets me," Odette said.

"Knock yourself out," Jack said, tossing her the keys. We have repairs on the kennels to make before dark."

"I'll go with you," Paula said. "Odette has told me about your place. I'd love to see it."

Odette, Paula, and Chief were soon on their way across the island. Coco, Old Joe, and Mudbug were in the back, barking, wagging their tails, and having the time of their lives. Paula's smile disappeared when Odette pulled to a stop in front of the Majestic.

"That place haunts me," she said.

"Tell me about it," Odette said. "You've lived on this island your entire life, Chief. What's the story on the Majestic?"

"It's haunted," he said, "But you already know that."

Coco and Mudbug were sitting in Chief's lap, both vying for his attention.

"You know more about it, don't you?" Odette said.

"Oyster Bay was a destination for the rich and famous during Prohibition; a place where they could drink, gamble and commit sin. It was also a haven for gamblers, mobsters, and bootleggers."

"Jack said you own the island. Did your family sell it?" Odette asked.

"A bogus deed appeared in the parish courthouse, the Atakapan writ of ownership disappearing in the process," Chief said.

"That is so wrong," Paula said.

"White men have never had problems stealing from the Indians," Chief said.

"There must be someone who can help right the wrong," Odette said.

"I've tried," Chief said. "The island has been deserted my whole life. It hasn't seemed that important."

"Jack says that's about to change," Odette said. "What'll you do?"

"I learn things every day I live here," Chief said. "I believe this island is a sacred portal between this world and the netherworld. The white man comes and goes. Doesn't matter because Oyster Bay will always belong to the Atakapas."

"What else?" Paula said.

"I had a vision the night the rougarou first appeared on the island. Jack and I performed a sweat lodge ceremony to try to figure out what it meant."

"You had a vision?" Paula asked.

Chief nodded. "Yes."

"Tell us," Paula said.

"I was asleep and smelled smoke. I didn't awaken. Instead, I floated out of the teepee and down the hill."

When Chief paused, Odette said, "Please, go on,"

"The Majestic was on fire, flames licking the sky through the broken windows. The head and upper body of a beautiful young woman with long red hair were poking out of an open window. Though she was incapable of speech, I could tell she was begging for someone to help her. No one did."

"What do you mean, incapable of speech?" Paula asked.

"I could read her thoughts," Chief said. "She had a damaged soul that rendered her mute. That's all I can tell you."

Odette and Paula waited for Chief to continue the story. When he didn't, Odette said, "Is that all?"

"I probably wouldn't have remembered that much if the rougarou's claw ripping through my teepee hadn't awakened me," Chief said.

"I didn't know the Majestic had ever burned," Paula said.

"It hasn't," Chief said.

"Maybe it was just a dream," Odette said.

"There are dreams, and there are visions," Chief said. "What I experienced was very real. A dream vision."

"If what you say is true, then I understand why the vision worries you," Odette said.

"It left me with many questions," Chief said.

251

"You didn't find the answers when you and Jack performed the sweat lodge ceremony?" Paula asked.

Chief shook his head. "I passed out. If Jack hadn't dragged me into the healing waters of the Magic Fountain, I could have died."

"Sounds like the ceremony was a waste of time," Odette said.

"For me, maybe. Jack saw his deceased parents, and they blessed him with a message of hope."

Odette parked the ATV at the foot of Chief's hill, and they hiked up the sandy trail to his teepee. Mable, his favorite hen, heard them coming and flew into Chief's awaiting arms.

"Hey baby," he said. "Miss me?"

It was easy to see she had. They spent the next hour feeding the chickens and Buttercup, Chief's cat. They sat on the bluff staring out at the black clouds forming out over the Gulf when they finished.

"I love it here," Paula said. "It's both enchanting and magical."

Chief was holding Mable in his lap. "J.P. and I have to deal with the rougarou."

"You're too involved," Paula said. "Let Jimmy go with J.P. They can handle it."

"Something or someone is trying to tell me something important about the rougarou. I don't know who or what. It's troubling," Chief said.

Trying to lighten the conversation, Odette said, "Let's show Paula the Magic Fountain."

Chief left Mable with the other chickens. Old Joe, Coco, and Mudbug followed them up the sandy trail to the artesian well bubbling from the limestone and flowing into the cobble-bottom pool. Paula stuck her finger beneath the water flow and touched it to her tongue.

"My, oh my!" she said. "This is the best water I've ever tasted."

Odette cupped her hands and let them fill with the water. "It is wonderful."

Paula began unbuttoning her blouse, pulled off her shorts and panties, and then stepped naked into the water.

Paula smiled when Chief's eyes grew large. "Don't act so surprised. You've seen me naked. Join me."

Paula didn't have to ask twice, Odette stripping off her shorts and blouse and then tip-toeing into the water.

"Chief," she said. "Are you going to stand there gawking or join us?"

Chapter 30

The shallow pool of artesian water was neither too hot nor too cold, the distant sound of waves crashing the shoreline backdropped against water gushing from the wall of limestone.

"This pool is truly magical," Paula said. "I can feel the energy surging through me. Have you ever had a mystical experience here?"

"Maybe," Chief said.

"Tell us," Odette said.

"Private," he said.

If he were capable of that particular phenomenon, he would have blushed when Paula asked, "Did it happen the night Miss Millie spent with you?"

"How do you know about that?" he asked.

"Jack put the love potion in your rum, but I was responsible for mixing it. Remember? Why are you looking so unhappy?"

"I'd forgotten about the love potion. I thought Millie liked me because of who I am, not what I'd slipped into her drink," he said. "Did Miss Millie tell you about the fountain?"

"You must have made an impression. Millie told someone, and that someone spread the story.

By now, everyone in Chalmette has heard it."

"No wonder Millie moved away," Chief said.

Paula squeezed Chief's hand. "She had her reasons for moving from Chalmette, which didn't involve you. You were simply the catalyst."

"Story of my life," Chief said.

"You have no reason to feel blue," Paula said. "You showed Millie a slice of existence she never knew existed. Give her a chance to explore it."

"You think she'll come back to Chalmette?" Chief asked.

"Probably not. You could visit her in Santa Fe."

"Maybe," Chief said.

They were silent a moment, listening to the Gulf and the sound of artesian water.

"There's more magic to this pool than just its name," Paula finally said.

"Is that just you feeling wonderful, or is it the traiteur in you talking?" Odette asked.

Paula didn't answer. "Let's sit in a circle, hold hands and close our eyes. Maybe we can summon an oracle to give us the answers to all our questions."

They clasped hands and closed their eyes, so close to each other that Chief had to bend his knees to keep from putting his bare foot where it didn't belong. Deep euphoria soon took control of their senses, their minds melting into unthinking protoplasm.

Chief's mind began to reel as shrill noise rattled his brain. Though he tried to will it away, it captured his psyche, conveying him into a realm of unusual dreams. When the resonance of wind chimes and perfume of wild sand roses supplanted the clamor, he was too far displaced from reality to know where he was or to care. Paula was experiencing the same exotic sensation.

255

Odette was also out for the count though she experienced none of the voices Chief and Paula heard. When they opened their eyes, darkness had cloaked the sky.

"Dammit!" Chief said. "I'm late, and J.P's going to be pissed."

"Did you hear the voices?" Paula asked.

Chief opened and shut his mouth, trying to pop his ears.

"I heard," he said.

"What voices?" Odette said.

"Straight from the ether," Chief said. "I was wading in it."

"What voices," Odette asked again.

"Beautiful voices," Chief said. "They were so resonant and peaceful. I wanted to cry."

"You're talking gibberish," Odette said. "Were you hallucinating?"

"A lucid dream," Chief said. It told me what I need to know about the rougarou."

"Then you've found the answer to the question you sought," Paula said.

Chief bowed his head. "There's a patch of land in the middle of the swamp," he said. "A Cajun trapper's house sat in an open field on the little island. Grandpa took me there once."

"He took you there for a reason?" Paula asked.

"Maybe," Chief said. "The island is where the rougarou lives."

"You saw the beast?" Odette asked.

"Yes," he said.

"Did you hear voices, Paula?"

"Different voices than the ones Chief heard."

"Am I the only one who didn't hear anything?" Odette said.

"If you'd have had a question, baby, the oracle would have answered it," Paula said.

"It's late," Chief said. "I need to get the

256

pirogue and head back to Jack's before J.P. decides to take my scalp," he said.

"We're ready," Paula said.

Odette raced across the island, Jack, Jimmy, and J.P. waiting when she stopped in front of Jack's house.

"Where the hell have you been?" J.P. asked.

Chief didn't answer, dropping the pirogue into the back of J.P.'s truck and then following Odette and Paula inside.

"It's too dark to go looking for the rougarou," Jack said. "You'll have to do it tomorrow."

"Tomorrow will be too late," Chief said. "We have lights. The time couldn't be more perfect."

"Are you drunk?" Jack asked.

"Drunk on magic," Chief said.

"You're drunk on something though I don't know about magic," Jack said. "What the hell are you babbling about?"

"I had a vision, and now I know where to find the rougarou," Chief said.

"Where?" J.P. asked.

"When I was a kid, Grandpa took me in the pirogue to a spot of land in the swamp. A hermit trapper named Antoine lived in a house on the island."

"You think your Antoine is the same person who had the buckshot removed in the emergency room?" J.P. asked.

"Antoine was old fifty years ago," Chief said. "Could be his son, though, or maybe his grandson."

"How could he have had kids if he was a hermit?" Jack asked.

"Things can change in fifty years."

Jimmy gave Paula a stern look. "Where have the three of you been? We've waited here all day."

Paula rubbed her breasts against Jimmy's chest and humped his leg in a show of wanton affection.

"Baby, I missed you so," she said. "I can't wait to crawl beneath the covers with you."

Embarrassed by Paula's bawdy expression of affection, Jimmy's frown morphed into a silly grin. Pulling away from her embrace, he poured himself a mug of rum from the half-empty bottle on the counter.

Paula smiled and nodded when he said, "Rum?"

"Don't dirty a mug because of me," she said. "I'll share with you."

"I don't mind dirtying Jack's dishes," Chief said.

Taking two mugs from Jack's kitchen cabinet, he filled them with rum, handing one of the mugs to Odette.

"Damn, I needed that!" he said after a deep drink. J.P. and Jack were still giving him dirty looks.

"Your Antoine story doesn't quite hold water," J.P. said.

"Visions don't lie," Chief said. "You'll have to trust me on this one."

"Then let's go now," J.P. said.

"Too early," Chief said. "I'm starved and still thirsty."

Coco and Mudbug had joined Oscar by the fireplace, and Old Joe had gone out the doggie door to check on the other dogs. It wasn't long before Jimmy's eyes began to close.

"I've had enough to drink," he said. "I'm heading for the camper and some shuteye. Are you coming, Paula?"

Paula grabbed his elbow and followed him to the door. As if she'd forgotten something, she let go of his arm and hurried back into the house. Instead of retrieving something she'd forgotten, she cupped her hand to Odette's ear.

"Pick me up in the ATV in thirty minutes," she said. "I'll wait for you at the camper."

J.P. didn't notice the exchange between Paula and Odette.

"Those two are off for a night of marital bliss," he said.

"I'm heading for the beach to set up my new tent," Odette said. "Can I leave Mudbug here for the night?"

"You bet," Jack said.

"Mind if I take the ATV?" she asked. "The tent is in the back, and it's pretty heavy."

Jack tossed her the keys.

When Paula exited the camper thirty minutes later, Odette was waiting for her in the ATV.

"You must have put some awesome sex on Jimmy," Odette said.

"What I put was something in his rum," Paula said.

"You spiked his rum?" Odette said.

"We have work to do. I couldn't take a chance on him waking up."

"You're bad, girlfriend," Odette said. "What are we going to do?"

"Witch work," Paula said.

"Tell me."

"Drive us to the Majestic," Paula said. "I'll tell you when we get there."

Odette pulled the ATV to a stop in front of the Majestic.

"What?" she said.

"Chief wasn't the only one to have a vision in the Magic Fountain. The Oracle told me what I needed to know."

"Which is?"

"The lighthouse keeper's daughter," Paula said. "Members of the mob killed her parents and kidnapped her. She was only fifteen when they took her to the Majestic."

259

Paula nodded when Odette said, "Laurel?"

"They made Laurel a prostitute. She never left a ten by ten room for years and was forced to service one drunk after another."

"Horrible!" Odette said. "What became of her?"

"We're going to find out," Paula said. "We need to bury and consecrate her bones so her soul can cross over."

"Her soul is trapped in the Majestic?" Odette asked.

"We have to release her. There's no one else to help her cross over." Paula handed Odette a swath of black cloth to wear. "First, we dance."

Odette had danced in a strip club for money. Now, her movements had an essential purpose as she and Paula danced beneath a moon cloaked in lacy clouds. Odette felt one with the earth. A humming rhythm flowed from the mantle straight to the marrow of her bones. Though the weather was chilly, Odette was sweating when Paula grabbed her arm.

"It's time, baby," she said. "We're about to see some crazy shit. Don't freak out on me."

Waves coming in from the Gulf roiled the water in the bay. Odette felt as if she were on a boat in the ocean as she followed Paula up the wooden walkway to the doorway of the Majestic. Paula lit her black candle, pushed open the door, and stepped into the darkness.

Pulsating luminescence lighted the walls. Images of people trapped in agonizing despair cried out in silent pleas for help. When Odette tried to touch one of the images, her hand disappeared into a broken mirror. Closing her eyes, she pulled her hand from the mirror, hoping it wasn't a stub she would see when it appeared. That wasn't all Odette could see.

"Don't touch the walls," Paula said. "The

spirits will grab you and pull you in. I won't be able to save you."

Odette's heart raced as she nodded and followed Paula into the Stygian darkness. She almost suffered sensory overload when a high-pitched wail began rattling the walls and her nerves. Odette placed her hand on Paula's shoulder.

"I've never smelled anything so putrid. I think I'm about to throw up," she said.

"Dead souls and decomposing flesh," Paula said. "Don't think about it, or it'll suck your soul out of your body."

Broken glass cut into Odette's bare feet, blood oozing between her toes.

"There's glass all over the floor," she said.

"No, there isn't. The spirits are trying to protect themselves by manipulating your thoughts. It isn't real."

"Damn, sure feels real," Odette said. "Protect themselves from who?"

"You and me. Even spirits of darkness hate change."

"What are we going to change?" Odette asked.

"Destiny, baby," Paula said. "If they don't kill us first."

"Paula," Odette said. "I'm scared."

"Me too," Paula said.

Music began to play. It sounded like background music to a horror movie Odette had never entirely forgotten. Paula's voice sounded distant and unreal when she called out.

"Laurel, where are you?"

Skull faces flew in lazy circles around the darkened room, blood dripping from their empty eye sockets. Odette screamed when one of the skulls banged into her face.

"Stupid pussy," the skull said.

"Ignore it," Paula said. "The spirits will say

261

horrible and repulsive things. They have no power
to harm you, so don't let the words get to you. At
least most of them don't."

"Some of them do?"

Paula didn't answer her, calling again.
"Laurel, where are you?"

The music had become overwhelmingly loud,
the stench stomach-turning. Paula didn't waver,
moving ahead through the darkness. She stopped
in front of a door in the hallway of the third floor.
Gaseous demons appeared to block their way.

"Get thee hence," Paula said.

A monstrous demon, molten sulfur oozing
from its thick, decomposing skin, continued to
block their entrance into the room. Brilliant cuts
marked its body, reeking of death.

"Go back to where you came," the angry
apparition said. "You aren't welcome here."

Paula began to pray aloud. "Yea though I
walk in the valley of the shadow of death, I will
fear no evil. . ."

The demon's image flickered and disappeared
as Paula grabbed the door handle and pushed it
open. A glimmering light of pale green illuminated
the room with an unearthly glow. A girl with red
hair was in the middle of an unmade bed, crying
as she sat cross-legged on the sheets. Paula went
to her, trying to hug her. The girl kept moving
away from Paula's embrace.

"Laurel, we're here to help you cross over,"
Paula said.

A voice behind them said, "She doesn't
speak."

Chapter 31

When Paula and Odette wheeled around, a young man with light brown hair and clear blue eyes was smiling at them. Though short, his shoulders, exposed by a sleeveless tee-shirt, were muscular and covered with tattoos.

"Who are you?" Paula asked.

"Christopher," the man said. "Why are you here?"

As Christopher glided past them, both Paula and Odette realized he wasn't exactly human. Sitting on the bed, he put his arms around Laurel, who rested her head on his shoulder.

Christopher smiled again when Paula said, "To help Laurel cross over."

"Maybe she doesn't want to cross," he said.

"Do you, Laurel?" Paula asked.

Laurel's expression remained unchanged. She neither looked at Paula nor answered her question.

"Laurel is non-verbal," Christopher said.

"Her parents didn't know," Paula said.

"She became that way because of the abuse she suffered in this room."

The tiny bedroom was on the upper floor of

the Majestic and faced the beach. Through a window with a dirty pane, Odette and Paula could see flashes of lightning out over the Gulf.

"You are not one of the men who abused Laurel," Paula said.

"What do you know of Laurel's abuse?" Christopher asked.

"In a vision I had, I saw what the endless procession of lustful men did to her," Paula said. "I didn't see you."

"This room was Laurel's prison. She never left it."

"How do you know all this?" Paula asked.

"I was a janitor. I brought Laurel's food, cleaned her room, and took care of her needs," Christopher said. "We became friends."

A storm was moving in from the Gulf, rumbles of thunder beginning to rock the Majestic's old wooden frame. Laurel's willowy arm wrapped across Christopher's broad chest.

Christopher nodded when Paula said, "Looks as if Laurel thinks of you more than just a friend."

"Our relationship is complicated," he said.

He smiled when Paula asked, "Are you a ghost?"

"As I said, it's complicated."

"Then maybe you'd better explain," Paula said.

Lightning, much closer this time, flashed outside the window. Wind blowing through a broken pane in the window whipped the tattered curtains.

"You don't seem like a person who would condone such abuse," Paula asked.

"The people who owned the Majestic had little regard for the rule of law. Armed men protected their interests. Every conceivable vice was readily available to the rich guests who stayed here.

Some prostitutes got money for their work. Laurel was a slave and had no choice. Gangsters forced her to participate in the vilest of perversions."

"You saw all this and did nothing?" Paula said.

"It was the Great Depression, money and food in short supply. Intense hunger changes a person's perception of right and wrong," Christopher said.

"I never really connected Prohibition with the Great Depression," Paula said.

"People with good intentions often create the direst of situations," Christopher said.

"What do you mean?" Paula asked.

"Prohibition was supposed to protect people from the horrors of alcohol. Instead, it resulted in even more crime and violence."

"You sound like a college professor and not a janitor," Odette said.

"I was in my final year of medical school at Tulane when the Depression began," Christopher said. "Though I managed to eke out a living for a few years, things kept getting worse."

Christopher grinned when Odette said, "Most doctors don't have tattoos."

"Souvenirs of time I spent at Angola."

Odette's hand went to her mouth. "Angola has a horrible reputation."

"Hell on earth," Christopher said.

"What did you do to get sent to prison?" Paula asked.

"Robbed a bank, got caught, and sentenced to twenty years."

"You don't look old enough to have served twenty years," Paula said.

"I escaped," Christopher said.

"No one escapes from Angola," Odette said.

"There was a mass escape in 1933. Horrible living conditions became progressively worse

265

during the Depression. People facing poverty and the possibility of world war had little concern for the prisoners when the State cut its budget. The mortality rate was already high. The prison system became even more brutal and corrupt. We finally rebelled, killed some guards, and broke out."

"You didn't get caught?" Odette asked.

"I'd heard about Oyster Island in prison. The gangsters and rum runners who lived here had lots of food and money and didn't care if the people they hired had tainted pasts."

"And you became Laurel's caretaker?" Paula said.

"I was warned the job required me to be deaf, dumb, and blind," Christopher said. "After a while, listening to Laurel's screams, I could take no more. I killed a man who was torturing her."

"The gangsters killed you?" Odette said.

"Laurel and me," he said.

"Why did they kill Laurel?" Paula asked.

Lightning flashed outside the little room, the burst of intense illumination combined with the green glow from Christopher and Laurel.

"I told you the story is complicated," he said.

"I can understand why they killed you," Paula said. "Why would they kill a person who isn't dangerous who provides them with so much profit?"

"Who says Laurel isn't dangerous?" Christopher said.

When lightning flashed again, Laurel raised her head off of Christopher's shoulder and opened her mouth, her long fangs glinting in the momentary illumination. Christopher also had fangs.

"You're vampires," Paula said. "How did that happen?"

"Lots of vampires in New Orleans,"

Christopher said. "A visitor to the hotel infected Laurel, and she infected me."

"Vampires are undead. How can you now be ghosts?" Paula asked.

The pulsating green light flickered and died. When it returned, Laurel and Christopher were gone. Lying on the bed in an embrace of death were two skeletons, wooden stakes still piercing their chests. Again, Odette's hand went to her mouth.

When the light flickered again, Laurel and Christopher, still locked in an embrace, had returned.

Christopher nodded when Odette said, "They killed you in your sleep?"

The wind had picked up outside the old hotel, an approaching storm rattling the windows and lighting fixtures hanging from the ceiling.

"We're here to help Laurel cross over. We'll help you too," Paula said.

"Vampires can't cross," Christopher said.

"Yes, they can. If you let us, we'll take your bones to the beach and bury them. Odette and I will perform a burial ceremony and consecrate the grave. Once that happens, you are free to cross over."

"How will we know?" Christopher asked.

"You can see the beach from the window. When the ceremony is complete, we'll light a bonfire. When you see the fire, your souls will be free, and you can cross over."

"The ghouls and demons will never let you leave this place," Christopher said.

"Then you must protect us until we escape," Paula said.

"How are we going to carry the bones?" Odette asked.

"Put them in pillowcases," Paula said.

"Won't they be too heavy to carry?" Odette

said.

"Bones only make up about ten to fifteen percent of a person's body weight. My guess is there are no more than thirty pounds of bones for us to carry."

"Then let's do it," Odette said.

"Christopher?" Paula said. "It's now or never."

Thunder shook the Majestic as the light flickered and revealed the bones. Odette stripped the cases from the two pillows on the bed and filled them with bones. When she finished, she handed one of them to Paula.

The light had disappeared from the room as Paula and Odette pushed through the door into the dark hallway.

"Christopher," she said. "Are you coming with us?"

When no one answered, Odette, said, "We'll never make it down the stairs in the dark."

"We have to try," Paula said. "All I have is what's left of my black candle, and we'll need it to perform the consecration ceremony."

"There won't be a ceremony if we don't make it out of here," Odette said.

"Take my hand," Paula said. "I think I can get us to the stairway. We can hold on to the handrail and make it to the bottom floor if we go slow."

"Christopher," Odette called as she followed Paula down the dark hallway. "Why have you abandoned us?"

"Don't know, baby," Paula said. "We'll just have to trust ourselves."

They were halfway down the first flight of stairs when the monsters began coming out of the walls. Odette screamed, almost dropping her bag of bones, when a gelatinous hand stroked the back of her neck.

"Don't stop," Paula said. "At least now we can

see."

Green light glowing from the monsters leaking from the walls provided pulsating illumination as Paula and Odette hurried down the stairs. When one of the demons popped out of the wall, Odette swung her bag of bones at it.

"Christopher," she called again. "Please help us."

Tentacled beasts with glowing eyes and razor-sharp claws grasped for Paula and Odette as they descended the stairs.

"Drop the bones," an unearthly voice boomed.

"Fuck you!" Odette cried out.

A colossal demon, blocking their exit and stinking to high heavens, awaited them when they reached the bottom floor.

"Drop the bones, and I will spare your lives," the demon said.

"Christopher," Odette called again. "Please help us."

As the demon approached them, something came screaming down the stairs behind them. Odette and Paula had only a brief moment to see it was Christopher, stripped to the waist, his muscles bulging and his vampire fangs bared. He wielded an old Confederate saber as he flew past them and attacked the demon. For a moment, it wasn't readily apparent which of the supernatural beings was getting the best of the violent confrontation.

Demon's blood and decayed flesh splattered as Christopher backed the monster against the wall and succeeded in dicing it up. Moving aside, he let Odette and Paula pass by him. He began slicing up the glowing monsters coming down the stairs with his back to them.

"Get out the door," he cried.

The wind blew their scanty black garments as they pushed through the door to the wooden walkway leading to the shoreline. It slammed behind them as they hurried across the wooden slats undulating in the waves whipped up by the wind.

"Hurry, baby," Paula said.

"What about Christopher?" Odette asked.

"He's already dead," Paula said. "He can't die twice."

Instead of getting into the ATV, Paula headed straight for the beach about a hundred yards away. Waves crashed over their bare feet as they reached it.

"How are we supposed to dig a grave?" Odette asked.

"On our hands and knees," Paula said. "It only has to be deep enough to cover the bones. The waves will uncover it anyway and take them out to sea."

As Paula and Odette began clawing a hollow in the damp sand, light rain sprinkled their shoulders. When lightning flashed, Odette thought she saw two figures in an upstairs window.

"The waves are filling the hole almost as fast as we dig it," she said.

"It's deep enough," Paula said. "Dump the bones. We can't leave them in the pillowcases, or the spirits won't connect."

The rain was falling harder as Odette shook the last of the bones into the makeshift grave.

"What now?" she asked.

"Cover the hole as best you can," Paula said.

Paula cupped the black candle in her hands and mouthed a secret incantation. The candle lighted and continued to glow brightly even amid the heavy rain pelting them.

"Is this good?" Odette asked.

"It'll have to be," Paula said. "Ashes to ashes, dust to dust. Dear God, please consecrate the bones of these two souls and allow them to cross over. Get driftwood."

"No fire will start in this downpour," Odette said.

"Faith, baby. That's all we have left."

Paula and Odette began scouring the beach for wood and soon had a pile laid in front of the shallow grave. Lighting the black candle again, she tossed it on the pyre as Odette held her breath.

The driftwood exploded into flames, rising ten feet into the air. As the fire burned brightly, Paula turned to the Majestic and waved. In a moment, the Majestic exploded, flames rising from the roof. They heard a roar like a low-flying jet.

Above them, Christopher and Laurel were holding hands, smiling and waving before disappearing forever into the deluge soaking Paula and Odette.

Chapter 32

The weather had turned damp as Chief and J.P. unloaded the pirogue and eased it into the water beside the road. Drizzling rain peppered their shoulders as J.P. climbed into the front of the little boat. Old Joe followed him into the pirogue as Chief pushed away from shore.

Chief's grandfather had hollowed the pirogue from the trunk of a single tree. More than a hundred years old, the coat of bright yellow paint made it look brand new.

Chief and J.P. wore headlamps that cast narrow light beams into the darkness as they paddled through the murky swamp. Rain dimpled the water, and Chief tried not to think about the cool breeze blowing through his damp shirt.

Refusing to let Chief go after the rougarou alone, J.P. had the pneumatic gun cradled against his chest. Chief trusted no other person on earth more than J.P. to take the critical shot except for himself. Chief's headlamp glinted in the yellow eyes of an alligator floating like a log in the water.

Above them, tree bats chasing insects

stirred up by the drizzle darted through the beams of light cast by their headlamps. Bats can fly in light rain but take shelter when it becomes a downpour. As yet, it wasn't that way. Chief was thankful for every mosquito the bats ate and kept from sucking his blood. The bellowing of a bull gator diverted his attention from the bats and returned it to the job at hand.

Many years had passed since Chief's grandfather had taken him to the little plot of dry land in the middle of the swamp. Time didn't matter because he remembered the pathway to the island as clearly as if his first trip there had only been yesterday.

Old Joe, his gaze locked on their watery path, seemed to realize the gravity of their trip into the swamp. His sudden throaty growl signaled they were nearing the island and that there was something there the big dog didn't like.

Chief guided the pirogue through a channel cut in the fallen logs and cypress knees, landing the little boat beneath a giant tree with Spanish Moss draping from its branches. Old Joe jumped into the water and paddled to shore.

J.P. and Chief stood on the little patch of land surrounded by dank swamp. Old Joe didn't shake the water off his back, lying instead on the damp bank and awaiting directions. Chief and J.P. turned off their headlamps and exchanged hand signals. When Chief put his big hand on Old Joe's shoulders, the dog knew what to do.

J.P. and Chief followed behind Old Joe as he crept into the darkness. They halted when a barely audible growl came from somewhere deep in his throat. A light shined through the

273

bushes. J.P. and Chief dropped to their hands and knees and nestled up beside the dog.

A wooden cabin sat in the middle of a clearing, a man sitting in a rocking chair on the cabin's covered porch. The shotgun in his lap glinted in the dim light of a coal oil lantern hanging from the rafters.

"I don't know who you think you're hiding from out there in the bushes. I can see you plain as day. Come out with your hands up, or I'm going to give you a taste of buckshot," the man said. "Both of you, and take hold of that dog's collar. I don't want him anywhere near me."

"The shit just hit the fan," J.P. said.

Chief held on to Old Joe's collar as he followed J.P. into the light of the coal oil lamp as the rain continued. The man wore a pair of old overalls over a dirty flannel shirt that didn't entirely cover the gang tattoos on his neck. Despite a Mississippi twang, he spoke good English.

"Comment ça va, Antoine?" J.P. asked.

"I ain't a Cajun, and I ain't Antoine," the man said. "Don't you remember me, Lieutenant?" the man asked.

"Should I?" J.P. said.

"You ran me in once."

"I've run lots of men in," J.P. said. Give me a hint."

"Tank Johnson."

"You've aged a little since I last saw you, Tank," J.P. said.

"Unbuckle your sidearm real slow," Tank said. "Let it drop to the ground. If you come within an inch of the handle, I'll blow your damn head off."

"Yes, sir," J.P. said.

His .45 and holster thudded as they hit the damp earth.

"You got two holsters," Tank said. "Drop it."

J.P. unbuckled the holster with the pneumatic gun.

Tank watched it fall and then grinned when Chief asked, "What happened to Antoine?"

"The old fucker put up a fight. Looked as if he was about a hundred though still strong as an ox, or maybe a wolf. He'd have killed me for sure if I hadn't surprised him in his sleep. Almost did anyway."

Tank touched what remained of his left ear.

"Did Antoine do that?" J.P. asked.

"The old fucker bit my damn ear off," Tank said. "Didn't think it was ever going to stop bleeding."

He grinned again when Chief asked, "Where did you bury his body?"

"He was lucky I didn't just let him rot. I tossed his body in the swamp. The Gators took care of it."

"We think he may have been a rougarou," J.P. said. "We brought a serum to cure him. If he bit your ear off, then you're infected."

Tank glanced at the sky as the full moon peeked through the rapidly moving clouds.

"I don't need your serum. I like the power being a wolf gives me."

"You're not immortal. Antoine was a rougarou, and he's dead," J.P. said.

"He was human when I killed him, or it would have been me feeding the gators," Tank said.

"Let me give you the shot," J.P. said.

"For what?" Tank said. "So you can take

275

me in easier? I guess you both know neither of you or your dog is going to leave the island alive."

Tank had a dog chain on the porch and tossed it to Chief.

"What's this for?" Chief asked.

"Chain the dog to that tree," Tank said.

"He doesn't like chains," Chief said.

"And I don't like him. Last time I saw him, he tried to tear my throat out."

"You don't need to chain him," J.P. said. "He doesn't attack unless someone commands him to."

Tank grinned again. "You and the big Indian won't be around to give him orders, and I have special plans for the dog."

Tank kept his shotgun pointed as he backed up to the porch, retrieving a bloody flour sack. He dropped it at J.P.'s feet.

"What is it?" J.P. asked.

"Shot me a swamp hog the other day," Tank said. "I always give what I don't use to the gators. Take it down and dump it in the swamp. Don't try to escape. You won't make it, and the dog and Indian will be dead before you are. When you finish dumping the carcass, put your hands on your head and wait for us."

Chief patted Old Joe's head after chaining him to an oak tree.

"Sorry, big boy," he said.

Seeming to know what was about to happen, Old Joe didn't struggle or bark.

After J.P. had dumped the bloody remains of the hog into the water, Tank began banging the butt of the shotgun against the porch.

"The gators come running when they hear me pound the porch," Tank said, pointing the shotgun at Chief. "Put your hands on your head and join your buddy."

The drizzling rain continued as J.P. and Chief stared at the alligator feeding frenzy that had begun in the water. The big males were bellowing as they fought over the bloody hog carcass.

"What now?" J.P. asked.

"You got a choice," Tank said. "You're both going into the water, either dead or alive. I'll enjoy the spectacle whichever you choose."

"Don't you want our wallets and watches first?" J.P. asked.

"I don't trust you any farther than I could throw the big Indian into the water. Keep your hands on your head. Big boy here can get your wallet for me."

Chief handed the two wallets to Tank. "He has a solid gold St. Christopher's medal on a solid gold chain around his neck. Want me to get it for you?"

"Why hell yes," Tank said.

Chief unhooked the dog whistle around J.P.'s neck. He put it in his lips, his back to Tank, and blew. Tank didn't hear the silent whistle. Old Joe did. They heard a loud pop as the chain around his neck parted. The shotgun flew out of Tank's hands when the big German Shepard hit him with the full force of his weight square in the back.

Terrified of dogs, Tank scrambled to his feet and dived into the shallow water away from the wild gators. Chief had to grab Old Joe's collar to keep him from going after him. Turning around, Tank stood up and began transforming into a rougarou.

J.P. dived for the shotgun, pointed it at Tank, and pulled both triggers. The blast knocked the partially-transformed rougarou back with a loud splash. The gators, smelling

277

blood in the water, attacked, finally managing to pull the struggling man beneath the surface. Tank didn't come out of the water as J.P. and Chief watched the feeding frenzy.

When the water finally stopped churning, Chief asked. "Can a rougarou drown?"

"Don't know," J.P. said. "He wasn't fully transformed because the buckshot bloodied him."

Chief put his arms around Old Joe and hugged him. "You saved us, big boy. Sorry I had to chain you."

"Hell, Chief," J.P. said. "That dog's smarter than both of us. He knew you didn't have a choice."

"You think he would have broken the chain and saved us even if I hadn't blown the whistle?" Chief asked.

J.P. gave Chief a high five. "Glad we didn't have to find out."

They waited on the bank of the swamp long after the gator frenzy had ended.

"You think he's dead?" Chief asked.

"What's left of Tank Johnson is digesting in the bellies of a half dozen gators," J.P. said. "Tomorrow, the police and F.B.I. will be swarming this place. Let them deal with it."

"You want to check the cabin before we go?" Chief asked.

"This island's a crime scene. We don't want to destroy any clues. Let's get the hell out of here."

"If you're waiting on me, you're backing up," Chief said.

After J.P. and Old Joe had taken their places in the pirogue, Chief pushed off from shore, stepping gingerly into the boat so as not to step in the water. The wind blowing up from the Gulf whipped the tree branches and Spanish Moss hanging from them. The rain was falling in bucketloads as they reached the road to Chalmette. They pulled the pirogue out of the water, loading it into the bed of the truck.

Old Joe's tail never stopped wagging as J.P. reached around the bucket seat and scratched his ears. They reached the bridge in time to see and feel the explosion lighting the sky over the Majestic.

J.P. slammed on the brakes. "What in Holy Hell was that?" he asked.

They found Jack, dressed in his red flannel nightshirt, staring in the direction of the Majestic. Old Joe, his tail wagging, jumped out of the truck when Chief opened the door for him. Lucky, Oscar, and Coco, their tails also wagging, met him.

The three men watched as the ATV pulled up in front of the house. When Paula and Odette exited dressed in only the tiniest swaths of black cloth, Jack went into the house to fetch a couple of bathrobes.

"What the hell's going on?" J.P. asked.

"Witch work," Paula said as she slipped the white bathrobe over her shoulders.

"Did you two just blow up the Majestic?" he asked.

"The Majestic is fine," Paula said. "The ghosts and ghouls are gone. At least the bad ones."

"Maybe you'd better explain," J.P. said.

"Tomorrow," Paula said. "I need to get to the camper before Jimmy wakes up."

"You're a day late and a dollar short," Jack said. "The sun's coming up, and Jimmy just stepped out of the camper."

Chapter 33

Jimmy glared at Paula and followed her and the others into Jack's little house.

"I couldn't sleep, baby," she said with a hug. "Sorry I wasn't in bed when you awoke. I promise I'll more than make it up to you."

The smile on Jimmy's face as he pulled up a chair at the plank table indicated Paula's show of affection had soothed him. Odette and Paula went into Jack's galley to help him cook breakfast.

They were all at the table, enjoying Jack's grits, shrimp, and eggs when J.P.'s cell phone rang. He returned to the table, grinning broadly.

"Who was it?" Jack asked.

"Junior Portie. He was at the Frenette's house checking on Latrice and the doctor."

"Are they okay?" Odette asked.

"Dr. Frenette's cancer is in remission, and he's up and walking," J.P. said.

"Hallelujah," Jack said.

"That's not all," J.P. said. "They'd talked about our dog training facility with Junior.

Latrice just told me they're good for however much money we need for the project."

Jack got up from the plank table before the applause stopped, returning with two bottles of rum.

"Time to celebrate," he said.

"As an officer in our new company," Chief said, "I make a motion we head up to Rockie's and continue the celebration there."

"Not so fast," J.P. said. "In a few hours, this island will be swarming with cops. We can hit Rockie's when they finish their investigation."

"Then let's get started," Jack said. "We have lots of rum, and it doesn't drink itself."

End

Eric Wilder

Book Notes

I hope you liked reading Oyster Bay Boogie as much as I enjoyed writing it and that you liked all the eccentric characters. Though fictional, many of its historical details are factual. Like the other states bordering the Gulf of Mexico, Louisiana has barrier islands. Rum running was rampant in the Gulf during Prohibition, along with gambling and speakeasies.

Louisiana's Angola Prison has a long and sordid history. The vampire Christopher could have escaped from Angola in 1933 because an actual massive prison break occurred that year.

Are there rougarous in south Louisiana? A friend of mine confided in me that "At night in the swamp, you hear lots of sounds; some you recognize and some you don't want to know."

Please consider leaving a review and reading the second book in the series, *Oyster Bay Tango* coming in the summer of 2022. You may also like my French Quarter Mystery Series and Paranormal Cowboy Series.

Thanks for being a fan. My stories would be little more than morning fog wafting across a forgotten lawn without beautiful readers like you. Thank you.

About the Author

Born on a sleepy bayou, Louisiana Mystery Writer Eric Wilder grew up listening to tales of ghosts, magic, and voodoo. He's the author of fourteen novels, four cookbooks, many short stories, and Murder Etouffee, a book that defies classification. His first two series feature P.I.s adept in the investigation of the paranormal. He lives in Oklahoma near historic Route 66 with wife Marilyn, three wonderful dogs, and one great cat.